I0748419

THE VERNORE GENE

SHADOW REIGN CHRONICLES

J.T. WHITESELL

Library of Congress Cataloging-in-Publication Data has been applied for.

ISBN-13: 978-0-578-03151-4

First Edition. Printed in the U.S.A.

15 14 13 12 11 10 9 8 7 6 5

Cover design by Richard Whitesell
Chapter heading from ClipArt.com
Book design by J.T. Whitesell
Edited by Bess Johnson

www.jtwhitesell.webs.com

The text type was set in Times New Roman at 10 pt.
The title type was set in Eccentric STD at 40 pt.

For Lin,
I am the kerosene and you are the match.
Separately we are nothing, but together we ignite!

GRUNDAGON

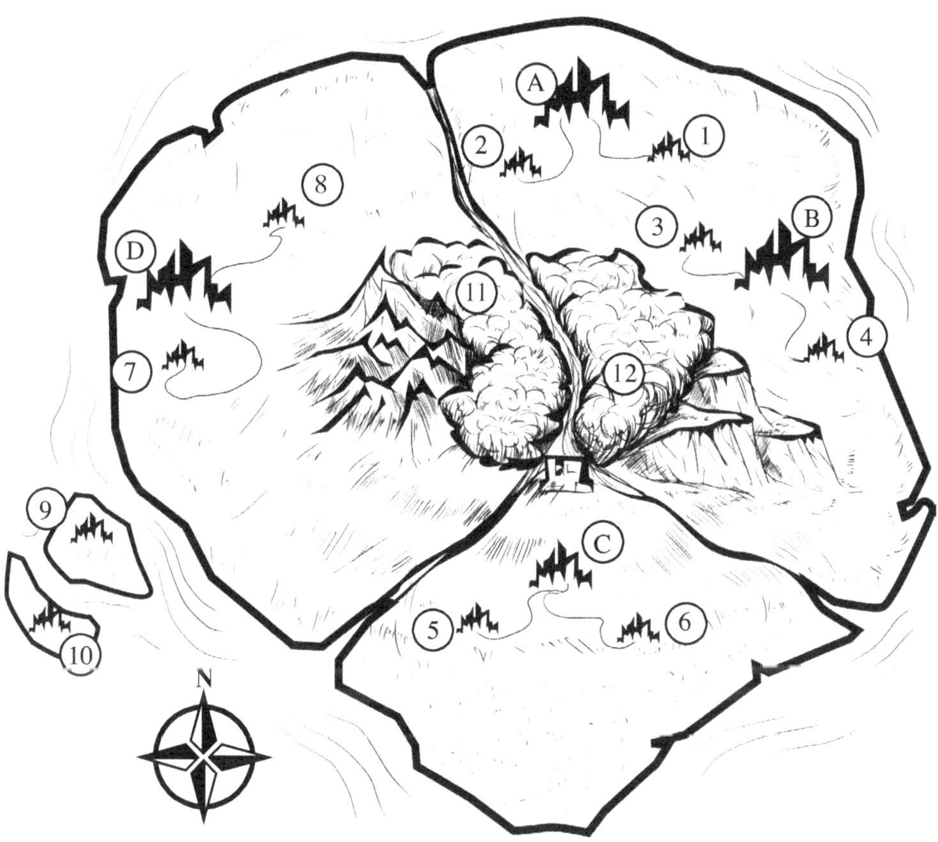

Major Cities
A. North Central City (NCC)
B. East Central City (ECC)
C. South Central City (SCC)
D. West Central City (WCC)

Minor Cities
1. Bynnin
2. Joryn
3. Eucin
4. Clavanor
5. Klut
6. Cluce
7. Postana
8. Glyfe

Islands
9. Rhomahr Isle
10. Ecnamor Isle

Tribes
11. Maimugg
12. Taimugg

Prologue

A little girl sat in a field surrounded by a sea of flowers. The colors of sweet white violets, springcress, and blue eyed grass united in a fragrant blanket. A rain tree shaded her from the jungle's intense sun. She giggled when a bushy striped tail tickled her bare legs as it ran around her. Without warning, it bounded off toward a large rock in the distance.

"Socks, come back! We can't play over there!" she thought as she pulled herself to her feet and ran after the ring-tailed lemur.

Silently, she approached the boulder and heard two older boys murmuring on the other side of the rock. One boy spoke in a language close to Maimuan. His voice was recognizable, but oddly sweet-natured. It teased her often, but she was too young to understand a ten year old's infatuation. "Do you think she's crazy?"

"Of course, Contardo! She won't eat the meat the hunters bring home and she fights with anyone who looks at her the wrong way."

The little girl didn't understand every word. She was still learning the language her foster family spoke. It had been three years since the life she had known had come to an abrupt end.

"Anaba! I told you not to play over there!" A woman's voice echoed through the clearing as she approached the boulder.

The two boys scurried around the boulder. The largest one grabbed Jailin's long pony tail. "Jailin, are you spying on us?" She tried to worm her way out of his grasp.

"Contardo! Don't make me tell Darwishi what you've been doing." The woman who'd entered the clearing had a long black braid contouring one side of her robust face and her long brown dress swept the field clean. She approached the boys with determination.

"Sorry, Meovi. Please don't tell my father!" The boy let go of Jailin's hair. "She's just so strange." He surveyed the little girl from head to toe. "Why don't you do something about it?"

"What do you suggest, my future Primary?" Meovi scoffed at the boy by using the title of the individual who rules the tribes.

"She cries about her parents and someone named Benny and how the world swallowed them up. It's so annoying."

"She's eight years old and has a big imagination. She certainly doesn't need to hear from a ten year old about the Global Quake. It scares her."

"History is very important, Yenena." Contardo addressed Meovi by her tribal title. "She should know what caused a civilization to change so drastically almost 800 years ago."

"You're a smart boy, Contardo. I would think you'd know how to speak to your elders." Meovi took Jailin by the hand and led her back to the tribe, leaving the two boys in the clearing.

"Tell me about the Global Quake, Meovi." Jailin ran to keep up with her foster mother's quick pace.

"Are you sure, Anaba?" She spoke Jailin's tribal name with endearment.

"Yes!"

Meovi scowled. It would be another night filled with tears. "In the year 2152, the whole world shook. The continents divided, then realigned, and civilizations broke apart. New cultures arose and people constructed new cities and towns. Those who were poor either became rich or starved to death while the rich got richer or killed each other for power."

"Do you know which continents make up Grundagon?" Jailin interrupted.

"Some wise-men say it was Africa and a part of North America, called Brazil. Others say it's too hard to tell."

"Tell me what happened to the animals!" Jailin prompted.

"They ran for shelter. Somehow they knew the Global Quake was coming. When the soil cracked and combined with other soil, each animal had to create a new home and a new way to survive."

"Sarana told me about that. She said her parents have told her their history over and over. One day she'll pass the story on to her cubs."

"Who's Sarana?" Meovi glared down at Jailin.

"The cougar I play with, the one who hunts the Markhor and Gemsbok in the clearing. She's the only cat who's not scared of those horns!"

Meovi didn't like to hear from Jailin's wild imagination concerning her ability to talk with animals. "Anaba, what did I tell you about that?"

"I'm not making it up! I can hear them."

"You're lucky GIA let you live with me instead of some city folk who would put you in military school."

"Why?" Bewildered eyes gazed up at Meovi's sour face.

"Because then you would end up in a mental hospital, Anaba." Meovi slid her hand over Jailin's dark hair.

"Like Daddy?"

Meovi grimaced. She didn't want to remind the poor girl of those unbearable times.

1

Jailin peered between the openings of the leaves. She crouched on the highest limb with her back against the tall teak tree. It was dark but the cloudless sky lit the ground like a spotlight out of heaven. Clutching her necklace, she watched a man slither across the ground on his chest. He wore black boots and a thin grass-stained white tank top which stretched over his broad shoulders. He had on camouflage pants with a belt full of assorted weapons and tools around his waist, and a white lustrous fur was tied over one shoulder.

"What he doesn't know may kill him tonight," Jailin whispered. There was no reply except for a twinkle in a pair of eyes that showed out of the shadows above Jailin's shoulder.

She made her way down the tree using the interlocking braches of the neighboring teaks. It was done smoothly, effortlessly, and with enough speed to be almost a blur to common eyes. She was on top of the man without a single sound.

"Crouched in the brush. Three o'clock from the boulder." Jailin's thoughts indicated the man's location.

Peering just above the tall blue-eyed grass, Jailin watched the man lift his head and gasp. He wasn't as skillful as he thought. Yellow, dark-rimmed eyes locked with his and the man held his breath, heart pounding. The cougar snarled.

"Can I attack?" the cougar thought. Even in the darkness, the sandy-brown fur glistened. Its feet kneaded the soil with its head slouched just below its shoulder blades—ready to pounce. The oval eyes displayed no fear.

"Not yet. He hasn't engaged. Let's see if he makes the first move." Jailin returned the thought. Three pounding hearts drummed in her ears. Each raced at a different speed and they mixed harmoniously. Jailin knew the cougar's heart rate was fast, but normal. The one pressed against her shoulder was slightly elevated even for its naturally quick pace. The third was rapid too. Way too fast to be caused only by fear. This man couldn't be the source, could he? That didn't make any sense, but no one else was around and it certainly wasn't Jailin's heartbeat.

The man began to try soothing the cougar by talking to it as if it were a mere infant. "It's okay, big guy. I won't hurt you… yet." He slowly reached for the large knife tucked into the belt at the small of his back. As he raised it out and was about to make a quick slash at the cougar's neck, Jailin grabbed his wrist and in the same movement turned him to face her.

"You shouldn't have come alone." She leaned in close enough so that her nose almost touched his. Her face was so intimidating that the growling could have been coming from her instead of the cougar.

"Who said I'm alone?" the man retorted. He couldn't possibly think that arrogance would help him survive. Jailin backed up, crossed her arms and clenched her teeth.

"I followed you. I know that you were exiled. Do you honestly think they'll take you back if you bring them *another* fur?" One arm unfolded so she could swing an irate finger at the fur draped over his shoulder. He jerked his head sideways to see what she was pointing at. He'd forgotten about the fur.

"Well, honestly, I wanted to find something worth more, but diamonds are harder to come by these days." Jailin only returned a stare of disgust. She found no humor in harming the wildlife. The man's face hardened. "Who do you think you are? A new animal rights junkie? Saving the Grundagon Jungle one animal at a time?"

"Oh no, I won't actively *do*… much." One corner of her lip curled into a smile. She looked off into the darkness as if to see something that no one else could.

"Huh?"

"I'm not the one you need to be defending yourself against." Her head spun back to look at him. "I give you the options and you choose your own fate." Her eyes were the first part of her face to express her feelings and she was livid.

"What are my options?" His hand reached up to scratch his jaw bone under his ear. This motion always helped him to think out his next step.

"Now that she knows you are here and what intentions you have, I can let her dismember you *or* you can change your ways and walk away now." Jailin pointed to his choices: the cougar and the road.

"Hmm… female. I misjudged that tonight," the man mumbled under his breath.

"Well?" Jailin heard what he said but it didn't matter to her. She wanted him as far away from here as possible. Deep down, she wanted to believe anyone could change, but it wasn't her place to decide who could and couldn't. No one was punished for their first offense.

"Those are my only choices?" He sounded hopeful. Jailin figured the choices were pretty cut and dry. He was just wasting time, but she couldn't figure out why he would bother.

"Yes," she hissed. This was getting annoying.

"What happens if I kill her instead?"

"Instead?" He couldn't possibly think he could win. It was two against one. She would help the cougar if needed. "I never said she was going to kill you, I said dismember. You can live in agony the rest of your days."

"Maybe I want to fight back. I'm the hunter, not the prey, here."

Jailin rolled her eyes. "You have been prey ever since you left that camp. Or did you forget?"

"All right, perhaps I'll go, but just because I'm no longer hunting."

"Poaching." Jailin corrected.

"Call it what you will. You'll be better off following a different path in life after a stunt like this." He was getting fed up with her. It was one thing to threaten him. He was used to that, but her hatred for someone she didn't know based on false information was another thing. Granted, she didn't know the truth.

"Are you threatening me on their behalf?" she questioned. He couldn't scare her if he tried. Poachers were men with childish fear for real work. Fear of being seen as weak for working a desk job in the city.

"I'm just telling you the truth. Take it however you like," he said in a nonchalant manner.

There was a long silence. The man thought she was contemplating his future. Jailin remained still. Her eyes glassed over, deep in thought. The cougar let out a low growl that almost sounded to the untrained ear like a sigh of frustration.

"What should we do with him?" the cougar thought as she turned her back on the two of them and peered out into the wilderness, anticipating another attack.

A slight rustling sound came from the underbrush. "Did you tell anyone where you were going tonight?" Jailin asked the man. She was anxious for his answer. Whether he told the truth or not, she couldn't know for sure.

"What's it matter? I'm either dead or a brand new man because of you." The lightness in his voice surprised her. He sounded sad. Nothing like the proud man she had loomed over moments ago.

She searched for stray thoughts as the man's eyes slowly met hers. "Do you see anything, Socrates?" Jailin thought.

"There is some movement in the brush. I cannot confirm from this perspective whether it is animal, man or apparition. Are you not able to break the barrier?" The voice she heard was a masculine tone. Not deep, but soothing in a father knows best sort of way.

"I'm not picking up any thoughts. It's either man or a true hunter with abilities like mine or better." She paused to smile slightly. "Besides, you don't believe in the unknown," she quipped. He didn't believe his own words either and she could tell. If he had, he would have been halfway across the jungle by now.

"In this case I have an inability to explain the white in the brush," Socrates thought. He didn't like to be ridiculed.

The cougar crouched and Jailin squatted down into her fighting stance, ready if needed. "Do apparitions smell like dirt?" the cougar thought.

The man saw Jailin look past him toward the cougar. He looked over his shoulder and saw that the cougar was stalking her way toward the underbrush.

"What's going on?" he asked, looking entirely confused at what had transpired.

"I suggest you change your ways *right* now and take the road to freedom before you regret it," Jailin advised between clenched teeth. She didn't know what was coming for them and she didn't want to have to defend someone who'd only just proved himself worthless to her.

Just as the man turned to go, a white cat jumped out of the brush. The cougar, looking like a domestic dog in comparison, went for its neck and slashed with its claws. The bewildered man staggered backward and then turned to run into the jungle.

"Follow him, Socrates." Jailin thought as she reached for the stick strapped across her back. It was a four-foot wooden bo staff. She spun it in a circle on her right, and then making a figure eight across her chest she made another circle on her left. Then she lunged toward the white beast.

As the man ran, his panic dissipated and he regained his thoughts. "What's going on here? I should go back. That was a big cat. Could it be *the* panther? It was white after all. Apparently it exists—it must be the one from the myth." He touched the fur at his shoulder and shuddered. "He's definitely bigger than a normal panther!"

The man had stopped running at this point and was pacing. "Jailin, he appears to be considering his return. What do I do?" Socrates thought in a fretful rush.

"Stop him. I'll come as soon as I can." She grunted and gasped as if her advancements on the white beast weren't quick enough.

"Any suggestions on how you expect me to achieve success?"

"Do what you do best." The words in her thoughts were increasingly ragged with exhaustion.

"My logic has no effect on a subject that cannot hear me," he said, annoyed.

"I know that. I meant throw rocks at him or something else annoying. I'm busy here." Jailin jumped down from the boulder and landed on the back of the giant cat. Her bo staff popped open into a thin wire and she looped it around the cat's jaw, then under the muzzle and pulled back on it like a harness. "Open your mind. I know you can hear me. Answer me! What are you doing here?" She prodded at the black wall the white cat had built in his mind. Not many animals were like this. This was like the human minds she couldn't penetrate.

The thrashing and head bucking began to slow. Jailin still held on. She felt his body slow and his mind wavered slightly. "Back away. We need room," Jailin said aloud to the cougar.

The cougar stopped pacing around the fight and reluctantly began to back away.

"I was after that man and you let him go. He killed my cub and my mate. I'm all alone. I have nothing!" The giant cat fell to the ground with grief. He had seen the fur on the man's shoulder.

"Beg your pardon, Jailin, I could not stop him," Socrates gulped.

Jailin turned to see the man standing on the boulder holding a ring-tailed lemur by its scruff. The man appeared as if he'd been struck across the face with a repressed memory at the sight of Jailin wrestling with a giant cat.

"Put him down!" Jailin yelled across the short distance as if she were miles away. The look on his face confused her. He'd come back, but it didn't make sense for him to have done so.

"Now, now, let's not get huffy, my girl," he said as the ring-tailed lemur wiggled in his hold. Socrates was desperate to get away.

"I'm not *your* girl." She didn't appreciate his little moniker. What had caused this sudden arrogant tone?

"So much anger for such a petite body." His eyes traced her curves and he grinned as if he had given her a compliment.

"Put him down or else." She put one foot forward and the hand that was hidden behind her clenched. He wasn't about to take control over what happened in *her* jungle.

"What a grown-up threat," he mocked. "You still have no idea what the world is like. You live in this jungle like a tribal woman who looks nothing like one. Born into wealth without a care in the world… no, I suppose you have cares, but you don't have your priorities in the right order. You think you're doing good, but evil is relative." Socrates stopped moving around at this point. He was intrigued and willing to hear this man out.

"Oh please. I get enough insights from Socrates. I don't need your input too!"

"I know more about you than you think I do." He stared at the ring-tailed lemur in his grip. The man wondered if it understood what was happening.

"Oh? And what is it you think you know?" Jailin had heard it all before. The lies this man would think up in fear might be interesting. Her body relaxed and she was a little less aggressive.

He looked up to the sky as if to recall the exact words in an article posted for all of Grundagon to see. He smiled and said, "You are Jailin Munrow, daughter of Dr. Theodore and Dr. Kathleen Munrow and born in this jungle. Your mother mysteriously died when you were five and your father is in a mental hospital in North Central City." He lowered his head and gazed into the mahogany trees, longing for that past.

"So you can read a newspaper about the most intelligent, loving, and giving wildlife veterinarians in all of Grundagon." This guy was good, but she wasn't about to fall for his ability to over-prepare for every situation.

The man turned to look at her, and then shied away to a spot where nothing but trees stretched out before him. This frustrated Jailin. She didn't want to recall those days. She had so many nightmares of that night. Every year that went by she recalled more and more. She despised whoever it was that was responsible, but finding them was hard. Her eyes welled with water. She shut them tight to conceal her hurt.

"Aw, did I hit a sore spot?" His cockiness returned as his eyes grazed over the ghostly cat.

"Do you want me to end this?" the giant white cat thought as he walked up next to Jailin. She tilted her head the way a dog does to understand his master. Then she remembered why he was here.

"I can fight my own battles," she snapped out loud. She never looked at the cat. This gave the man the idea she was talking to him. Suddenly, she sprang up the boulder with hardly any bend in her knees. Before the man could fully turn around Jailin was on the ground behind him with Socrates at her shoulder.

"Dawn is coming in a few hours and I haven't found food for when the cubs wake. I need to go," the cougar thought. She was still a little tense from the fight with the white beast. Every movement was watched, every scent was inhaled, and every sound was noted that this creature made while near Jailin.

"Everything is fine. You can go. Be safe, Sarana," Jailin thought as she turned to head home, leaving the man on the boulder.

"Hey! Where are you going?" the man shouted at her. He marched down the slanted side of the boulder and rushed around the front so as not to lose sight of her.

"Home," she said softly. He'd already ruined more than she had planned on tonight.

"I think we have unfinished business here!"

She didn't believe they had any dealings at all and certainly didn't prefer to elongate the evening. "That doesn't mean I can't leave you here."

"Don't you want answers to your questions?" His question sounded as if she had just told him his beloved dog had just been hit by a car.

Jailin stopped before she disappeared into the darkness of the trees. She was just a shadow with two heads, from what the man could make out—hers and Socrates'.

"You can't answer my questions. So I'm not going to waste any more time on you." Her reply was quick and direct. It didn't hold any anger, but it stated that she wanted nothing more than to be alone right now.

"No? I thought we were having fun here. Although, if the information I have confiscated from the camp you think I'm exiled from is correct, then I know of someone who might be able to help you." He leaned against the boulder as if he could wait there forever for her answer.

Jailin was back at the clearing in a blur, surprising the man again with her abilities. "What are you talking about?" Instinctively her hand flew to her neckline and gripped down hard.

"I think this giant monster has some interesting information running through his veins and if not, maybe this disc I have has some answers." He waved a small shiny circle in the air. "I may also be able to explain that necklace you clutch when you are anxious or nervous."

"My necklace? What do you know of it?" Her face flushed at his casual recognition of such a delicate object.

"More than you'd probably like to hear. That symbol shows up more often in North Central City than you could ever conceive. And it's spreading through Grundagon fast." She could see his muscles tense and hear the revulsion in his words.

Jailin looked to the giant cat, then to her necklace, back to the man still holding the disc, and then back to her necklace again. "What do you think Socrates?" she thought.

"You have always followed your own path, no matter what I tell you. But if your curiosity is as great as your pulse conveys, I suggest you watch your back throughout this ordeal." His head rested on her shoulder and he curled his tail around her neck lovingly.

"Oh, lord, do you think I should believe him or not? Stop avoiding the subject."

"I cannot tell you what will or will not make you happy. Much of this could be difficult to bear. You may get answers you do not want to hear."

"I have questions too." The giant cat strode up next to Jailin. "And I'll watch your back, if you don't mind?"

"I have Socrates for my back," Jailin thought rather rudely. Then she smiled and looked at the cat. "But I can always use the extra strength."

"As well as another source of locomotion," Socrates deadpanned, which was unusual for him.

"I can hear you, you know," the cat thought to Socrates.

Jailin was caught off guard. "Really? I've never experienced direct interspecies communication before. I'm usually the one to interpret, but this makes sense because you were able to block me from your thoughts earlier. You must have a great power."

"That disc the man holds is full of experiments on my kind as well as information on numerous species.

"Unfortunately, that information may translate into what has been happening to you. Also, I believe that your control over your abilities is lacking due to the fact that you can't open your mind enough to concentrate on multiple languages at once. That's why you stopped searching my thoughts to ask the cougar to back away."

"So does this mean that you can answer my questions?" She looked hopeful. This cat could be her reason to believe that all was not lost. She promised herself she wouldn't turn her back on this.

"No. Not all of them. Only what I know about myself, which is probably not enough to satisfy you about your past. Socrates is right. This will be hard to bear."

"Let's start this journey. All three of us: you, Socrates, and me." Jailin turned to the boulder and saw that the man had disappeared. She cursed herself. "Where did he go? I should have noticed. I never lose a human."

"This is exactly what I meant about your control over your abilities. You need to listen to all that your senses have to tell you." The cat sat down on its haunches and licked his paw.

"Remain calm, Jailin. He does not voyage too far too hastily. He has gone into the brush over there." Socrates pointed to the other side of the boulder. He looked tired and in desperate need of sleep.

"*Socrates*! This is why you are supposed to be watching my back. You should have told me sooner."

"I no longer believe he is the threat we originally characterized him to be." Socrates was usually right and Jailin knew that, no matter how many times over the years she had argued with him about who knew more.

"Oh no? What about his family?" She pointed to the cat. She wanted to believe Socrates would be wrong about something this one time.

"I presume that is a different matter altogether."

“What do you mean?” the cat asked. He stopped cleaning himself and stared at Socrates in confusion. The dark outlines of his eyes narrowed. One ear twitched backward as if to pick up a sound from behind him, but it didn’t deter his attention.

“I am suspecting either that extremist animal rights group: PAAL or …”

“Or what?” Jailin and the cat asked in unison.

“One of us against their own subconscious.”

“Interesting. So you’re saying that he has the same aim as the cat and me, which is to find out how and why we are like this, but he doesn’t know it yet?” Jailin couldn’t believe that someone would be completely unaware of theirself, but then again, she didn’t know all that much about herself.

“My family’s fur is on his shoulder. How do you explain that? No PAAL member would be caught dead with that in a one-mile radius.” The cat was incredulous.

“With the equivalent, I can clarify any human garb. If one comprehends that they are to be observed but still must conceal a truth from others who perceive them: how might one accomplish this task?”

“What is he talking about?” The cat was utterly confused. Even with his ability to hear Socrates without the help of Jailin, he still needed her to translate his meaning. This was a complicated creature.

“He’s saying that a person may choose clothes suited to fit in with a certain crowd. When another type of crowd, which wears different clothes, can see that you still don’t fit in due to a secondary issue such as personality, you may no longer fit in with that original crowd.”

"What does it have to do with that guy?" The cat's head shook as if to clear his mind.

"He's just saying that even though he's wearing the fur it might not have been him who killed your family. Like a costume. He's undercover."

"He couldn't just say that? Wait here." The giant cat bounded off into the brush.

"Do you think he'll hurt that man?" Jailin asked.

"Is your emotional standpoint on this man altering due to my observations?"

"What? No!" Jailin unwrapped Socrates from around her shoulder and neck and cradled him in her arms. She slumped down against the boulder and Socrates nestled into her lap. They waited in silence for the cat to bring the man back.

"His name is Bailey. Benjamin Bailey." The voice came into Jailin's head just as she was about to fall asleep against the boulder. The trees were glowing and the springcress glistened with the bright orange of the sun dawning on them. "So?" She said groggily as she started to stand up.

"When I caught up to him he was recalling a time when he was a boy of about six, and your parent's home was ransacked. The two others that died were his parents. It's a very sad story. I'm sorry to have overheard it."

"Oh my!" Jailin hung her head between her hands. "Are you sure? If this is true then he knew my parents! His parents worked for mine. We used to play in my sandbox. Why don't I remember him?" She shut her eyes and tried to remember the boy's face.

"Give it time. It may come back. It will all come back." He tried to sound reassuring, but a strange guilt was hidden behind his words. Socrates heard it, but he wouldn't make any comments. Jailin had enough on her mind.

"I don't know if I can remember anything before the incident. I need visual cues." She rubbed her temples and tried as hard as she could to generate some memory of her childhood.

"I'm bringing you one now."

"What do you mean?"

"I'm bringing Bailey back."

"But I've already looked at him and got nothing. How do you expect anything to be any different this time?"

"Listen this time. Look deeper."

3

"It's almost dusk, dear." Dr. Kathleen Munrow stood over her husband, who was sitting at his desk writing furiously. Her dark hair was tied back into a short ponytail with wisps of hair sticking out like she had just woken up, even though she had her clean, perfectly pressed lab coat on. Her face was small and round and her eyes were as dark as night. A baby lemur sat on her shoulder.

"I know. I'm almost to a stopping point." Dr. Theodore Munrow was a diligent, hardworking man. He almost never slept, but always looked wide-eyed and excited for new information. His hair was unkempt and his eyes were set deep and appeared hollow. He was so thin that anyone who saw him would think he had never eaten a day in his life. "How is your research going?"

"Not as well as I had hoped. I know it's only been two days, but I'm not getting Socrates to imprint on the other females." Her finger scratched the little chin and his head went up, indulging in the pleasure of it.

"Well, if you name him and let him ride on your shoulder all the time what do you expect?" Ted didn't look up from his writing, but his tone was all Kathy needed to understand his implication.

"I know, but he's special somehow. He listens to my philosophy readings. Jailin falls asleep and you're always so swamped. What choice do I have?" Her excuse sounded distant. More like she had thought it up for her husband's sake than for her own. She didn't regret treating him like her own child.

"I'm sorry, dear, but once I have this strain cured I will have more time for you and our daughter." She'd heard that excuse before. It was true for about a month until something else showed up on a diagnostic slide in the mail from some university asking for help.

"Jailin doesn't see either of us anymore. Johanna is busy taking care of her son as well as our little girl. Nicolas is out with you every day, putting Johanna and her son in a stressful position. I'm afraid our daughter will grow to hate us." Kathy scooped Socrates off her shoulder and cradled him. He cooed in her arms and she silently wished for a simpler life.

"Take a break tonight. Spend some time with her." Ted picked up his messenger bag, threw three books into it and kissed his wife on the cheek. "I'll try to be home early tonight."

Johanna Bailey was listening at the doorway. Her blonde hair with glints of red was pulled back into a high bun and her beautiful blue eyes sparkled. She always wore a pale pink dress with a white apron. She was reluctant to knock due to the conversation she had overheard, but Ted saw her as he headed to the already open door.

"Hello, Johanna. Can we help you?" He smiled and beckoned her inside.

"No. I was just...um, Jailin..." She looked around as if she had been led into a trap and was being served for dinner to a hungry lion.

"What's wrong with Jailin?" Kathy was at Johanna's side in an instant. Her round eyes grew and she patted Socrates' ribs as if comforting him would ease her distress.

"Nothing. She's just asking for both of you." Johanna looked down at her feet and watched her toes wiggle in her thin shoes.

"Go to her Kathy. I'll be home soon." Ted put his hand on her elbow for encouragement.

"Excuse me, Doctor, but will Nicolas be home early as well?" Johanna continued looking at her feet. She was embarrassed of her eavesdropping even though she was the only one aware of it.

"Yes. I suppose he would be unless I leave him tied to a sycamore fig." Ted laughed alone at his humor. It was a deep rumbling laughter. Kathy smiled. It had been such a long time since she had heard him laugh like that. "That man hardly gives me any personal time." He smiled at Johanna.

"Yes. He adores you." She returned the smile but avoided eye contact and a strand of pale strawberry-blonde hair fell into her eyes.

"Let's go see Jailin and Benny. They're playing in the yard, yes?" Kathy took Johanna by the arm to escort her back to the children.

"I'm at the same place as usual!" Ted yelled over his shoulder and was out the front door.

"Madam, I was wondering if I might take a personal evening?" Johanna was still watching her feet.

"Oh? Plans? It's going to be a beautiful night. I suppose I could allow that. Would you like me to watch Benny?" Kathy eyed the woman for her reaction to see if she was sincere. Johanna was always so bashful and nervous. Not to mention overly polite. The woman never said "no" to anything.

"That would be wonderful, but I already asked my sister to watch him pending your approval." Her eyes glanced to Kathy. She didn't believe in getting her hopes up. This way she could never be let down.

"That sounds fine. I might as well send that bio-engineer home, although he pays the lab fees so I can't force him. He won't tell Ted what he's working on. I find him a little... creepy. Is that the right word?"

"Oh yes, madam. Hit the nail on the head. He makes me..." Johanna hesitated and blushed. "Nervous."

"You're always nervous, my dear." Kathy and Johanna laughed together at the thought. Kathy laughed harder and louder. She assumed Johanna's laugh was always so light and airy due to her mcck naturc. "Arc you going out tonight?"

"No. Staying in. I miss the quiet nights alone with... Nicolas." She winced a tiny bit, but hoped it went unnoticed.

"I understand." Kathy had witnessed the strain on a marriage before due to one's dedication to work and didn't bother to pursue Johanna with unnecessary questions.

They made it to the double glass doors that led into the back yard. Jailin was making piles in the sandbox while Benny was pretending to be a monster knocking them down. This made Jailin laugh and clap with excitement. Her dark brown hair swept over her shoulders. Her round cheeks were red from the sun and her smile couldn't have spread any farther across her tiny face.

"How cute they are," Kathy noted and Johanna stared at her blonde little boy having the time of his life. She nodded with a smile of contentment.

"May I take Benny to my sister's now? It's past nine," Johanna asked Kathy after finishing the dishes. She was wiping her hands on her apron. Kathy was sitting at the table helping Jailin draw animals and keeping Benny's hands on his own paper instead of coloring on Jailin's.

"Oh my, it's late. I hadn't realized the time. If you could just put Jailin to bed and I'll go up and say goodnight after I record observations in my lab." She scooped Socrates off the table. He had found an interest in the spoon left on the table after dinner.

"Of course, Madam." Johanna picked up Jailin and took Benny by the hand. They went up the large staircase and turned left into Jailin's room, which had everything a small princess could ask for. Benny always looked amazed every time he entered the room. He was awestruck at all the stuffed animals, toys, and abundance of color that splashed the room. He never budged from the doorway.

Johanna tucked Jailin into bed, kissed her forehead and said, "Mommy will be up in just a moment."

Jailin looked up at her, played with the flower pendant dangling from her neck like a kitten, then pouted and pulled the covers over her head. "No." She didn't yell. She just didn't want the day to end.

"Say good bye to Jailin, Benny." Johanna took the amazed little boy's hand.

Benny followed his mother's order while still gazing around the room. "Good bye, Jay-Jay." A little hand, in return, stuck out of the covers and grabbed at the air in an attempt to say farewell.

Outside the lab, where Kathy was writing the last observation and putting Socrates in his cage, she heard a loud bang.

"That must be Ted's car door." Kathy lit up and forgot to latch Socrates' cage. She flew outside the back door of her lab which led to the driveway.

Jailin was still in bed waiting for her mother to come up like Johanna had promised. She heard her mother's voice outside and stood up on her bed to peek out the window.

"What are you doing here this late? Why do you have Ted's Jeep? And who's in the back seat? Oh my God, please... *NO*!"

Jailin never saw anyone but her mother outside her window. The Jeep was veiled in darkness and whoever was near it was also invisible to her little eyes. She watched her mother fall, after hearing two loud pops. Getting out of her little bed, she made her way down the hall. A door that was left open distracted her and she was surrounded by a new sight. There were tall counters, stools, microscopes, beakers, cups, and bottles scattered around the room like someone had rushed to take what was important and leave. The door to a mini fridge, that was about the same height as her, was open a crack. She pulled it open and saw a test tube with blue liquid in it.

"Wata!" Jailin pulled out the test tube and drank it. Immediately she got drowsy and fell asleep on the floor.

The two gun shots startled Socrates after Kathy left the lab. In his fear, he ran circles in his crate until the unlocked door swung open. He jumped down and found his way through the hallways of the house and before he knew it he was in the room with Jailin curled up on the floor. He considered continuing his hunt for a hiding spot but instead snuggled up on top of her and fell asleep.

At one in the morning, two unidentified agents had found Jailin and Socrates in the lab. The one man woke Socrates when he lifted him, but Jailin was still asleep.

"Agent Levin, it looks like she's been drugged," a stocky agent announced as another skinny senior ranked agent came in the room.

"Find any ID on the blonde out back, Reilly?" The skinny one with a bushy mustache asked. He hadn't had the mustache on his face for long. He kept rubbing and scratching it.

"Yeah. She's the housekeeper and nanny. Her name is Johanna Bailey. No criminal records. Husband was Nicolas Bailey, we found him viciously mauled to death not far from the house. According to Mrs. Bailey's sister, he went out with Dr. Munrow on research frequently." The stocky agent rubbed the back of his neck. He still had trouble adjusting to the heat of Grundagon.

"I take it the brunette is Dr. Munrow."

"Yes, but not *the* Dr. Munrow. That doctor was his wife, Kathleen."

"Ah, yes, Ted. I've read about him. Have you found him?" He walked around the room, picking up a paper here, moving a test tube over there.

"No. Not yet."

"Might be something to look into there. We should get this marked as a crime scene. Try not to move anything around." He wiped his fingers on his pant leg, and then scratched his mustache. "Find anything else of significance?"

"There's some strange cat prints in the dirt outside. You want to look?"

"Sure. Did you check with the sister about caring for the little girl, since she's watching the boy until the grandparents come get him?" He opened the small animal cage another man had dropped off and waited for the stocky man to put the ring-tailed lemur inside.

"She said she would until either Dr. Munrow is found or a will declares a legal guardian." The stocky man turned and picked up the little girl. Without waking she snuggled herself against his strong build.

"Charming." The man roughly smoothed his facial hair with his thumb and index finger. The two agents left the room. The thin one was holding the cage with Socrates and the other held Jailin asleep in his arms.

Jailin had listened intently while Bailey told the story of that dreadful night. There was a lot to think about while she waited for him outside the tent. When he called to her, she pulled the flap to the tent aside and peered in cautiously.

"Welcome to my humble abode!" he said with a smile and held his arms out to his sides in an inviting way. During the time she was waiting, he had changed his clothes. He wore loose, stonewashed jeans with a black muscle tank under an unbuttoned gray shirt. His belt was now a simple black leather one with no weapons or tools. In fact, she didn't see those items anywhere in the tent at all.

"You live *here*?" She peered around at the small area. A sleeping bag was rolled up in one corner. There was a small portable radio and a solar energy coffee maker. Two black bags were piled in the corner and a cell phone sat on top of a few manila folders.

He laughed in response to her question. "No. This is just temporary."

"What do you mean?" She had never heard of a home being temporary. This was so secluded she felt sorry for him. He must be so lonely.

"I do what I must to fulfill my needs. Then I quickly move on. If I stay in one place too long someone's sure to find me out." This comment made Jailin raise one eyebrow at the different interpretations his words implied. "For work! That's all. I didn't mean…" He trailed off now that he understood the sexual implication that his word choices had made.

"So how do you know about… *that* night? You were six and staying with your aunt."

"First of all your house is… let's call it decaying. Not that it isn't still standing, it is, but anything of any importance or value is gone. The inside has been gutted and destroyed, possibly by angry poachers, passers-by, animals, and or thieves." While he talked, he moved some things around. It appeared as if he was cleaning up for company and embarrassed by the few things he had lying around.

"I know. I've gone back a couple of times. All I found was my mother's necklace in the sandbox." She traced her hand along the side of the tent. She hadn't felt a fabric like this before. The Maimugg tribe didn't have anything like this. It was smooth and strong, but not strong enough to keep out a determined hunter.

"Ah, yes, the necklace." He smiled over the edge of the coffee cup he had filled. Sitting on the ground, he watched her inspect her surroundings. He could tell she was resilient and that impressed him.

"You said this symbol is all over North Central City. Why?" She lifted the pendant up so he could see it.

"It's a logo for a company called Vernore Biotech and Pharmaceuticals. I'm not sure what they do exactly, but by way of that symbol it's more like, what don't they do?"

"How come I only remember living in the Grundagon Jungle with the Maimugg Tribe? I don't recall living with your aunt." She was back to rubbing her hand up and down the tent wall. She liked the texture against her palm.

"That's because you didn't. Coffee?" Bailey got up from sitting in the middle of the tent and went to fill his cup.

She sat down and waited for him to come back and sit where he had just stood up from. "No, thank you. I just want to know what you know."

"Well, how about we start with what you know about yourself?"

Fists firmly placed on the ground behind her, she leaned back to look up at the poles that formed the top of the tent. She rattled off her abilities like she had told numerous people this over and over, and yet she had to tell it again. "I have the speed of a cheetah, the strength of a lowland gorilla, the farsighted vision of a hawk and the night vision of a cat, the agility of an acoughi, the reaction time of a viper, the memory and acute hearing of an elephant. I can smell and taste anything individually like a wolf and lastly…"

"Good lord. What's left?"

"The mating season of a Hoatzin. One night a year, I seek… during the rainy season. Well, I'm supposed to, but luckily I'm sedated through it."

"Ma… mating season? What do you mean? You don't have to tell me if you don't want to. Maybe I could help or something, err, I mean…" He was caught off guard by her sudden mention of sexual behavior. Without thinking his mouth just rattled off what came to his mind.

"Why are you talking so fast?" she interrupted his rambling.

"Huh? I'm not am I?" He looked away and rubbed his jaw line. He took another swallow of his coffee.

"Yes."

"Sorry," he apologized faintly, searching for a new topic to distract her from his embarrassment.

"I can hardly remember my parent's faces." She changed the subject for him. "I only recall playing with this while my mother held me." Jailin was turning the pendant over and over between her fingers.

"Do you recall my face?" He turned to look into her eyes. He didn't know why he had asked that question of the many that were floating around in his head. Words kept rolling out of his mouth. There was no way to stop them.

"No." She hadn't looked up from the pendant.

"Oh." His shoulders slumped forward. The hope he had for restarting their friendship fell with them.

"I mean, maybe if I saw a childhood picture, but my memory recalls exacts, kinda like déjà vu. I can store twelve percent more in my memory than normal humans do." Her eyes finally came up to meet his.

"Sounds interesting to study." His eyes locked with hers. For the first time he noticed the detail of them. They were the color of fresh moss after the rain with a hint of yellow grass that sways in the wind—her eyes captured the specks of what the wind carried away.

"No it doesn't." She smiled and averted her eyes. "Tell me about yourself," she changed the subject.

"Hmm… well, my aunt never married. She never had children. She was hell to live with and she was…" He trailed off.

"What?"

"A bitch. Sorry. I can't come up with anything nicer. She thought if she raised the daughter of Grundagon's priceless zoologists, she might get money out of it. She didn't do anything out of the kindness of her own heart. We both only stayed that one night with my aunt." Bailey had made his way to a strong pillar in the tent and leaned against it.

"What happened to you after that?" She had caught Bailey off guard by the sympathetic tone in her voice.

"You were fostered, as you know, and I was sent to my grandparents. They were really regimented and sent me to military school as soon as possible. It was either that or home school and they weren't the teaching type. At eighteen, I got transferred to a different… um, department. I chose not to go to college, but I got the same education from GIA, maybe even better."

Jailin got up to open the flap of the tent and peered out at Socrates who was sunbathing on a rock. She loved the meditating posture of the little primate. The way his paws rested on his knees and his head, eyes closed, tilted slightly up, toward the sun. Usually she teased him about this—saying it was "an awfully girly thing to do."

The cat laid next to the rock on his back with his paws in the air and appeared to be asleep.

"How did you know I was living in the jungle—if we both only stayed the one night with your aunt?" she asked.

He glanced down at his feet and rubbed the back of his neck. "You think GIA doesn't know these things?" He decided to change the subject when he saw her scowl. "Tell me how you two got back together." Bailey was pointing in Socrates' direction with his other arm across his chest.

"Socrates? He never really left. My mother was his mother and we both miss her very much." She smiled at Socrates. "I meant after those agents had him in a cage that night. What did they do with him?"

"I don't know. He's never talked about it." Jailin closed the flap and turned back to Bailey with a slight smirk on her face.

"Never *talked* about it?" Bailey's arms collapsed at his sides. He didn't know what she meant.

"How do you know the specifics of that night? You never said." It occurred to her that he might know about the videos of her parent's research, but how he might have come to find them, she wasn't sure.

"Your parents documented and recorded everything except the man who rented the lab. I only found sound recordings of his work. He never appeared on any of the videos." His brow was still furrowed—trying to comprehend why Jailin would say Socrates never talked about it.

"Mm-hmm and you only *took* the tapes? Perhaps you have information you shouldn't have."

"It's my job to snoop. Besides you didn't answer my question."

"Which was?" She picked at her finger nails.

"Socrates never *talked* about your reuniting because…" He prompted.

"Oh, that!" Jailin started laughing. "I forget about outsiders sometimes. I can speak with animals telepathically." It rolled off her tongue as if she were describing something as simple as tying a knot.

"What? How? That can't be possible!" This bit of information had never come up in any of his field reports.

"It's one of those many side effects to the notorious drink. Sorry, I forgot to mention it earlier." She waived one hand in the air as if it didn't matter.

"Side effect?" Bailey questioned under his breath. He had begun to pace the small area of the tent. While deep in thought, he rubbed his stubble. The nights in the jungle had been long and he couldn't remember the last time he had shaved.

Jailin was suddenly at Bailey's back. He stopped when her hands slid up his shoulder blades. She whispered in his ear. "Would you like to see? I can ask Socrates to come inside."

Bailey's pulse raced at the feel of her warm breath on his neck. He closed his eyes and took a deep breath. A slight tingle ran down his spine as he said, "Uh, sure."

"Socrates? Can you come in here?" she thought.

"Another trust game? Are you positive this is what you desire?"

"Just get in here!"

Socrates opened his eyes, slowly got to his feet, and proceeded into the tent.

"Yeah right! How do I know you don't have him trained to some kind of whistle or something I can't hear?" Bailey couldn't believe his eyes. He'd swear service dogs were trained to do more as public servants than to just enter a tent. This had to be a trick.

"Are you dense? Do you see a whistle?" Jailin got frustrated with the lack of belief. "Tell me what you think he should do and I'll tell him, how's that?"

Bailey walked over to the pile of black bags and picked a pen and paper out of the top one. He wrote: Refill my coffee cup.

Jailin rolled her eyes at this absurd request, but asked Socrates anyway. If this would convince him, so be it.

"Does he require cream and sugar as well?" Socrates rolled his eyes back to Jailin in agreement and walked up to Bailey to take his cup.

"He wants to know if you want cream and sugar." She giggled a little. Socrates could be funny in his own little way.

"Neither." He turned to watch Socrates with his cup and with a sudden reaction of unease, said, "Uh, can you read my mind?"

"No. Homo sapiens are too um… complex."

"What is complexity?" Socrates sat down with the coffee cup, as if to begin a deep debate. "Is it something that you do not understand or that no one understands? Does everyone believe the same conclusion if it sounds good? In the future you might want to choose your words carefully before you make an accusation that humiliates another."

"None of that right now!" Jailin snapped in her thoughts. She knew Socrates liked a good debate when he woke up from a nap, but she wasn't ready to put on a show today.

"But you can't hear my thoughts, right?" Bailey needed reassurance again.

"No," she said straight-faced. Then she smiled and thought she might give him something else to worry about.

"Good." He leaned back up against the rigid pole.

"Although I can hear changes in heart rates and sometimes smell certain chemical imbalances." Jailin turned to leave the tent. She'd let him figure that out on his own and see which was worse: hearing what he thought or sensing how he felt.

Socrates had trailed behind Jailin and stopped when Bailey yelled to her, "You can do what?" Socrates winked at Bailey as the tent flap closed behind him.

Socrates came out of the tent and looked around. No Jailin and no giant cat. "In view of the fact that you are out of my range of sight, I am still optimistic that you are capable of hearing me," he thought. There was no reply. Socrates stuck his nose in the air and found Jailin's scent. He scurried into the trees and lunged from branch to branch. The small ring-tailed lemur moved quickly through the dense leaves. He was used to walking on the ground, but in desperate times the higher the branch the quicker he could fly. Panic escalated and in his mind he yelled Jailin's name over and over.

"Quiet." Socrates halted when Jailin's voice sounded in his head. She came down a few branches from above him and dropped one arm to allow Socrates onto her shoulder. "Dierno says something has been unleashed in the jungle and we need to keep our minds clear."

Abiding with her request, Socrates said nothing. It was only about two in the afternoon by indication of the sun, and it was increasingly hot. Sweat pooled on Jailin's brow and ran down her temples. She wiped her face with the cloth that covered her forearm.

"Dierno, are you still out there?" She listened for any sound the jungle might make—a broken branch, crinkled leaves, or slow breathing. She even inhaled what the wind had to offer.

"I can hear her heartbeat. Can't you?" Dierno's voice whispered in her mind.

"I hear a lot of things, including heartbeats, especially Socrates'. Wait… what *is* that? It's so slow, so quiet." She closed her eyes and tried to listen harder.

"She's sleeping."

"Who is?" The skin between her eyes wrinkled. Jailin couldn't think of anyone or anything in the jungle she hadn't run into before.

"Digna, The Worthy." Dierno's words dripped with revulsion.

"I concur that that suffices as an answer, but it will not prevent the question from being asked again." Socrates informed Dierno of his vague answer.

"She is my sister. Due to our color we usually only go out at night. Unfortunately, when she wakes, she will hunt for new prey."

"What do you mean by new prey?" Jailin had found her way to the teak tree Digna was sleeping in. Digna was draped along one long limb. A mix of large deep green, decaying yellow, and ghostly blue leaves draped around her body. Jailin could see she was a little smaller than Dierno, but how much smaller was not evident due to her distance.

"She's been sent to locate us," Dierno said. He had known Digna wouldn't stay away long. It had been two years—not long enough, since he had last seen her. It wasn't a happy reunion then and he didn't expect it would be any different this time.

"Us?" Jailin inquired.

"You and me. We are special like she is, but her master wants more info, tests, money and power. He wants us."

"Can this master of hers help us?" Jailin was anxious about the possibilities and brought one hand to her chest to lie over the top of her necklace.

"No. He only wants to advance himself. I got lucky. I was thrown away and left to die as a cub. She is perfect. She is worthy. She is Digna." The words came out like a chant. He enunciated her titles as if she were a goddess and not a feral cat.

"I conclude that no matter what we endure, we will indisputably fail against her," Socrates deducted. He had a gift for pointing out the obvious.

"Only if we have to fight her. Though I don't know for sure, Jailin may be our only weapon in his game." Dierno sounded relieved to have finally found Jailin. Perhaps this journey wouldn't be a failure.

"Game?" Jailin squared her shoulders to Dierno and looked up into his eyes with her hands on her hips. "Who thinks this is all just a game?"

"Vernore."

Jailin's hand flashed up to her necklace again. "Vernore? Bailey said this is Vernore's company symbol. This was my mother's. How can this be evil?" She didn't want to believe that something so sentimental could have such a negative connotation.

"Bailey also said evil is relative." Socrates recalled the comment from only hours before. "It makes sense."

"Well then, I guess everyone has to choose a side once and for all," she said aloud to accentuate the importance of her fight against the one who had brought destruction to her family—her life.

"Which side do *you* choose?" A voice came from behind a cluster of trees. When Jailin turned around she saw Bailey leaning his shoulder into the largest teak as if to prop it up.

"*Min*e," Jailin whispered in agitation.

Bailey was unsure if she was upset by whatever had just happened between her and the giant cat or if she was upset with him. "Listen. I'm sorry if I said or did anything to piss you off back there, but I had to make sure you weren't... crazy," he whispered and hoped he hadn't offended her.

"How did you get here?" Jailin asked quietly so she wouldn't wake Digna.

"I've been a snoop in this jungle for a long time and I know how to track. See?" He held up a small device that blinked in the dead center of a screen with a bull's-eye on it. "You didn't think you'd get too far from me did you?" he asked with a wink.

Socrates, who was clenched to her back, reached over her shoulder to show her a small round flashing object. "This was on your shoulder." She took it from him, squeezed it and let it crumble to the ground.

"We must go now. We need a plan and more information. I think Bailey is important to this quest," Dierno thought.

"I suppose you're right," Jailin said aloud by accident.

"Good. I don't let harm come to any of my... friends," Bailey said thinking her reply was meant in return to his statement about not letting her stray too far.

"Shhh. Don't wake her," Jailin pointed up.

"Damn it, another steroid kitty," Bailey said but this time much quieter. He was surprised to see another cat. All this time, he had thought the White Shadow was a legend. Now he'd found two.

"Let's go. I know a place, at least for tonight." Jailin led them through the jungle. She was guiding them from up in the trees. The dense foliage hid her from Bailey's view. Since Socrates preferred to walk on the ground with Dierno, Bailey followed closely behind them.

"Could this cat, maybe, keep some of these branches and vines out of my face?" Pushing the plant life out of his way, he didn't intend to sound rhetorical, but no one answered him or acted as if he had said anything at all.

Water running through a narrow brook could be heard when they came to a wetlands swamp. A wet, almost moldy, smell filled the air. Dierno stepped into the soft dirt and created a deep hole, which Bailey stumbled into. He was covered in mud.

"Stupid cat keeps causing more trouble than he's worth," he mumbled and shook the excess mud from his hands, then looked at his legs for a clean spot to wipe them.

"His name is Dierno." Jailin was hanging upside down from a limb looking at Bailey while he tried desperately to get the mud off.

"Oh, yeah? He told you that?" He sounded sarcastic and this question was intended to be rhetorical.

"Yes." She flipped down from the branch landing in the mud on both feet. A little mud splashed up into Bailey's face.

"Right. Why do I even bother?" He wiped his chin on his bicep, which was the cleanest area on him.

"Why do you bother? You're so mean to him and I don't know how he ignores you so easily," Jailin said. She was fed up with

Bailey's whining. This was not the boy she remembered. This man was annoying and a complete baby.

"He killed *my* parents and *your* mother." His eyes burned and his teeth clenched together.

"A man killed my mother with two bullets and *you* have no proof of what you say. There are no recordings of that!" She prodded his chest with her finger. She was stronger than he had realized. It felt like iron was being jammed into him.

"I have mention of a giant cat print outside your house! Indisputable." He pushed her hand away from his chest and pointed to the hole in the mud he had just picked himself out of.

"Didn't you see the giant cat in the tree back there?" She pointed in the direction they had just come from.

"Yeah, I did and that means there are two! And a female no less, so now we can breed them, right? Make more monstrosities!" Both their tempers were flaring. Dierno and Socrates looked at each other and would have continued on without them had they not cared for the safety of those two.

Jailin slapped him across the face. "Be a man and stop whining." His head flew to the side. She had such force in it for such a small body. He was amazed at the pain radiating through his cheek.

"Excuse me?" He slowly turned his face back to hers. An outline of her hand was painted on his cheek. Jailin's back was already to him and walking away into the swamp. Bailey sighed and rubbed away the pain. "Why are we walking in this swamp, anyway?"

"The man must be suffering from acute memory loss. Did he not say he was in the military at one point?" Socrates was looking back over his shoulder at Bailey who was sloshing through the mud looking like a stubborn child.

Jailin stopped. "Are you serious?" Everyone stopped and looked at her. She turned to Bailey. "You're not military, are you?"

"What? Why do you say that?" He watched his feet slosh in the thickening mud.

"You just asked why we are walking in this swamp. You also said that you knew this jungle. If so, you know this leads to a stream and that an animal can't track a smell in flowing water."

"I know that." He didn't sound convincing and Jailin heard the lack of confidence in his statement.

"Best to keep in mind, Jailin, that he is full of various insights and knowledge of the past and abilities unbeknownst. Must we press him anymore before we reach home?" Socrates tried to keep Jailin calm and avoid regrets for what her temper might cause her to do.

"Fine," Jailin thought. "Never mind," she said to Bailey.

They made their way deeper into the swamp. The water started to run clear and Bailey stopped once to wash the remaining mud from his hands and face. By dusk, the trees had parted and revealed a small clearing with a few small huts. They continued to follow the stream as it led to the smallest isolated hut off to the side. In the dark it didn't look like much of a home. It was drafty and uncomfortable in appearance—almost eerie.

"Finally." Jailin relaxed and a smile hinted across her face.

"You live *here*?" Bailey's voice reflected the same tone Jailin had used in regard to his tent.

"Hello, brother," the thought came out of the shadows and eyes glowed like fire.

6

Everything was still. A strange feeling washed over Bailey. He turned around when Jailin didn't answer him. Her face was pale and she stood so motionless that she might as well have stopped breathing. "What's wrong?" He had no idea that next to the hut eyes were burning out of the darkness.

"Digna," was all Jailin could whisper. Bailey turned to look—her eyes were locked on her hut. One foot stepped out of the darkness. It was white and huge. Large round eyes reflected and then the black nose and white muzzle appeared. The head towered over a long gap of darkness above the displayed foot. It waited, paused for impact. Then it slinked out of the darkness, showing everyone a profile of strength and tenacity. As it crossed in front of Jailin's hut, the tail curved down, then back up at the ankles. It sat in front of the door and squared its body to everyone.

"My dear brother, Diega. It's been a long time." Digna purred and licked her paw, then rubbed it across her face. Until now it wasn't visible that the only differences between the two giant cats were their eyes. Both of the cats' eyes were outlined blacker than night, but Dierno's one eye was a beautiful forest green and the other was blue like the ocean on a stormy day. Digna's were bright red like the fires of hell. Her right eye had an elongated black spike stretching out of the corner toward her ear. From the top and bottom, spikes extended out from the slim pupil and were connected by a half circle that dissected the spike at the corner. Her eyes were enchanting, even if they were evil.

"It's Dierno now… *sister.*" His voice gave away the anger he had been storing up over the years.

"Oh? When did you decide this?" She seemed to be enjoying this game of catch up.

"As soon as I no longer had a master and the name he gave no longer suited me." Dierno sat back on his haunches and waited for her to process that night from so long ago.

"It will suit you for as long as we both shall live." The heat in her eyes increased. Jailin thought she noted a quick change in a heartbeat, but whoever it belonged to, it slowed just as quickly as it had started.

"You mean as long as you live, Worthy One."

"Ugh, she sounds more like a wife than a sister." Jailin pretended to hold back vomit as she thought this to Socrates who was now crouched on her shoulder.

"Wait, why did you do that? What's going on?" Bailey was feeling left out since he couldn't hear any of the conversations. Especially one that caused Jailin to exhibit an action which portrayed disgust about what had been said.

"Now is not the time to explain. Keep an eye out for others." She figured that giving Bailey a job would keep him busy. And keep him from annoying her.

"Mmm… fun." Bailey was less than thrilled, but looked around anyway.

"You found the girl. Such a good brother. And to think my master thought less of you." She was squinting at Jailin as if to assess her enemy and gather information.

"I did not find her for you. I was looking for him. I mistook him as one of yours." Dierno glanced at Bailey as he mentioned him.

"Do you believe you are an avid hunter now? Did you learn something we could not teach?" Digna insinuated that no one was better off without Vernore. She'd experienced enough of his genius to know better.

"Yeah, it's called honor, friendship, and love."

"Touché, brother." Digna got up and sauntered over to them. Bailey took a few steps to the side, searching for an escape if needed. Jailin and Dierno stood their ground.

"You two know something I don't? She's gonna kill us, isn't she?" Bailey's voice was alarmed, but he noticed that neither Jailin nor Dierno followed him.

"It's called courage, you wuss." Jailin spat back. She didn't understand how someone so muscled would be so quick to run away. It occurred to her that he was either a fantastic actor or he was hiding something.

"Enlighten me. What is courage? Is holding our footing really wha…"

"Not now, Socks!" Jailin cut off Socrates with the nickname he hated most. She couldn't see him perched on her shoulder, nor would she take her eyes off any potential danger, but she knew Socrates had made the same abashed face he always did when she cut him off from his debates.

"I am not your kitten nor do I share any of the biological makeup of one. So, as I have stated before, please refra…"

Jailin cut him off again. "Stop it!"

"And she said I sounded like a wife." Digna turned Jailin's own joke against her. Jailin in return got frustrated and put her hand to her bo staff as a passive threat. "Now, now, pet. We don't need to go to that extreme, do we? I'm just here to talk."

"Talk?" Jailin was suddenly confused and unsure if she should trust this. Too many adversaries had told her they were just going to talk before they made their moves.

"We're okay," Dierno reassured her.

"Yes, of course, brother. No need to fear me." Her tail whipped side to side as if anticipating a game of cat and mouse.

"Who should I worry about?" Jailin knew nothing good ever came of pretending creatures lived by their words.

"Hmm." Digna looked up at the stars. "I will show you something and then you can decide who to worry about. Who, in the end, will be your friends and who will be your enemies?" Digna walked around Jailin as if to size her up, taking in everything she could. Finally, she sat in front of Jailin and they were eye to eye.

"What is it you want me to see?" Jailin asked as Digna's paw slowly came up off the ground.

"Don't touch her!" Bailey who had been watching this whole silent charade from the sidelines, came up behind Digna to hit her in the back with what looked like a tree branch compared to her size, but was rather large for Bailey. As his arms came down, Digna turned her head, caught it in her mouth and snapped the branch in half.

"Tell your boyfriend to back off or I'll snap him like that stick." The fire in her eyes roared and Jailin again could hear that same heartbeat quicken as before and then die out.

"Ben, back up. I'm fine." Jailin cocked her head to look around Digna to warn him as asked.

"Uh..." Bailey was stunned. It took him forever to take a few steps backward after hearing the use of his first name.

"This time it's purely psychological, but next time it won't be. Take my left paw and look at my pad." She raised her paw slightly.

As Jailin slowly reached for Digna's paw, a flash of the man who had rented the lab at her parent's house came into her mind. He was thin with dark hair and a long, drawn face. He looked starved and sleep-deprived. He was dressed in a black-collared polo shirt, khaki pants and a long white lab coat. He was on one knee in his neatly organized lab, teaching a small, white domestic-looking kitten to shake.

Jailin shook the memory from her mind and looked at Digna's paw. There, tattooed on the bottom, was the pendant. Vernore's symbol. Jailin dropped it and backed away. "Is this it? What you came to show me? Were you sent to kill me too?" Jailin's thoughts were rushed and nervous.

"Psychological tonight, physical another." The red eyes backed away slowly. This cat knew something and she wasn't telling Jailin what it could be.

"In that case go, sister," Dierno said as he stepped between them. Bailey saw this and got angry at the allowance of a cat to defend his childhood friend—even if it was a massive cat.

"Yes. It's about time. I'll see you later, little one," she whispered in Jailin's direction. "Brother." She nodded to Dierno, then took off into the shadows.

"What was that about?" Bailey was a little scared, and nervous, but especially angry. He didn't look as if he could contain himself any longer. He began pacing back and forth, which he did when he was anxious.

"I wish I knew." Jailin was staring at her feet. Her hand was placed lightly on Dierno's shoulder at the highest point she could reach and Socrates cuddled his head into the back of her neck.

"What did she say? Why did you get so scared? You still look frightened or sad. I can't tell which." Bailey was still agitated. Nothing was making any sense to him.

Jailin raised her head and looked at Bailey. Her eyes suddenly went darker as they dilated to reach deeper into the darkness behind him. "Not you!" Jailin bent down and then sprung on Bailey in one quick motion. He couldn't react quickly enough and she had stretched her arms around his chest, sending them both to the ground. "Dierno! Cover me while I get Ben inside!" She was squatting over Bailey's waist with her hands on his shoulders. He had passed out after his head hit a stump that was partially buried in moss and fallen foliage. Once she had him sitting up she pushed one shoulder under his arm and hoisted him up to take him inside her hut. Dierno had taken off in pursuit.

"Socrates, get Meovi over here to look after him. Stay here until I get back and be safe," Jailin ordered.

She emerged from the small hut after putting Bailey inside and looked deep into the woods. She closed her eyes and inhaled deeply. "This is the last time, Carlos," she yelled to the entire cruel world.

"Who are we chasing?" Dierno asked Jailin as she jumped through the trees from limb to limb, swaying under her massive strength and speed. Dierno was maneuvering his way through the trees, dead brush, and uplifted roots below her. The darkness of the night didn't slow down either of them. The trees became less dense as they made their way toward the tourist and camping grounds of the jungle.

"Someone with too much time on his hands," she thought in return.

"What's his purpose?"

"To catch and resell exotics in the city pet shop. He's been after Socrates forever it seems."

"Then we have no choice but to stop him."

They reached an area which had been cleared for parking the vehicles of those who were hiking or camping along the trails of the jungle. A large white van that read North Central Exotic Pets in bright bubbly letters intended to attract children into begging their parents for a new pet was parked under the cover of large flat leaves and branches. It hadn't been moved in some time.

"Wait here a minute," Jailin told Dierno. She climbed up one of the mahogany trees and turned off a camera placed at an angle to record the parking lot. When she finished she returned to Dierno's side. "All set. This should be fun!"

"What were you doing?"

"I monitor the campers, fisherman, and hunters who park here. I make sure they behave themselves."

"And this particular man doesn't?"

"Exactly." A sound of a breaking twig was heard in the distance. "Quick, hide! Here he comes." She hid inside the back of his van and Dierno hid in the trees just on the other side of the van. From over the ledge of the back window she saw Carlos emerge from the woods. He looked tired and a little worried. He dropped the duffle bag he was carrying and his tranquilizer gun on the ground and reached up to open the back door.

"Hello, Carlos," Jailin said as he opened the door. She sprang at him, pushing his chest to the ground with her bo staff in her hands. He was used to fighting with her and when they hit the ground he pushed her over his head. Jailin somersaulted up onto her feet but still remained crouched low to the ground. Carlos jumped up on his feet and as he turned to face Jailin, she foot-swept him and he was back on the ground. Jailin sprang up out of her crouch to pounce on him, but he was already crawling toward his tranquilizer gun. Jailin quickly got to her feet and ran past him. She picked up the gun and shot all the tranquilizers into the closest tree. Carlos' eyes bulged and he froze in place. Without having to look she unlocked the closest animal cage to let the few go that he had already caught that day.

"You've been selling animals that are illegal to own as pets due to their extinction rating. If I hand you over to GIA, you're finished."

"I get fine. I pay. I go. No more. You see." He acted cocky, trying to bluff his way out of being caught.

"Then I guess I'll leave you to the great outdoors that you *love* so much." As she said this she thought to Dierno, "Look hungry and angry as you show yourself."

"No! No! I go! Never sell again!" he said as he saw Dierno appear from out of the trees. He scrambled up to his feet and ran off into the trees, pushing leaves and vines out of his way.

"We have to finish this tonight or he'll be back. He's lied like this too many times. I'm tired of giving him the benefit of the doubt," she thought to Dierno as they ran off after him. "You're an illegal immigrant Carlos! You might live longer out here in the wild," she yelled out.

Jailin had taken to the trees again. She didn't like the obstructed views of running on the ground in the dense blackness of the undergrowth—if she could help it. She caught up and swung down on top of Carlos, putting all her weight on him as they fell to the ground. They rolled and when she pinned him down on his back his elbow came up and hit her in the jaw. A small drip of blood came down her lip. She brought one hand up to wipe the blood away but before she could Carlos twisted out beneath her and kicked her against a tree.

Jailin grunted at the impact, then quickly got up and ran after him. His run was like baby steps compared to her speed and she tackled him again. This time she grabbed both of his arms and then popped open her staff to wind the wire around his hands behind his back.

When she was sure the knot would hold, she wiped the blood from her mouth with the back of her arm and then lifted him to his feet. She felt his pockets for knives or anything he could use to get away. She found only his cell phone and held on to it as she guided him back to his van.

"What are you going to do with him?" Dierno asked.

"Turn him in," she answered.

"How's your jaw?"

"Stings. I've been through worse, though."

They reached the van and while Dierno held the back of Carlos' shirt, she opened the duffle bag that was on the ground. Out of the bag she pulled two ropes. She pushed Carlos down at the base of the tree she had shot the tranquilizers into and retied his hands behind it. Using the second rope as reinforcement, she again tied this around his torso and the tree. Once he was secure, she opened his phone and dialed the North Central Police.

The dispatcher answered and she dropped the phone into a pile of leaves while yelling. "Help! He's trying to hurt me!"

"No! No hurt!" Carlos yelled back.

She pulled out a videotape from inside her vest and said, "They'll like this tape. Maybe you'll remember this day. It shows you with three Shoebills and two Slow Loris'." She tucked the tape inside an envelope and found a marker in the duffle bag. She wrote I'm guilty on the envelope and then tucked it into the rope wrapped around his chest.

Carlos began to kick and thrash against the tree trying to free himself. "Let. Me. Go," he shouted over and over.

"Maybe *you* need a tranquilizer," she said with her arms crossed over her chest.

"My store, my family?" he questioned, trying to get her to feel some remorse.

"Oh, the animals will be put back in the jungle, *where they belong*. Your store will be sold to someone else who wants to abuse the system and if they are smarter than you, they won't sell exotic animals. And perhaps you should be more worried about your family than anything else."

"You no hurt them?"

"Heavens, no. *They* haven't been trying to catch and resell *my* family, have they?"

"No. They do nothing." He hung his head. Dirt fell from his hair onto his chest.

"I have advised you do the same in the past. You'd better hope they have their papers filed correctly or they'll be leaving with you."

"You be sorry. I know bad man. He help me. You see." Carlos' face showed the anger he felt toward Jailin. He raised his head and squinted his eyes with his bottom jaw jutted forward.

"Not if he's smart he won't." She tied a cloth around his mouth and then turned her back to him. "See you soon, Carlos. Oh, wait, no I won't," she said as she and Dierno were walking into the trees.

After she was out of sight she rubbed at her jaw line where Carlos had hit her. A small bruise was beginning to show and a small cut on her bottom lip where she had bitten it was still bright with blood. She stopped and looked up at one of the cameras in the tree.

"Where did you get those?" Dierno asked when he noticed where she was looking.

"My parent's house. They came in pretty handy for them, so I took them just in case. Little did I know that Bailey had already been there and taken the tapes that recorded what actually happened to our parents that night. I thought the missing numbered tapes were recordings of animal research so I taped over the ones I took to make sure the jungle was safe. That's how I found Carlos."

"You've been protecting the animals here for a long time?"

"As long as I can remember," she said, smiling up at the cloudless night sky through the break in the thick foliage.

"You're a good girl, Jailin. Strong-tempered, but still good."

"Gee, thanks, Dierno."

They headed back to Jailin's hut, feeling depleted of all energy. Jailin walked along side Dierno instead of using the trees this time.

8

Jailin emerged from the shadows of the trees to the small clearing where her hut was. The sun peeked over the horizon, casting a golden hue over her home. The beauty of this place was welcoming, but Jailin couldn't consider it home in her heart. Not when she felt like such an outsider—alone with no true family to welcome her.

The sun reflected off the pond next to the hut. It connected to a small stream that ran far back into the trees. The hut was constructed of logs and mud. One window was structured next to the front door and another faced toward the other huts concealed behind it. There was a smoking chimney in the far corner.

Jailin entered her hut. It had an open floor plan and standing in the entryway she surveyed the kitchen that contained a fridge, a wood-burning stove that exhaled smoke, and a small two-seater table. Off the kitchen on the left was a door that led to the attached bathroom. Dividing the room from the kitchen was a pulled curtain which concealed the bed from the view of the kitchen. Bailey was still sleeping on the single mattress lying on the floor. A small circular table was positioned next to the threshold.

Standing at the wood-burning stove was a stocky woman in a long brown dress with a black sash tied around her waist. She had a long black braid down her back laced with a single red ribbon.

"Morning, Meovi." Jailin didn't look at her while she took her bo staff off her back and propped it against the table by the door.

"Busy girl. You've been gone awhile."

"Yeah, a lot has been happening lately."

"And the man? It's not the rainy season yet." She watched Jailin fidget out of the corner of her eye.

"Oh, lord no, nothing like that, Meovi."

"He's cute. I know, I know. It's none of my business anyhow." She held up her hands admitting defeat to a stare of anger.

"Has he woken yet?" Jailin turned to stare down at Bailey, watching his bare chest slowly rise and fall.

"Tossing and turning through the night. Nothing that says he's been conscious enough to make sense of anything."

"I found Carlos." She tried to hide her smile, knowing how Meovi felt about her crusades. "I think we're finally rid of him."

"Please don't get in over your head. I don't want to hear that you…"

"Meovi, please."

"I know I'm not your mother, but I still worry."

"A little too much. Keep an eye on him while I take a bath, will you?"

"Of course, Anaba."

Jailin turned back outside to bathe in the pond while Socrates and Dierno curled up on the floor at the foot of the bed and fell asleep.

Meovi brought a warm towel, a cup of tea, and Bailey's cleaned clothes over to him at the bed. She wiped his face with the towel and he began to stir. She lifted his head and held the tea to his mouth. He drank slowly and laid his head back down.

"What *is* that?" Bailey's voice was hoarse as he experienced the aftertaste of the tea.

"I know it's unpleasant, but it clears up any ailment in a jiffy."

"Where am I?" He looked around, but he didn't recognize a single thing before his eyes.

"This is Jailin's home."

"Jailin! Where is she? Is she okay?" Bailey sounded desperate.

"Calm down." Meovi wiped his brow with the towel. "She's outside. She'll be back in in a minute."

Bailey got up out of the bed feeling a little weak. He threw on his newly cleaned jeans and tank, then snapped his knife back around his waist while he headed to the door.

"Where are you going?" Meovi shuffled after him.

"I need to know what happened last night." He closed the door behind him.

"Where does she find these guys?" Meovi asked herself and went back to the stove.

"Jailin!" Bailey yelled to the surrounding jungle.

"What are you yelling about?" Her voice came from the pond next to the hut. Only her head was visible above the water. Damp hair was piled up on top of her head which she rested on a rock, while the sun tanned her face.

"Uh… what are you doing?"

"Taking a bath. What do you want?" Jailin's hands came out of the water to adjust her hair as she lifted her head.

"I… I just… What happened to your face? Are you okay?" He saw the slight bruise on her jaw line and the gnash in her lip.

"I'm fantastic. And how are you? How's your head?"

"Actually, it doesn't hurt now." He patted his head in amazement. "What happened last night?"

"Well, first I was passively threatened by a cat and then I chased down the man I've been after."

"Oh… I see. So, you really like this guy?" He ran a finger along his jaw to indicate her bruise.

"Good lord, I'm not dating him. I finally got him arrested or deported for illegally selling exotics. Geez, what kind of girl do you take me for?" Jailin turned her back to him then rose up out of the water to get her towel that was folded a little farther away from the water. Her back glistened in the sun with the water pooled at her waist. Bailey could see a small tribal tattoo at the base of her neck above her shoulder blades. He gulped and turned away. Trying to rid the images of the slender curves of her body was difficult enough. She wrapped the towel around herself and let her long wet hair fall down her back. Her bangs fell over her eyes.

"Sorry, I just thought that…" He began to rub his head, scrunching up his blonde hair at his forehead. It looked disheveled, as if he'd tossed and turned in his sleep non-stop.

"That what?"

"That you might not be living *alone* out here."

"I'm not. I have Meovi. And no, I'm not into girls, jerk!"

"I didn't say that!" Bailey watched her pick up her clothes and walk back into the hut. He sighed and followed her back in.

Meovi had two bowls of vegetable soup placed at the table. "Come eat. You both must be starving." She grabbed Jailin and Bailey by the elbows and escorted them to the table.

"Please, Meovi. I need to get out of this towel." She tiptoed around Dierno, who took up most of the floor, grabbed new clothes from a small chest by her bed and slipped into the bathroom.

"You sit here and don't anger her." She plopped Bailey down at the table.

"I don't do it on purpose."

"I know, but you could at least think before you speak."

Bailey's lips tightened into a hard line as if he knew she was right and had no other way to show his concurrence.

Jailin came back out in a black v-neck vest trimmed in baby blue. She wore her usual tiny black shorts and the same black arm gauntlets that wrapped over the web of her thumb and pointer fingers. On her feet she wore the same black slipper-like shoes and leg gauntlets that stretched over her knees. Her hair was still down as she went through a drawer by her bed for the five clasps she used to tie her long dark hair back. Three were for her pony tail and the others were for the untamed strands by her ears.

"You're going on patrol? You should rest first." Meovi's concern always made Jailin feel as if she were still a little girl.

"I'm thinking about it. I'm at least going to take Socrates and Dierno with me."

"Not my place to ask, but is that huge cat safe?"

"Safer than this man so far." Jailin threw her head in Bailey's direction.

"For someone so unsafe, why did you bother getting him out of harm's way last night?" Meovi interrogated.

"Yeah!" Bailey popped up in his chair. He was thrilled someone was on his side. The smile revealed his glee to the entire room.

"I don't need this right now." Jailin felt defensive and looked toward an empty corner in the room.

"Eat first. Then do what you want." It was an order, not a suggestion.

"Can I patrol with you?" Bailey's eyes widened with hope.

"You wouldn't be of much help and probably more of a liability."

"Those two look like they can use the rest. Doesn't that make them a liability? You look like you could use the rest too."

"Thanks for the concern, but I've got research to do."

"Maybe I could help?"

"Oh yeah? And when you feel like telling me the whole truth then maybe I'll let you help."

"I wish I could, but I can't."

She rolled her eyes. He was still playing this game. "Why not?"

"I don't have the clearance to tell you. I joined that ridiculous poaching group to find answers about my childhood. I've never killed anything except a fly or mosquito."

Jailin smiled at Bailey's failed attempt at sincerity. "Ben, listen."

"Ben? This is the second time you've called me that! Except when you were five and it was Benny then. What's changed?" A smile came across Bailey's face, which replaced his concern about Jailin's detachment from him.

"Don't question a good thing, boy!" Meovi swung a hand towel against the back of his head. He smiled over his shoulder at Meovi. When he looked back to Jailin her smile was gone.

“I’m sorry. You were saying?” Bailey said while trying to conceal his bliss.

“Forget it. I’m going out.” Jailin turned and walked over to Socrates and Dierno. “Either of you coming with me?” she thought.

Socrates turned his head up to her. “I will resolve to sleep on your back.” He jumped onto her outstretched arm and up to her back.

“Dierno?”

“He is still asleep. He has a communication block that he cannot control when he falls asleep.”

“Fine.” She grabbed the shoulder sling holding her bo staff that she had propped against the table earlier and walked out the door.

“She’s not a normal girl. You can’t treat her like one,” Meovi suggested to Bailey.

“What am I supposed to do? Mark my territory?”

“Cute. Not a genius though.”

“I don’t even know why I’m here. This is ridiculous. I should just go back to the city and forget all of this.”

“She doesn’t know it yet, but she needs you.”

“Then tell her to come find me when she figures it out. I’m going home.”

“Where is home?”

“Vernore Manor Apartments on the south side of North Central City. She can send a bird to get me if needed.” Bailey tried to make it sound like a joke, but it came out sounding sadder than he intended.

9

Bailey turned the key to the lock on his one-bedroom apartment and crossed the threshold. Throwing his keys in front of the TV, he collapsed on his blue, fluffy couch. To block out the light, he covered his eyes with his arm.

"Lord, I could sleep for a year." Just as the words had left his mouth the phone rang. "Hello?" he asked drowsily.

"O.M.G. Benji! Where have you been? I've been calling and calling and calling. Why haven't you called me?" The high, flighty voice spoke so quickly Bailey didn't need to know what had been said. The quick voice was enough.

"Hey, Tabitha. What's up?" He couldn't have sounded any less enthused.

"*What's up*?! That's what you say after you've been gone for like ever?"

"Listen, I just got in. Can I call you later or something?"

"Oh, oh, oh, it's *leg* night tonight! You didn't forget did you?"

"Uh, yeah, I did… so?"

"So? Baby, you love leg night and their catchy phrase: '*Bring long lady legs and all you can eat chicken wings are on the house*!' We haven't gone out in so long. I thought this would be perfect!" Her shrill, high voice was giving Bailey the headache of his life.

"I'm exhausted. I'm staying home."

"What will you eat? You don't cook, Benji."

"Stop calling me that! I'll figure something out, maybe a salad."

"Salad? Are you sick?"

"Nope, not yet."

"Not yet? Are you starting to feel sick?"

"Sure feels like it." He had intended to say "sick of you," but thought better of it.

"I'll come right over. I'll be your little nurse. Give you everything your heart desires." He could hear the innuendo through the phone and rolled his eyes.

"No, thanks."

"Why not? Come on baby, it will be fun. Are you ignoring me?"

"Things at work aren't going as planned, okay? I may lose my job when I check in and I don't have time to play games with you."

"Okay, but you'll call me, right?"

"Yeah, sure."

"All right… bye-bye, Benji."

Bailey didn't bother to say goodbye. He hung up and reattempted to fall asleep on the couch.

"What do you mean he left?" Jailin's voice was raised in anger at Meovi.

"You acted as though you couldn't have cared less, Anaba."

"I'm not upset he's not here. I'm pissed off because he had that disc on him. Now what?"

"You may not want to hear this, but he did say you could send a bird to get him." Meovi hid the smile with her cup of tea.

"A bird! Like a carrier pigeon? Ridiculous! I still have no idea who he really is, other than someone from my childhood. What kind of man is he? What was he really doing with the poachers? Why was he after that cougar if he didn't intend to hurt it? God, I have so many questions that no one can seem to answer!"

"Choose your questions wisely, Anaba."

"I can answer most of those." Dierno lifted his head off the floor and looked at Jailin.

"How do you know him so well?" she said aloud to Dierno, indicating that the conversation with Meovi was over.

"Unlike you, I can read human thoughts, as long as the human is unaware of it, anyway. I can block my thoughts and so can a human if they become aware that there is trespassing going on in their minds, so anything he's thought, I've heard."

"Tell me what you know."

Dierno stood up and slowly stalked toward her, which for his size was only a couple of steps. "He's a member of the Grundagon Intelligence Agency, also known as GIA. Basically, he's a spy, but they prefer to be called snoops. He's only employed to gather data and report back to GIA. He's not extensively combat trained. Self-defense mostly. He was told my sister and I were myths and now he knows better. You saw him caught at the poacher camp as a snoop. Surprisingly, they didn't kill him."

"And the cougar?"

"Bailey was looking for blood samples to cross-reference those that GIA had acquired from your parents' house that night."

"What about the disc he has?"

"That holds information on animals in the jungle and the prices of hides for poachers. The disc is mostly of no importance, although there may be some slight info on me or my sister, who knows?"

"He does! What a jerk!"

"Well, you asked what kind of man he is. A stupid jerk around you, but a genius investigator according to GIA."

"Stupid around me? What's that supposed to mean?"

"I believe humans call it a crush."

"He has a what?"

"I said, I think..."

"I heard you. I just don't believe you!" she said aloud.

"Anaba, Anaba, Anaba." Meovi shook her head. After all her years of raising Jailin, she always knew what kind of conversations she was having with the animals.

"What? Do you have something to add too?"

"Always so blind for someone with such heightened senses."

"Geez. I feel so… so… cornered."

"You have questions that frustrate you. Why not send that bird now?" Meovi smiled.

"Birds become confused too easily. I'll go myself. Dierno, please do my patrol tonight. Socrates is coming with me."

A loud knock came at the door. Bailey jumped up off the couch, unsure for a moment where he was and then yelled, "Coming! Hold on a sec." He glanced at his watch. Eleven.

He opened the door and saw a familiar face. His green-eyed friend peered back at him with black shaggy hair almost in his eyes and covering his ears. He wore his old, ratty Green Machines Unite shirt, which had a screen print of a rain tree on it, and a long-sleeved white shirt under it.

"Hey, dude, what's up?"

"Hey, Gabe. Come on in." Bailey stepped back and opened the door wider for his friend to enter.

"Tabby called and asked me to check on you."

"No, she didn't, did she?"

"Yeah, but what really got me here was the salad remark. What happened at work to curb your love of meat, or should I say to avoid *leg* night?"

"You wouldn't believe me anyway."

"Try me."

"Well, I didn't get the info that work wanted. If I check in I might be fired and the job they gave me has everything to do with my past."

"Okay, and you think GIA won't forgive you, Mr. Genius? Unbelievable! You must have really screwed yourself or you're holding out on me."

"I met a girl."

"Now, this is more interesting. Explains a lot too. What's Tabby gonna say about this?"

"I don't know, besides, there's nothing to tell."

"But you wish there was. I can tell." A knock suddenly came from the patio sliding doors. "Who's that?"

Bailey repressed his smile the best he could. "Hopefully a bird, Gabe, hopefully a bird."

10

Bailey slid the glass door aside and stepped out. There was no indication that anyone had been there.

From inside, he heard Gabe yell, "Is it a bird, wise ass?"

Bailey turned around to head back inside the apartment. When he stepped on the mat, he heard a paper crinkle under his foot. Lifting his foot to inspect the cause of the sound, he saw the corner of an envelope flutter in the breeze. Picking it up, he walked back inside, staring at the writing on the front—he didn't recognize the fine script.

"Is that a love letter from your bird girl?"

"Not exactly," Bailey muttered.

"Another job, huh?"

"No. They don't know I'm back and I'd never receive a job in this manner."

"Creepy," Gabe insinuated. "Anyhow, are we goin' out tonight or what?"

"No. I've got work to do."

"Always on the clock, man."

"Hopefully."

"Dude, you need a vacation."

"I'll take one later."

"You always say that."

"I'm always working."

"Take a breather for a sec and tell me about this girl." Gabe's body gave way and landed on the couch. He propped his feet on the coffee table.

"Huh? Oh, yeah. Not much to tell."

"Oh sure, gonna play it like that, huh? I saw the look on your face when that knock came. You want some hot bird and won't tell me who she is. Dude, I'm telling little Miss O.M.G. Tabby. Then you'll get what's coming to you! HA! Not tell ol' best bud, Gabe, will you?"

"Who's O.M.G. Tabby?" A voice came from the patio door, which had been left open.

Both Gabe and Bailey turned around to look at the open door. Only darkness loomed in the threshold.

"Who's out there?" Gabe picked up a magazine off the end table and rolled it up, holding it behind his head, ready to attack.

"Gabe, put that down, you idiot!" Bailey grabbed the magazine, knocked his friend in the head and took one step toward the patio. "Jailin?"

"Who's Jailin?" Gabe asked.

"The hot bird apparently," she said as she stepped through the doorway into the small living room. She wasn't wearing the patrol clothes Bailey had last seen her in. Her routine when going into any of the major cities, so as not to draw attention, was to look as casual as possible. She wore a cotton T-shirt with a white bodice and navy blue cuffed sleeves which hugged the curve of her shoulders. Her jeans were a faded blue low rise cut that flared from the knees. Instead of her usual pony tail, she wore her hair loose, but kept the clips in the sections of hair by her ears.

"Yeah, definitely the hot bird… well, not a bird, though," Gabe mumbled out as he dropped his jaw slightly.

"You look… different. Nice, I mean." Bailey stumbled over his words. He avoided eye contact with her in an attempt to regain his thoughts.

"Uh-huh, thanks." She looked around as if she hadn't really heard him and went to sit on the couch.

"What brings you here?" Bailey asked, acting as if he couldn't care less.

"Birds are pathetic to deliver a message," she hesitated and sniffed the air. To help her think she squinted her eyes. She knew something was off, but this place was full of new smells and she couldn't pinpoint what it was that she didn't like. "Even if they remember where they're going, they forget why they're there once they arrive."

"I wasn't being literal. In fact, I didn't really expect to hear from you again."

"Fine. I'll go." Jailin stood up to leave, but was intercepted by Gabe.

"No. No. You just got here. We hardly know each other. Sit." He pulled her back down to the couch, sitting uncomfortably close.

Bailey looked at his feet and made a private plea for Gabe to disappear. Then he reflexively grunted, knowing that Gabe might be the one to get her to stay. The inner turmoil caused him to slouch into his recliner. Jailin cocked her head, looking toward Bailey. She was a little confused about how to interpret his grunt and detached posture in the chair.

"What's Socrates got to say tonight?" Bailey asked thinking her head tilt was an involuntary reaction to a personal conversation.

"He hasn't said a word. He's patrolling the roof."

"Ah."

"Whoa, you have an ancient dead philosopher on the roof? Awesome!" Gabe's eyes went wide with curiosity. He already knew too many GIA secrets.

Bailey softly sighed in frustration. He considered asking Gabe to leave, but was reluctant in case she became upset. Jailin smiled at Gabe's remark, which made Bailey feel alienated from them.

"Your friend here is funny," she said. "I like him."

"No, you don't. You don't even know him."

"Hey, that's not fair. She can like me if she wants." Gabe tried to defend himself. "And please do." He rubbed his finger over her hand.

"This one exhibits some irritating tendencies, Jailin. I must request, please do not pursue him during the rainy season." Socrates had been listening from the patio.

"I'm just testing Ben," she thought.

"Is there an explanation for regarding him on a first-name basis? I sense a fluctuation in your heart rate. His as well, while that one touches you. What are you hoping to achieve?"

"Information," she thought with delight. She turned to face Gabe. "Whatever you boys are planning for tonight, I'm in."

"Oh, sweet! You heard her Benji. Let's go, leg night here we come!"

"Uh… how much did you hear?" Bailey asked Jailin.

"Enough." She concealed her smile as best she could. "Benji, is it now?"

"That's a long, stupid, story and I'd be happier not having to tell you about it."

Jailin just lifted her eyebrows in interest, but gave no promises about asking or not asking, later on.

"Dude! Shower! Change!" Gabe clapped to enunciate each word. "It's still early. I'll call Tabby!"

"*No!*" Bailey shot out of his chair and grabbed the phone by the couch. Immediately he was back in his chair.

"O.M.G. Tabby?" Jailin asked.

"We're not going out. I've got work to do."

"Oh, right, so you don't get fired. I forgot." Gabe sat back down and Jailin got up from her seat. Towering over Bailey, slumped in his chair, she crossed her arms, cocked her hip and peered through her lashes at him.

"I should go," Gabe said. "Leave you two… birds alone." He snickered and made his way to the door. "Dude, you want a tie or a sock on the door knob or something?"

"Get out." Bailey answered him without taking his eyes off Jailin.

"What job are you getting fired from?" she tested his honesty.

Bailey hesitated. He wasn't sure where to draw the line between her and confidential information. Quickly, his eyes darted to the envelope on the side table. His intuition said to trust her. "I work for GIA. Heard of 'em?"

"Yeah. Go on."

"They have me gather data. Steal if needed."

"Like information from my parents' house and a poacher camp?"

"Not exactly, I had a job to gather anything I could on the mysterious white panther. It just happens to be connected to both of us."

"I see. Poachers would know that kind of thing, wouldn't they?"

"Seemed like a place to start. GIA also wanted blood samples from surrounding animals, but I didn't get anything significant."

"The disc?"

"Mostly useless garbage. It led me to a picture of the giant footprint and I got angry and thought I had it all figured out. I thought I had found the answer to both our parents' death."

"You mean *your* parents' death. I'm sure you haven't considered my mother in all these years."

"I've thought of you every day of my life. You were my best friend, my only friend. I thought you were dead, too, until I stole the tapes from your parents' house."

Jailin smiled a tiny bit, but revealed no real appreciation for Bailey's concern all these years.

"You are quite fortunate that he cannot hear the quick flutter of your heart rate," Socrates thought.

"Don't do this now," she thought in return. "How did you get caught by the poachers as a snoop?" she asked, in order to change the subject.

"I was in the middle of downloading information on a white panther cub. The DNA readout was amazing. How anyone could figure out a way to manipulate the DNA structure synthetically and then make it compatible with a common wildcat—it blows my mind. That's when I saw it."

"Saw what?"

"Your necklace. It's the symbol in the corner of the printouts, on the computer, and their uniforms. It's everywhere and on everything. Originally, I thought it made sense. Who else would be manufacturing these things?"

"They're his employees," she deduced on her own.

"Yeah. I made a real mess this time. No idea how I survived."

"You lied your way out, like you did to me at first."

"How did I know you weren't working for Vernore and playing dumb? That necklace implies that you do."

"He stole my parents' lives, their work, money… *everything*!"

"As well as mine, though they didn't have what yours did."

Jailin began to feel overwhelmed and sat down on the floor. "What do we do?"

"Perhaps we should start here." He handed her the letter he had found on the patio earlier. It read: *Come to Vernore Biotech and Pharmaceuticals, 7th floor at 6pm tomorrow.*

The scent from when she arrived suddenly got stronger. Closing her eyes, Jailin slowly brought the letter up to her nose. "We should go," she said, looking up from the letter. The paper smelled like home—her parents' home, especially on that dreadful night.

"No. You stay here. If he's the cause of your abilities, you shouldn't go near him until you know more about him. I'll go. The letter was sent to me anyway."

"But you don't know what he might do to you if you go."

"I don't see why he'd hurt me. GIA has been investigating him for so long that he'd have a huge problem if something happened to me. He's on thin ice."

"Fine, I don't like it, but take Dierno with you."

"All right." Bailey smiled at Jailin and was glad that they had come to this conclusion without another fight.

11

Bailey and Dierno entered an office on the seventh floor of Vernore Biotech and Pharmaceuticals. Bailey pushed open the large solid wooden doors and peered into the room. An elaborately carved wooden desk with a large black swivel chair sat in front of a wall of glass that displayed the busy streets and closely knit, tall buildings of North Central City.

"Hello?" Bailey called. "I received a message to come here at six. Is anyone here?" There was no reply. Digna walked out from the shadows, stretched her long limbs forward and dug her claws into the plush burgundy area rug in front of the desk.

The chair swung around and a man in his late sixties with salt and pepper hair was sitting before him. He wore a finely tailored black suit and a red silk tie. His face was long and angular. Crows feet and worry lines on his forehead aged the appearance of his face.

“Glad you came, my boy. I almost thought you wouldn’t,” the man said as he swirled a glass of red wine under his nose, pleasantly enjoying the bouquet.

“I debated about it for awhile,” Bailey lied.

“I heard about the encounter you and your friends had with my pet.” His eyes flashed to Digna. “Where’s the girl?” the man asked with one eyebrow raised.

“I didn’t know the invitation extended to her as well. Does it really matter?” He crossed his arms. This vile man should know Bailey wasn’t stupid—he was a member of GIA, after all.

“Perhaps not, but we’ll see. I’ve noted that you brought my trash back with you.” Dierno gave a short growl, knowing that the man meant him. “Very interesting. I guess when you take out one component and add another you get astonishing results. I should have kept you around longer.”

“You are one son of a bit…”

“Didn’t your parents teach you any manners, boy? Oh no, they wouldn’t have, always too busy with the Munrows.” Bailey couldn’t see the suppressed smile, due to the wine glass being pressed against those blasphemous lips.

“Who do you think you are?” Bailey sneered.

“Who am I? I am Adolph Vernore. I am the soul of this city, next to Godliness if I may, and soon to be King of Grundagon.” He stood up and walked around his desk. Sitting on the lip of his desk, with one leg up off the floor, he rested his hand on Digna’s head. She purred and rubbed her head against his knee.

“The people won’t stand for that, especially GIA.” Bailey wasn’t believing a word from this man’s mouth.

"They can't stop me. One day soon I will also own GIA. Maybe even change the name to Vernore Intelligence Committee, since a woman's name implies weakness."

"VIC. Very funny." Bailey was not amused.

"Join my team, boy, and become a man."

"Who are you to say what kind of man I am?" Bailey's fists clenched at his sides.

Vernore paused for a moment before saying anything. It was an interesting question. "For a long time, I thought I was to be your father. Unfortunately for me, you were born with blonde hair. Until then, your mother had no idea whether Nicolas or I was your creator."

"What? How in hell did you come up with that deluded notion?"

Vernore smiled at the remembrance of the private thoughts which he was about to divulge, "Your mother, Johanna, and I were in love, you might say. She would say that, anyway. Your father was always away, sometimes for a year at a time, which is why she saw me on a regular basis. They had no money, which was why she worked for Dr. Munrow. My son, Adrian, who's your mother's first son, and your brother, has special gifts like I do. Your mother was my first human experiment. I continued my work on Adrian and then your girlfriend, and let's not forget Digna and Diega."

"Dierno, now. He changed his name, and she's not my girlfriend." He balled his hands into fists. They were moist so he wiped them on his pants.

Vernore cringed at Bailey's display of nerves. "Well, of course not, not as of now anyway. You'll grow closer and then you'll be begging me for my help."

"I'll never need your help!"

"Is that what you believe? But I digress. The vial poor little Jailin drank was meant for you. You may be Nicolas' son, but I don't believe he ever treated you like it. Perhaps that's because he never trusted your mother's loyalty. I was upset when your mother chose him over me. Think of all the amazing children we could have created together."

"I was six when you took them from me and Jailin was five. Neither of us remembers our parents very well and it's your fault. How dare you?" Bailey was beginning to get even more furious. His face was turning red and his hands clenched harder into fists.

"I'm sure Jailin can remember more than you can. She's incredible, I hear." He looked down at Digna and petted her head affectionately.

"She says all she remembers is when her mother used to hold her as she played with the necklace. That's the only thing she has left and now it just reminds her of you and all she has to revenge." His voice seeped through his clenched teeth.

"Necklace? What necklace?"

"The one with your stupid logo—the V that looks like a flower on a silver chain." Bailey pointed to the gold logo on the wall. Vernore was guilty of pride and he didn't hide it.

"I gave that to your mother. Not Kathy." He sipped his wine and stroked Digna's head.

"Shit. She doesn't remember her mother…" Bailey rubbed his throat as if he'd been yelling for hours.

"No, she does not."

"She remembers mine." Bailey felt sorry for Jailin. He knew she didn't remember him too well, but now that he knew she didn't know her own mother, he felt even worse.

"To think I was going to make you invincible. A strong man who could have anything you desired. I could still give you all of that."

"With that liquid Jailin drank? How do I know it won't kill me?" Bailey looked at Dierno, he wanted to be as close to Jailin as they used to be so long ago. He wanted to minimize the gap between them in any way he could. Dierno shook his head. It was the only way to be sure Bailey would understand that this was wrong.

"The testing took forever," Vernore replied to Bailey's question. He couldn't see Dierno's influence on the boy. "There were many deaths, numerous failed experiments, and others which were quite interesting. You were getting older and less naive. Diega, err Dierno, wasn't showing any potential; little did I know it revealed itself in years, and Digna showed incredible results in higher volumes and more doses. It tires her and she has to sleep off the fatigue, but her gifts are increased tenfold. I gave up on… Dierno. I was sure that he would expire, which is why I named him Diega—to supplant. Now I know better."

"What will happen to Jailin?"

"Well, Adrian is fine, although he was born with his genes already manipulated. He is a pure Vernore. The vial from the lab was an alteration of his DNA segment primarily to fix the anger, hunger, and hormone issues. He can be a little uncontrollable at times, and the meat he eats could break a middle-class man's bank."

"He's not a vegetarian?"

"No!" A sinister chuckled escaped through Vernore's thin lips. "He won't touch anything but meat and requires supplements to balance his nutrition. Why do you ask?"

"Jailin won't touch meat. Won't watch anyone eat it either."

"That may just be her upbringing. I'd have to run tests."

"Well, you're not going to. She thinks you're evil and I'm not about to convince her otherwise."

"I consider myself a temperate man. I also agree that I want more than the average person and will do outlandish things to get it. If that is evil, so be it!"

"Why did you ask me here?"

"So you can give me what I want."

"Well, you've got it backward. You have to give us whatever we want."

"We? Meaning you and Jailin or GIA?"

"Does it matter?"

"No, you've done exactly what I needed you to do."

Bailey hesitated. He searched his mind for anything he might have said wrong. "What would that be?"

"You've been given information that you'll go back to your girl with. She'll have more questions and she'll come directly to me. Exactly how I want it."

"Then I won't tell her."

"You don't have to. It'll get out. She *will* come to me."

"I *won't* let her!"

"Eventually, she'll come to see her father or on an excursion during the rainy season. Perhaps she'll meet Adrian, unless you have the desire to stop that… *do you*?"

Bailey shook his head slowly, while looking at his feet. He wasn't sure it was right to talk about Jailin in this way and he felt heat flush his face.

"Denial." Vernore commented on Bailey's reaction. "You say she's not your girlfriend now, but you certainly won't stop what may happen between you two in the future."

"Stay away from her! Stay away from the Maimugg tribe and away from her father!"

"I own that facility and his illness. He stays as long as I want and it will eat away at him until Jailin gives herself up in exchange for his cure!"

"No! Originally you wanted me. Take me as your guinea pig. Give her her father back."

"Oh, how heartwarming—young love. It makes me sick." He looked down at Digna as if he could love no other but her. "Take back what I've said to your dear, little Miss Munrow. I know what a boy raised as poor as you sees in her." Vernore took a sip from his wine and stood to go back to his chair.

"What do you think that is? You don't even know me."

"I know her inheritance, and any man would love her for that."

"Whatever my mother saw in you, I'll never understand." Bailey was finished with Vernore's verbal torture. He turned to leave and Dierno followed right behind him.

Vernore took another sip from his wine while he peered out at the city—his city. It hadn't taken him long to acquire his high stature in North Central. Most of the enormous eminent businesses belonged to Vernore and if they didn't, they soon would. The narrow streets and sidewalks were filling with commuters as they made their way to or from work. The sun was setting behind the reflective building across the street and it glowed with an orangey-yellow aura. It was the only color that gave life to this monochrome city. When Vernore looked down from the thirty-fourth floor, he saw Bailey and Dierno running from the building. "Commence Experiment A-1," he thought.

12

At a coffee and pastry shop in North Central City, called Sweet Sip: A Vernore Café, a man sat reading the newspaper and drinking a macchiato. He rubbed his head as if he were nursing a hangover. He wore a red T-shirt and dark blue jeans. His short hair was black and tipped gold in a spiked, messy way. It appeared as if he had just woken up and only run his hands through it before walking out the door.

In his head he heard again, "Where are you? Get to the lab and prep the first experiment!"

"Now? I just got here and I had a crazy night. Let me relax."

"When you grow up, you can relax!"

"Damn, calm down!"

The door bell chimed, announcing that another customer had entered the café. Jailin walked over to the magazines and scanned the rack. The man was distracted from his mental conversation.

"She's new." He sniffed the air slightly. "I'd remember meeting someone who smells that good and is that hot." He intended to keep that thought to himself.

"None of that now. You can scoop up with girls later."

"It's hook up. Geez, you're lame."

"Get back here *now*!"

"Get out of my head!" He stood up to walk out the door, but then chose otherwise and went over to the magazine rack.

"Hey there. You like animals?" he asked with a sly smile, noticing the *Grundagon Zoology* magazine in her hands.

"Some more than others," she shrugged.

"Why that one?"

"It's for… someone."

"I certainly find *biology* interesting."

"What about it do you find so interesting?"

"The female part." He jutted his jaw at her.

"Oh great, another one," she said to a little old woman flipping through a gardening magazine. The woman looked toward Jailin and then to the man and smiled.

"Sorry, force of habit," he confessed.

"I'll try not to hold it against you."

"Thanks. I've never seen you in this city before. Do you live around here?"

"No. I come into the city about once or twice a month."

"Are you from one of the local towns, such as Bynnin or Joryn?"

"Not exactly."

"Oh, well, you should check out this club called Dance Zoo. It's awesome."

"We'll see."

“You want a drink? You seem like a chai tea girl.”

“A little redundant, isn’t it?”

“What is?”

“Chai means tea, so your saying tea tea is redundant. Like people who say ATM machine.”

“True, although it doesn’t stop people from saying it. Maybe I’ll start just saying chai from now on.”

“Don’t do anything on my account.” Jailin was beginning to enjoy this man’s company and she certainly didn’t mind the view.

“Tell the barista what you’d like. It’s on me,” he offered.

“Thanks, but you don’t have to do that.”

“I insist.”

“Can I get two?”

“Uh, sure, why not?” He shrugged. It wasn’t like he was pressed for money anyway.

“One goes with this.” She held up the magazine.

“No problem.” He smiled and Jailin thought he seemed familiar.

Reluctantly, as if she was imposing, Jailin told the barista she wanted a chai and a black coffee. The man turned to the barista and said, “Here you go,” as he flipped a credit card out and handed it to her.

“Oh, Mr. Vernore, your purchases are always complimentary,” the barista said as she leaned toward him over the counter to make her cleavage under the edge of her apron more apparent.

“Uh… thanks.” Jailin picked up her two drinks and held up one in appreciation. With the magazine under her arm, she turned to walk out the door as quickly as she thought a normal person would. He was behind her before she was two steps out the door.

“Where to so fast?”

"You're Vernore!" She spun around, almost spilling the drinks.

"I know. I'm sorry. I'm so used to people already knowing that. Can I start over? My name is Adrian."

As she gazed into his eyes she saw something familiar in them. They were a beautiful blue with glints of sunshine. Happiness and comfort. She shook the thought away, "You think you own all of Grundagon!"

"Well, no, not exactly. You're confusing me with my father. I'm actually surprised you feel this way. Most girls flock to me, not from me—you saw the barista in there." He threw his thumb over his shoulder to indicate the café. "I admit the attraction is probably because I'll inherit everything my father owns, but that doesn't mean I *am* him." He pushed his hands into his pockets.

"I'm leaving now," she said, and began to walk down the sidewalk away from him.

"I didn't get your name!"

"You didn't earn it!" she called back.

"Feisty. I like that. It's a whole new change to my life," he yelled down the street to her as she continued to walk away. "Okay father, I'm on my way," he thought.

"Where is she?" Bailey paced back and forth. Dierno was scrunched on the patio, thankful that Bailey lived on the ground level. Socrates was sitting on the couch with the remote for the TV. The only button he liked to hit was "channel up."

"Tell him, Socrates," Dierno insisted.

"All the information I possess has come from you. You are more than welcome to inform him if you desire."

"I can't. I figured since you have thumbs, you might write it out for him."

"My instruction with Jailin on writing has not been completed. And we only execute it in the dirt."

"Well, find a pen and try something. Anything."

Socrates got up off the couch and went over to the kitchen table. He jumped up and grabbed a pencil and an old envelope.

VRNO COMNTY MENTIL HOPSTL. Socrates wrote on the envelope, and Bailey looked at it with a furrowed brow. After a few moments he said, "To see her father? When did she leave?"

TO HORS GO.

"Two hours ago? When will she be back?"

DO NOT NO.

"So we're stuck waiting?" Bailey's hands closed into fists. Usually he was so patient, but this late in the day he was restless.

I ASK ER he wrote, then thought to Jailin, "I am attempting a disappointingly constructed conversation on paper with Bailey. As difficult as it is, it is progressive. He wants to know when you are returning."

"I'm on my way. Ten minutes."

COM NOW.

"Wonderful," Bailey said sarcastically. "I need to figure this out before she gets here. Dierno, please don't speak or think or whatever it is you do, about last night. I need to protect her and if it means leaving some things out, then that's what we've got to do. That includes you!" He pointed to Socrates. Dierno nodded in return.

"Dierno, I require that you divulge any information you have to me."

"I will when the time is right."

“Conspirator.” Socrates got down from the table and went back to the couch. He resumed hitting the channel up button.

Bailey was still pacing when Jailin came in the door. She had intended to return after telling Socrates she was on her way, but she had had one more errand.

“I thought you were coming right back? It’s been two hours since Socrates told me you were heading over.” Bailey was a little on edge—more out of concern for Jailin alone in an unfamiliar city than anything else.

“I tried to see my father. The first time they wouldn’t let me in. I walked around a bit, stopped at a café with the intent to try again. That’s what took me longer than expected,” she said sadly.

“Oh… how is he?”

“Catatonic. The nurse says he seems to get that way occasionally after some of the medicine he takes.”

“It’s not permanent?”

“Doesn’t sound like it, but since I couldn’t talk to him I walked around town. You want this coffee I got for him? It’s black and cold now, but I’ll reheat it if you want.”

“Sure. Put it in the fridge and I’ll reheat it in the morning. Are you okay?”

“I think so. How’d the meeting go last night?” She used her hands to form quotes in the air as she said meeting.

“More like a huge waste of time.”

“Why is that?”

“He didn’t have a lot to say about anything that could help us. He just knows a lot about my mother and that I have a brother.” Bailey was clutching the counter and pushing all his weight onto it. Jailin watched as the muscles flexed in his arms. She knew he couldn't break the counter and wished she could hear his thoughts to find out what was bothering him, but then thought better of it.

"Wow, really? That must be so exciting for you. Did you meet him?"

"No, and I don't want to! Vernore had an affair with my mother. I don't want to think about how my bloodline is connected to that asshole." He let go of the counter and turned around to face her. Jailin saw the brilliant blue with glints of light in his eyes and she realized why Adrian's were so familiar.

"Vernore's not really your father though, right? I mean, Nicolas was…"

"No, Vernore is *not* my father! Thank goodness."

Jailin considered changing the topic, but she had too many questions to just let this go. "You must have talked about other things. Did I get mentioned?"

"No, nothing of any real importance," he lied as best he could. It was the only way he could insure that she didn't run off to Vernore the way he wanted.

"Oh." She sounded disappointed. She pinched the bridge of her nose then extended her fingers to rub her eyes while she yawned.

"When was the last time you slept?"

"I don't remember."

"Stay in my room tonight. I'll be up working for awhile. This way I won't keep you up. And I can just crash on the couch."

"Thanks." She averted her eyes due to the intimacy of the idea of using his bed. "Goodnight."

"Night," he said as he sat at the table and booted up his laptop.

In his room, she borrowed the smallest shirt she could find from his dresser then crawled into bed. The smell of him was in the sheets and on the pillow, though she couldn't describe the smell, it was comforting in a way that made her feel safe like the jungle did. Her mind began to wonder if he would be able to smell her when he next slept in this bed. Her face moved deeper into his pillow as she drank him in.

"May I come in?" Socrates asked from outside the door. She got up to let him in. "I must say, listening to some of your thoughts is not always a sought after-privilege of mine."

13

When Adrian entered the lab on the thirty-fourth floor he walked across the long, dark open platform. A tanned woman with black, red, and white dreadlocks wearing a red running suit sat in a chair. She balanced it on two legs with her feet on the table. Under the chair, her prehensile tail whipped back and forth across the floor.

"Afternoon, Honovi."

"Evening," she stated, correcting him on the time of day. Her attention was solely directed to the tiny TV on the table.

"Yeah, well, long… everything," he said defensively.

"I heard. You didn't bother to block me." Her eyes flashed from the TV to Adrian and her lip curled slightly. The events of the day rifled through his mind.

He swallowed hard and stared at her for a long moment until he realized she was hinting at his night of careless drinking instead of his new acquaintance. “Did my father brief you?” He changed the subject.

“Yep.” Her hand crunched into a bowl in her lap. Adrian hadn’t noticed she was eating.

“We’re starting with A-1.” Adrian couldn’t remember the last time he had eaten. Staring at the bowl of snack mix, he licked his lips slightly.

“Sakuna’s ready and hungry,” she said between mouthfuls.

“Good.” He turned back to look across the platform he had crossed over when he entered. It was dark against the far wall. A few murmurs could be heard across the unlit distance. He didn’t bother to find out what they were thinking.

“Something on your mind? You don’t seem like yourself.” Honovi’s head dropped back so that she could see Adrian upside down. The same smirk was still on her face when he turned around.

“Nah. Well yes, but I don’t want to talk about it.” He ran his hand through his hair, then cursed himself for the possible disheveled look he might have caused. He looked around for a mirror, but decided not to bother worrying about it tonight.

“Fine by me.” She set her chair back on all fours and the bowl clanged when it hit the table.

“Are you all set?” He blinked away the unnerving sound of the bowl wobbling to find its equilibrium.

“Put Sakuna on the platform and I’ll be there after I change.” She stood up and switched off the little TV.

Adrian followed her out and went to the platform while she went up the metal staircase. “She’s got to stop naming the experiments,” Adrian mumbled under his breath. He put his headphones on and blasted music into his ears. When he had set all the switches and knobs in place on the monitoring system he looked up. Honovi was making her way down the stairs. "Why do you gotta wear that? It's so… distracting," he thought.

A smile crossed her face. She was wearing her knee-high stiletto black boots and a straight red mini skirt, cut like a loin cloth, over even smaller shorts. The red triangle bikini top didn't cover her enough and the red sleeves with a high stiff collar only accentuated her protruding chest. "Keep your pants on sugar pie. I'll be home late," she thought in return.

Adrian looked down the panel in front of him and switched one toggle up. A light came on in the far corner of the room, revealing a full-size cage from floor to ceiling. A six-foot-tall vulture with a wing span of fifteen feet squawked and flapped in distress.

"Quiet down, love," Honovi thought as she approached, and the bird began to relax. Adrian flipped another switch and the cage opened. The bird hopped out to the center of the platform and Honovi jumped up onto its back. She swung her legs around its large neck and grabbed the reins which were already harnessed to the bird's neck.

"Ready?" Adrian thought.

"Always ready for you, sweet lips," Honovi replied in her head. Adrian flipped the last flashing red switch at the far end of the panel. The door in front of the vulture rolled up to the ceiling. The large wings spread when the talons gripped the edge of the platform. It took flight after plummeting a few feet.

"A-1 has left the building," he thought as he switched off the lights in the large room and took a seat to enjoy the music drumming in his ears. The door remained open for the return of Honovi and Sakuna.

"Perfect," he heard his father reply in his head.

Gabe was talking so fast that pieces of his description were missing. "Then it swooped down from the building and headed south." When he saw a black form swoop out of the tallest building in North Central City his first thought was to tell a GIA operative. He only knew one.

"Wait. What swooped?" Bailey asked. He always had trouble getting Gabe to focus on the main objective.

"I think it was a bird. A huge bird. I mean it's not that dark out. The sun is going down, but dude, it wasn't a plane." He shook the kitchen chair that he gripped in his hands to get his point across.

"Dierno, do you see anything abnormal?" Jailin thought. If any pair of eyes could see something abnormal and as big as Gabe had described, it would be Dierno.

"Something has definitely gone south. Heading for the jungle it seems. I can't say for sure what its intentions are, but it sounds hungry."

"I have to go now!" Jailin said to Bailey as she turned toward the door.

"Hold on! Is everything okay?" He got up and grabbed her arm.

She was surprised that he had caught her and she looked at the large muscular hand wrapped around her forearm. He hadn't gripped her hard enough to actually keep her from leaving, but she didn't fight it either. "I don't know, but I have to get home." She gazed into the beautiful blue sky of his eyes.

"I can drive you." He pulled her toward him ever so slightly without knowing that he had. Gabe had caught the subtle gesture and even though her feet didn't move, he saw Jailin lean forward slightly.

“I’m faster alone. Thanks, though.” She turned away and he dropped her arm. As she closed the door behind her, she glanced back at Bailey.

“How is she faster without a car?” Gabe asked completely confused.

“That’s a long story, but I gotta go. Things could get ugly.” He snatched his light-weight black jacket off the chair.

“Did you figure out that work thing?” Gabe was following Bailey from room to room.

“Yeah, I emailed Northpost with something interesting so I’m in the clear for now.” His words were quick and short. He wanted to find his keys and get going before it was too late.

“Then what’s your excuse for avoiding Tabby? She’s killing me with all the calls. She’s even stopping by now. I can’t take it!”

“Uh… tell her I, umm...” Bailey was back in the kitchen rifling through papers on the table.

“What? Tell her what?” Gabe wanted an answer. He couldn’t believe his best friend was this distracted. Never before had Mister Focused, Benjamin Bailey, ever been this diverted in his entire life.

“I don’t know. Anything. I gotta go. Lock up on your way out,” he said once he remembered that his keys were in front of the TV, which was the same place they always were so that situations like this could be avoided.

“You think it’s coming here?” Meovi asked. She was sitting calmly at the little table in Jailin’s hut.

Jailin had already put on her patrol uniform and was clipping her pony tail back. She was ready to run out the door to continue the chase. “I didn’t say that!”

"You said be ready." Meovi sipped her tea and then threw her long braid with the red ribbon over her shoulder.

"Careful. You know, keep an eye out. That kind of ready, just in case." Jailin was pulling her arm gauntlets up past her elbow. She worked her thumb through the hole in the side and then pulled it taut at her elbow again. As a ritual, she would always grind the knuckle padding into each hand.

"I'll tell Masou to prepare," Meovi said while gazing at her reflection in the tea. She envied Jailin's perfect face. Not an ounce of fat in those cheeks, no stubby chin, and certainly no large round forehead. She sighed lightly to herself and ran her hand around the plump contours of her face.

"Good idea." Jailin slipped her bo staff into the sleeve on her back, dropped her arm for Socrates to climb up, and ran out the door to take to the trees.

They reached a clearing where a dam had been erected to divert the heavy flow of water away from South Central City and the surrounding towns of Klut and Cluce.

"Can you see that?" Dierno thought.

"Yeah. What's it doing?" They watched as a large black object kept diving down toward the dam. Suddenly, a faint scream was heard in the distance. Jailin, with Socrates on her back and Dierno at her side, ran toward the sound.

They came up to what they realized was a giant vulture. When it saw them it picked up the man who'd already lost his limbs and carried him to a higher spot, continuing its feast. "Mine. Sakuna, so hungry. Mine," it kept thinking, over and over.

Suddenly, they heard a loud thump. Jailin peered over the side to see a man holding onto a pipe that lined the wall of the dam. His feet repeatedly kicked and scaled the wall to find leverage.

"You'll be okay. Hold on, I'm coming to get you!" Jailin called down to him. Their eyes met briefly and the horror she saw proved to Jailin that he didn't believe her.

"No, you won't," a voice behind her said.

Jailin spun around and saw a tall, lean woman standing in front of her. She cringed as the man screamed. He was right. She couldn't save him. "Who are you?" Jailin asked through clenched teeth.

"I'm your worst nightmare," she said and sprang at Jailin. Her nails—stronger than iron—extended out a foot and ripped the shoulder of Jailin's vest, grazing the skin beneath it.

"Ow. Bitch!" Jailin lowered herself to the ground—away from this woman's deadly nails. Her good arm supported her weight, one leg was bent beneath her and the other extended to the side. She pulled her bo staff out of its sling and twirled it above her head at the woman's face. When she backed up, Jailin used the opportunity to stand and regain her ground.

"I hear ticking below. It could be a bomb. I'll see what we can do," Dierno thought as he lifted Socrates up with his teeth and swung him onto his back. Quickly he was off toward the lower levels of the dam.

"What do you think you're doing?" Jailin demanded of the woman as she swung her bo at the woman's face. The woman was flexible. She bent backward with the bo staff and it missed by millimeters.

"Destroying a dam. What's it look like?" The woman swiped at Jailin's face with her claws, but Jailin was just as fast as the woman was flexible. Jailin used this moment to jump, trying to slam the staff down on the woman's head. As she descended, she hadn't noticed that the woman had wrapped her tail around Jailin's foot, jerking it to the ground.

She landed hard on her hip and elbow which reinforced the pain in her shoulder from the woman's claw marks. She exhaled a grunt of distress, but quickly got up. The woman continued slashing at her with extended claws. Jailin dodged her and then made her advance. Every attack only scarcely missed each other. Their movements were fast and agile. The woman bent her body in ways Jailin thought impossible. She looked like a contortionist in fast forward.

Just as the woman's left arm jutted out, Jailin slapped her staff at the exposed arm. It shattered open and wrapped around the woman's wrist. She pulled swiftly on the unbroken end of the staff to bring the woman towards her, pulling her off balance. Jailin kicked the right shoulder of the arm that wasn't tethered. The woman swung sideways and Jailin used her momentum to push the woman to the ground and hold both arms behind her back. "What's your purpose here?" Jailin applied all her weight onto the woman sprawled against the dam floor.

"To make Vernore look like a hero," she grunted out between breaths.

"By blowing up a dam?" Jailin couldn't understand how destroying something made you a hero. Unless, of course, you're destroying evil. Which was what Jailin thought she was doing right now.

"He's got the whole thing planned out. He'll look like a savior. Like a god!" Her laugh was evil and unmistakable to Jailin.

"*Honovi*!" Jailin gasped in shock. She punched her in the face, knocking her unconscious.

Honovi's head hit the ground and Jailin ran down to find Dierno and Socrates. When she found them, Socrates was just putting his teeth around the red wire.

"Wait!" Jailin yelled, but she wasn't quick enough. Socrates snapped the red wire on the bomb and the clock stopped at five seconds. Jailin exhaled, grabbing her chest with relief.

They returned to the top of the dam and saw the vulture heading north, carrying Honovi.

"What happened?" Bailey said as he ran up to them on the walkway of the dam. Then he saw Jailin's shoulder, "Holy shit! Are you okay?"

She looked at her shoulder and saw the blood pooling up. She applied pressure to it and starting walking the rest of the way off the dam. "Nothing Meovi can't fix."

"Who was that? What was that?" Bailey jogged to catch up to her.

"Not sure anymore, but things are definitely getting complicated." She winced as a shock of pain traveled through her arm.

"Come on. I'll take you home." Bailey put his arm around her waist and supported her by putting her good arm around his shoulders. He helped her get into his black truck. It was a Honda, the everlasting company of an endangered race, and they had reissued their Ridgeline model exclusively for GIA operatives. Once Bailey had her seated comfortably in the truck, he gave her a quick bandage to help apply pressure to the bleeding shoulder.

14

Honovi grunted as the vulture put her back down in the middle of the platform on the thirty-fourth floor. The room was dark and quiet, except for Adrian's slow breathing of a deep sleep and the muffled static of the music coming from his headphones. A surge of pain quickly ran through her body. It had been a long time since she had had to fight someone. She knew she should have kept up with her sparring routine—now she had a reason to.

"Why are you back so soon?" Vernore was at the top of the stairs. Half of his face was veiled in darkness. He looked disappointed while he stroked Digna's head.

"Perhaps I should have gone instead of her," Digna purred. She relished every opportunity to upstage Honovi, but she knew her master wouldn't let her out of his sight for long.

"So the dam didn't blow up. You have a million chances. It's not going anywhere!" Honovi was peeling herself up off the platform.

"The importance of this experiment was not to blow up the dam for my sake. I always accomplish my goals. You and A-1 were the test. You've failed."

"That damn bird was no good. How do you expect me to finish a task without proper…?"

"That's enough! You're the trainer. Get yourself together. I will review the tape." Honovi watched Vernore disappear into the shadows at the top of the stairs. She growled under her breath and then led the vulture back to his cage. From the food locker, she shoveled two heaps of a special bird food she always made especially for him into his cage.

"It's not really your fault, big guy," she cooed, feeling the crisp cold on her forehead pressed against the metal bars.

"Everything all right?" Adrian asked. He cracked his fingers as he strolled up behind her. His voice sounded pompous and composed. The simplest sentence from him condemned her failure.

"No, everything is *not* all right." Honovi turned around and met Adrian face to face. "I failed because of Anaba." The name rolled off her tongue like acid.

"Who?" Adrian could have sworn she had just cursed him, instead of mentioning some girl he'd never heard of before.

"A white girl adopted by my old yenena. She's… she's strong." She looked to the side and Adrian could see the bruise forming on the side of her face.

"So? You've got a voice no one can reckon with." He pushed her shoulder back in playfulness.

"Don't," she winced. "She kicked me there." Rubbing her shoulder, she thought she could invoke some compassion from Adrian.

"Oh, sorry." He actually felt a little guilty, but also a little amazed. Never had he seen anyone best Honovi at anything.

"Adrian?" She looked up at him through her lashes.

"What?" There was no need to ask. He already knew what she wanted and it caused him to take one step back.

"Can we? Please?" She inclined her body toward him. She didn't have enough faith to believe he would catch her if she fell forward.

"No. Not tonight." He angled his body to the side, as if that would deter her.

"But…" She bit her bottom lip, withholding her biggest weapon.

"No, Honovi." His voice dropped an octave and his eyebrows narrowed. Fists clenched in anger. He wouldn't let her do this.

"Please?" Leaning closer to him she put her forehead to his. She gazed into his eyes and begged again, "Please?"

"Honovi." He averted her gaze so that her forehead was now touching his temple.

"Want to review the tape? Watching me fight always seems to get you hot." She ran her hand across his chest under his unbuttoned shirt. He grabbed her hand to stop the motion.

"Mmm," his voice was deep, almost throaty, because even though she wasn't the girl of his dreams, she was right and she was easy.

"Socrates, go get Meovi, please," Jailin thought as she slid herself slowly out of the truck. Bailey was there to guide her to the ground and help her inside. A tender bruise had formed on her hip. Her shoulder was soaked in blood and hung low at her side. The cuts were thin but deep and the loss of blood was making her weak.

As Bailey walked her through the threshold, Dierno jumped out of the bed of the truck. He had Jailin's staff in his mouth. "This could use some work," Dierno thought as he dropped it to the floor in pieces.

"I have a lot of those. In fact, it's time I upgrade it." Jailin knew from past experiences that the hollowed wood didn't last. It was surprising that it had held up this long.

"What happened back there? Who was that with that bird thing?" Bailey needed to know. He wanted to help her, and with GIA on his side, perhaps he could make that possible.

"Vulture," Jailin exhaled roughly as her bruised hip rested on the end of the bed.

"Who calls themself Vulture? That's stupid." He smiled as he kneeled down on the floor to meet her eye level. She smiled back.

"I kind of like it," Dierno thought as he stuffed himself into a corner by the bed.

Jailin glanced at Dierno then said to Bailey, "Her name is Honovi. When she was a child, she went missing from our tribe."

"Her name sounds just like Meovi's. Is that a common occurrence in your tribe?" he asked as he moved from the floor to sit next to her on the bed.

"Honovi means strong. And Meovi is our wise woman and healer. We call her our yenena. Many new parents ask her to name their children when she delivers their child. When Meovi brought

Honovi into this world, she was so strong her mother didn't survive."

His hand crossed his body to rest on top of her hand. "She can't be stronger than you though, right?" He was leaning back on his other arm. He truly believed Jailin was unstoppable. Watching the pain contort her face, he knew she wasn't unbreakable.

She shrugged. "With Vernore's help who knows, but that's not my real concern." Her body shifted away from him.

"What is?" He sat up when she withdrew her hand. A twinge of concern ran through him. He hoped that she wasn't withdrawing her hand because he had offended her somehow.

"Maimugg legend says that there once were certain individuals born with a gift." Slowly she lay back on the bed to relieve the pressure on her hip. As her face relaxed, she smiled and motioned with her finger for him to come closer. He was relieved that she hadn't been intentionally pushing him away a moment ago. He stretched out on his side next to her and listened. "They're called Minowa, or singers. If they were to sing anything, a simple sentence or even a hum, anyone or anything that heard them would be enchanted."

"Enchanted?" His brow furrowed. He didn't understand the implication.

"Under a spell that lasts a long as eight hours, or perhaps longer, according to the legend." She slid her good arm under her head to hold it up.

"What happens?" Bailey was captivated by the legend. This was one he hadn't heard before, one that actually sounded true coming from Jailin's lips, versus actual snoop jobs from his commissioner.

"You become hopelessly in love with her. You'll do anything, and I mean *anything* for her." She looked at the ceiling as if to remember something from the past.

"Isn't there a way out of it?"

"Each interpretation of the legend is a little different. Some say no, there isn't anything anyone can do but wait it out. Others say if you've already found your true love then it has no effect at all."

"I see." He looked around the room, trying to avoid the awkward feeling in his stomach, or maybe it was just nerves. "Can Socrates and Dierno be affected?"

"I suppose it's possible. I don't know anything about their love lives, but to be on the safe side, if you have ears, cover them."

Meovi came in the door with a small pouch of herbs and went over to the stove. Either she didn't see them or pretended not to in order to avoid any interruption. It was difficult for Jailin to decipher which it was, so she pushed herself up from the bed, wincing at the pain, and went over to the stove. Meovi began using her native tongue, which only Jailin and Socrates understood. "What's going on?"

"I found Honovi. She's altered, but still a nuisance." The Maimuan words rolled together so quickly Bailey couldn't tell where one stopped and the other began.

"Will she come back here?" Meovi's face looked concerned, but not for the tribe's safety or her own. It appeared as if Meovi longed to see her and welcome her home with open arms.

"I don't know. She didn't say much." Jailin knew she wouldn't come back. Honovi had hated being a child without a mother and disliked by a father who would have preferred a boy. There was no possibility of a return with the intent to stay, but Jailin wouldn't tell Meovi that. She wouldn't break her heart.

"Go take that vest off so I can apply this to your shoulder." Meovi was grinding a fine powder and water in a bowl with a stick that was rounded at one end to the shape of the bowl.

Jailin went to her bed and pulled a clean powder blue tank top from her clothes chest. "Be right back," she said to Bailey and he watched her lightly limp into the bathroom to change her shirt. Even though her gait was unsteady, he thought she was the cutest cripple he'd ever seen.

When she came out, Meovi had a brown paste spread on a white bandage. She applied it to Jailin's shoulder and then wrapped a bandage around Jailin's arm and across her chest to hold the paste in place.

"Anything else hurting?" she asked in the universal language, as she studied Jailin. She had seen her limping and knew something was wrong with one of her legs.

"Just some bruises." She rubbed her hip. The paste was warming her shoulder and it already felt looser and easier to move.

"I'll get you some tea. It's already made at my hut." Meovi headed to the door and stopped to look at Bailey.

"Hello," he said.

She nodded then reverted back into her native tongue to speak only to Jailin, "I'll only be a few minutes."

"Okay," she said. There was no word in Maimuan for that. Jailin walked back over to the bed and sat down. She ignored the pain that shot down her leg.

"How come you don't have a tribal name?" he asked her, supporting the weight of his torso by propping himself his elbows on his knees.

"I do. I'm sure you've heard Meovi use it." She rubbed one hand up and down the thigh of the throbbing leg.

"I don't remember hearing it." He tried to recall the words that he had heard Meovi use since the first time he had met her.

"It's Anaba," she said humbly.

"Pretty." He found it harder to swallow than usual. "What's it mean?"

"She returns from battle." She sounded embarrassed by it, as if the name had condemned her to a fate she hadn't asked for.

"Meovi named you that?" he asked, thinking that it suited her.

"Yeah, I often fought with the other children, but always came out on top." She smirked quickly, then her face turned to the side to stare into nothing—remembering another childhood pastime.

"What name would she give me?" Bailey elbowed her lightly, making sure not to press against her hip.

"Probably Epimaco." She tried to stay as straight-faced as possible, but he was asking for it.

"What's that mean?"

"Easy to attack!" She quickly knocked him in the back of his head with her good arm and then leaned away in hope of avoiding any retaliation. Wrapping his arms around her waist, he playfully began to tickle her. He was gentle enough to avoid her injuries.

"Is that what you think of me? As beautiful a name like Anaba is for you, I only get some cheap joke?"

"You… don't… ha-ha… *stop*!" She tried to squirm her way out of his hold while gasping for air.

"I want something cool. Then I'll stop." He began to laugh with her. Dierno let out a low grunt to show his annoyance, but it went unnoticed.

"Okay… how… about… Gu… Guariruna?"

He stopped, but still held her around the waist. This felt better than he ever thought. “I don’t think I could spell that, let alone repeat it. What’s it mean?”

“Untamed wild man.” She felt his warm breath on her neck when it escaped his nose in disappointment. The tickling began again and she said, “Okay. Okay. Stop. I’ll make you… a deal.”

“All right. What’s the deal?” He kept his arms around her waist and rested his chin on her good shoulder. While listening to her offer he noticed the luscious smell of her skin. Closing his eyes and slowly inhaling, the fragrance of morning sunlight on dew-caressed leaves invaded his senses.

“I’ll give you a choice of two names. You can research the meanings or ask Meovi. Then you can have your silly, unnecessary name.” She tried to turn her head when she heard him inhale longer than necessary for regular breathing, but something inside stopped her.

“Deal,” he said, before he opened his eyes.

“Igashu, which would be Meovi’s choice, or Ryduen.” She felt the warmth of his body wrapped around her. It was comforting and made her forget her pain.

“Ryduen would be your choice?” He sounded hopeful.

“Maybe.”

“Maybe?” He loosened his grip around her waist in order to look into her eyes and read the meaning that might lie there.

“Could turn into Enyeto.” She popped up when she felt the release in his body and took two bounds into the bathroom and locked the door behind her.

“Oh, you have to come out eventually,” he yelled across the small room as if the door could silence him.

“I will. When you fall asleep,” she teased.

"I've got forever to figure out these names, you know." He stood up to walk over to the door, but didn't get as far as he had planned.

"Not when you have to get the door," she laughed at him. He could feel her gaze through the door. And suddenly there was a rapping on solid wood.

Bailey turned to look at the front door. "I hate it when you do things like that." He walked over to open it, but wasn't sure why he needed to when the tribe didn't have locks on their front doors.

"Things going well?" Meovi said when Bailey opened the door.

"Why did you knock?" He had to know why of all the times she'd entered she would knock this time.

"Didn't want to interrupt," she replied. "Are you going to let me in or are you not decent?" Her arms were crossed but one hand held out a cup with dark liquid swirling to escape its enclosure.

Bailey averted his gaze briefly before meeting her eyes again and said, "What's Ryduen mean?"

15

The little TV screen displayed Honovi and Jailin's fight. One black bar kept rolling through the screen every few seconds. The two girls fought with stealthy grace.

Adrian's heart pumped wildly and he found himself continuously reaching for the nape of his neck. "That girl is Anaba?" he asked.

"Huh? Oh yeah, that's her." Honovi wasn't watching the screen. She was sitting so close to Adrian while fingering his hair that she might as well have been sitting in his lap. The spikes of his hair had fallen flat, so he didn't mind that Honovi was mussing up his usually perfect hair.

"This is the test subject from the jungle?" He couldn't believe this was the enchanting girl from the café.

"Yeah, what'd you expect?"

"Well, like you, but… uglier." He winced. He knew better than to speak before he thought.

"Listen to me, little Vernore. I am ten times the woman she is and you'll remember that or you'll be as catatonic as her father."

"You mean Dr. Munrow? Father's been keeping him drugged like a mental case for almost fifteen years. Are you saying this girl is Jailin Munrow?"

"Yeah, and you'd better watch yourself around her. She finds out who you are and she'll kill you."

"Really? Fine." Adrian wasn't about to think of the meeting at the café. Last thing he wanted was Honovi or his father to know he'd already run into her. And lived through it.

Meovi stared at Bailey. She wasn't happy about what she was hearing. Tribal names were titles given to those who have earned it. "She gave you that name?" Meovi asked.

"No, she said I could choose." Bailey's eyes flashed toward the bathroom door Jailin was still hiding behind.

"What is the other choice?"

"Um… Ee… uh… Eegaw… I don't remember."

"Igashu?"

"Yeah! She said you'd have chosen that for me."

"Well, perhaps… although I won't do such a thing."

"Why not? It's just a 'What If ?' kind of game."

"This tribe doesn't play those games."

"Oh, Meovi, calm down." Jailin came out of the bathroom. She had changed from her shorts and leg gauntlets into a gray low rise yoga pant. Her perfectly sculpted abs were emphasized by the blue form-fitted tank top.

"This is why you shouldn't play these games," Meovi pointed at Bailey who was taken aback by the adorable girl before him. His lips parted slightly. His mind reverted to only a few moments ago. It felt like an eternity since his arms had been around her and he could smell the clean morning leaves of her skin.

"I didn't think it's a big deal. He was learning about our culture."

"He's learning about you."

"I'm sorry," he apologized. "Does it matter? I was just asking questions. I didn't mean to cross the line or anything."

"You didn't," Jailin corrected. "Something else is bothering her." Her eyes narrowed toward Meovi.

Meovi switched to the native tongue again to keep Bailey out of it. "Masou says Honovi's been caught sneaking around at night while you've been gone. No one does patrol like you and we may be in danger now because you're playing games like a lasowan. Did you really offer him Ryduen? What changed so quickly?"

"Hey, I heard Ryduen… I think. Will someone tell me what that means?"

"Jailin will tell you if she's going to play these games with you." Meovi spoke directly to Bailey. Her eyes filled with anger.

"There are too many ways to keep me in the dark around here," he mumbled to himself.

"You should go, Ben. She's right. I'm neglecting my people."

"But…"

Meovi gathered her herb pouch and grinding bowl. She left the tea she had brought on the table and walked out the door.

"I'm sorry. Here." She quickly wrote down the words she felt were important for Bailey to know and handed it to him. "Look up Maimugg translation and it will tell you what these words mean."

"Oh…" He glanced over the paper.

"Bye, Ben." Her voice was light as if parting ways was more difficult this time.

"Will Meovi be mad for long?"

"No. She thinks I got hurt protecting you. She thinks I'm distracted and doesn't want you to become Kafele."

"She said that?"

"No. Socrates translated for Dierno."

"Oh, right. I forgot that no mind is off limits to him."

She nodded once, kissed his cheek and walked out the door to find Meovi.

"Bye." After she was gone he opened up the paper she had given him to write down the last word she had used: Kafele.

Bailey entered his apartment and hit the power button to his laptop. The room was dark like his mood so he didn't bother to turn the lights on. On his computer he typed the first word, Enyeto. The computer spit back: Walks like a bear.

"Funny. Very funny," he said aloud.

He skipped down the list to Ryduen. The computer translated: He who has my heart. Then he entered the name Meovi was said to have chosen, Igashu. The computer gave him another translation: Wanderer or seeker. He knew she meant snoop.

"Interesting," he thought. "Don't see why this is a difficult choice."

Next he typed Lasowan, and it said One who causes fire in the heart. Bailey gulped, unsure how deeply he should read into this.

"What if I become Kafele to her?"

He couldn't figure out on his own what this could mean. Good or bad he desperately wanted to know. He typed it out and waited with his finger over the enter key. What was he waiting for? Worth dying for. He leaned back in his chair and put his hand to his cheek where she had kissed him.

"You always talk to yourself in the dark?" A hand rested on his shoulder, making him jump up out of his chair.

"Holy hell, Gabe. Don't do shit like that."

"Then don't sit in the dark, dude."

"Did you ever leave?"

"Nah, I ate your food, watched your porn and called Tabby for you."

"What?"

"Don't sound so upset. I put the porn back."

"I don't own any, so it's not even that funny. What did you tell Tabitha?"

"That you've got a new girl."

"Damn you. You didn't?"

"So what if I did? You blow it already?" Gabe playfully punched Bailey in the shoulder.

"Tabitha's manic-depressive, Gabe."

"You said to tell her anything. Besides, isn't she medicated?"

"I didn't think you were such an idiot." Bailey shook his head in bewilderment. Sometimes it was amazing how oblivious Gabe was to the world around him.

"Dude, relax. She's fine."

"How do you know that?"

"Because we uh…" Gabe's voice got quieter, "slept together."

"Oh…" Bailey was stunned. He couldn't think of anything to say to that.

"Don't be mad."

"I'm not."

"Are you sure?" Gabe was feeling guilty. Perhaps if Bailey were mad it would ease the pangs of guilt rushing through his nerves.

"Yeah. I'm okay with this."

"That's because you know you're free now to do crazy shit with that new hottie. What's her name?"

"Jailin. And it's not like that."

"Uh-huh, sure."

"It's not. It's different this time."

"Just because she's not a blonde bimbo doesn't mean it's different."

"What's that supposed to mean?"

"It means, dude, that you throw away any girl who gives it up too soon. The longer she holds out, the longer you stick around. It's like you're afraid that if you get too attached you'll get hurt again and lose everything—like when you lost your parents. You can't commit. Not that I think you should. I'm just surprised that you stuck with Tabby this long."

"You been holding this in awhile?"

"Nah, just a sudden epiphany."

Bailey looked back at his computer screen and read the words again. Worth dying for. "Well, this is definitely not like that."

"Are you committing yourself?"

"I think I have been since I was six."

"Dude!" Gabe's eyes grew wide. "You slept with her, didn't you?"

"No. I didn't."

"Yeah, you did!"

"I'm not fighting about this with you." Bailey wasn't about to get himself caught up in a childish fight of who did and who didn't. "When are you leaving?" Bailey walked over to the fridge and saw the coffee Jailin had left there. He took it out and reheated it.

"Hmm… maybe you didn't, but you've thought about it." Gabe knew when Bailey changed the subject it wasn't something worth fighting about in order to keep secret. "If you didn't sleep with her then what happened?"

Bailey slumped back down into the chair and closed his laptop. "She got hurt. I couldn't do anything to help. All I could do was watch it. She got beat so hard and just kept going." He dropped his head in his hands. He was so angry, so upset with himself for being so weak, so normal.

"Who beat her?"

He took a swallow of the coffee and let it burn down his throat. "Some woman dressed like a prostitute."

"Whoa, wait a minute. Why were you two out with prostitutes? I didn't know you did that kind of shit, dude." Gabe sat at the table with Bailey. This was getting more interesting.

"Not like that. It was some woman from her tribe." Bailey shook his head to clear the image. "She's evil and works for Vernore. They got into a fight. Yeah, Jailin could defend herself, but not against that freak show."

"So? You're GIA. Steal her some bulletproof vests or heavy artillery or somethin'. I know you've got the resources."

"It's not the same. Besides I don't think she's that inhumane."

"It's not inhumane to defend yourself."

"No, but I think I have another idea."

"What's that?"

"I could close the gap between us."

"Gap? You gonna change the tides? Move mountains? I need some specifics."

"She's special," Bailey smiled. "Incredible."

"Yeah, I've heard it all before, dude. Give it time and you might not feel that way."

"No. Let me explain..." Bailey told Gabe everything about the past few days. From finding her wrestling with a giant white cat in a small clearing of the Grundagon jungle up to the conversation he had had with Vernore. He told Gabe everything he wouldn't tell Jailin about her father and his illness in a mental hospital. He even made Gabe promise not to mention anything to Jailin about her father.

Lastly, Bailey told him about choosing Maimugg tribal names and the playful flirting with Jailin earlier that evening. He explained how Meovi believed him to be a liability for their whole civilization because of the time he was spending with Jailin, their best night watcher.

"So wait. Can you hear the wild cat and monkey thing?" Gabe said when Bailey was finished.

"It's actually a cross of a panther, tiger, and a domestic house cat according to blood samples I have at GIA's Northpost. I've learned that interbreeding is common among panthers so the different types of blood aren't rejected." Bailey moved a few papers around the table as he spoke, "It's not a monkey, by the way, it's a ring-tailed lemur. And no, I can't hear them but that's what I meant when I said close the gap."

"So by closing this gap you'd get super powers?"

"If that's what you want to call it, then yeah. If I don't die first, of course."

“Cool,” Gabe said dreamily as he brought his arms up to place his hands behind his head.

16

It rained the whole next morning and throughout the day. Bailey had been up through the night talking with Gabe and had only had a couple hours of sleep. He was tired, but had promised his boss he would meet him this morning with more information about Vernore's connection to the mysterious white panthers. Information that he couldn't put in an email. He was on his way there now and had no intention of leading them to Jailin.

Pulling into a reserved spot at GIA headquarters, he pulled up the hood on his zip-up gray sweatshirt with its navy blue GIA logo screen-printed on the back. He jumped out of the Ridgeline and sprinted to the large, reinforced tinted glass doors. When he got there, he waved his GIA key chain over the sensor plate and the heavy magnetic bolt slid free from the metal encasement.

"Afternoon, Sylvia," Bailey said as he ran by the receptionist.

"Afternoon," she replied but looked up too late to realize who had bid her the afternoon. He was already in his boss's office.

The room was empty and dark due to the rain. On the desk lay an envelope marked B. Bailey. He picked it up and read the contents.

Agent Bailey,

Thank you for contacting me about the visual on project V. Please keep this information confidential. It is of the top-most importance that we are not compromised. I have taken the responsibility to extract your personal items from your camp in Grundagon Jungle. You will find it all in bunker 17.

On a personal note—sorry, I could not meet with you as promised. I know you have more information. I will be outside Grundagon for an undetermined time, but I will contact you when I return.

Commissioner Levin

P.S. Take a vacation. You've earned it.

"Great." Bailey walked out the door and Sylvia finally noticed who had run past her.

"Oh, Agent Bailey. How are you? The Commissioner is out. Can I help you with anything?"

"No. Thank you, Sylvia."

"Okay, well you know where to find me."

"Oh wait, can you tell me who's in charge of running the blood samples I submit?"

"Let me look it up." Sylvia looked at her monitor and typed exceptionally fast. As she searched the GIA database Bailey kept re-reading the letter. "It's Jim Simon."

"You mean my old genetics professor?"

"Yes. It says here he's working on many different breakdowns of synthetic DNA strands. He's specifically assigned to your jobs."

"Thanks, Sylvia." Bailey smiled and stuffed the letter into the back pocket of his jeans. He walked out the door and back to his car before removing his hood.

When he arrived home, he plopped down in front of the TV with Gabe. "Anything good on?"

"Maybe if you owned some porn there would be."

"You're not going to let that go are you?"

"It's funny."

"No, it's not. Besides, don't you ever go home?"

"Yeah, but if I go home I'm afraid Tabby will be there."

"I thought you two were a thing now."

"Dude, how long have you known me? I just like sex and she's vulnerable right now."

"Damn it, Gabe. I didn't know you were that big of an ass."

A knock came at the door. Bailey got up to answer it as Gabe said, "Apparently I am."

Bailey was looking back at Gabe while he was opening the door and laughing with him. When he turned back he saw a woman with a large duffle bag. Wet jeans hugged her legs, a sweatshirt that read Grundagon Wildlife Refuge hung heavily on her body. Her hair dripped a river over the curves of her face and shoulders. Slumped over with her head down, she appeared to be lost. "Can I help you?" Bailey asked and she raised her head. Eyes, bloodshot from crying, looked back at him. His heart dropped into his stomach. "Jailin, what's wrong?"

"I don't have anywhere else to go," she said and he put his arms out to draw her in. She was trembling. He wasn't sure if her shaking was due to her crying or her being cold. Emotions twisted inside him. He was overjoyed to hold her, because he didn't know if he ever would again, but concern for the pain she felt had his heart splitting.

"Who's there, dude? You're missing out on the nudity!" Gabe laughed at his ongoing joke and Bailey grunted because for a moment he had forgotten Gabe was there. He was lost in her—in the smell and the feel of her against him.

"Come on," he whispered into her hair, "you can stay with me."

Her heart fluttered when she heard him say this. Perhaps Meovi was right and she was going to get hurt. Physically and emotionally. She just couldn't see it that way. Not with the boy who had played in the sand with her as a child. Not in the man who confessed thinking about her every day of his life and wondering about his lost friend. Could they be more than friends? Did she have the strength to accept his rejection? She forced herself not to think about it.

Bailey closed the door and released her from his arms.

"Oh, it's you." Gabe didn't intend to sound offensive.

"Maybe I shouldn't stay here. I can go to a motel or something." She was clutching her duffle bag tighter than before. She didn't want to go, but didn't want to cause a problem for Bailey either.

"No. Stay. He's leaving anyway."

"No, I'm not. I already told you. I can't go home."

"Then you can sleep on the floor." The irritation in Bailey's voice was inimitable.

"What for? The couch pulls out."

"I'm not sharing the couch with you."

"Oh, I thought you'd be sharing your bed," Gabe chuckled. "I'll share your bed, if you're not going to."

"Don't make me kick your ass."

Gabe made a childish face and mouthed Bailey's words back at him.

"Come on. I'll show you where to put your things." Bailey led Jailin to his room.

"Hey, hot stuff," Gabe said as they walked past the couch. "Cuttin' to the chase already, huh, Benji?"

As Bailey passed by Gabe he punched him in the back of the head.

"Ow! Dude, I was kidding." Gabe ran his hand through his hair to sooth the sting.

Bailey led Jailin through the doorway and she put her bag on the bed. The room was still the same as when she had slept there last. It looked as if it hadn't been used since. The bedspread was still wrinkled, the pillow she had used remained flat and some of Socrates' hairs were on the untouched pillow.

"Here." Bailey pulled four pairs of jeans out of the bottom drawer of his dresser. "You can put your things in here."

"Are you sure this isn't an inconvenience?"

"Of course not. Where's Socrates and Dierno?" Jailin opened her bag and Socrates popped his head out. "What else you got in there?" he joked.

"Dierno's patrolling the border of the jungle."

"Who's watching the tribe?"

Jailin sighed, "Not me. I talked Sarana, an old friend, into keeping an eye on them for me."

"What happened?"

"I got demoted out of patrol and ordered to leave temporarily."

"Did Meovi do this?"

"No. She fought for me to stay. Masou thought I was going to bring chaos to the tribe. Told me to get *it* out of my system. Whatever *it* is, I don't know. You can't fight your leader apparently."

"What if something happens and you're not there?"

"A friend owes me a favor. Sarana. You've met her."

Bailey shook his head. He couldn't recall meeting any of Jailin's friends. "I have? When?"

"You almost slit her throat a few nights back. I thought you were a poacher, remember?"

Bailey's forehead furrowed as he searched his memory. "The cougar?" Jailin nodded once. "I thought she was going to eat me, by the way. Otherwise, I would never had needed my…"

Jailin smiled at his attempt to defend himself, but interrupted him anyway. "She'll alert Dierno and he'll tell me if something goes wrong. I only have a two-mile radius for conversation, which is why we need her."

"I have a question." His eyes surveyed her from head to toe and he sounded concerned, yet sincere.

"Yes?" She squared herself to him and moved a step closer.

He swallowed and she could hear his heart beat louder with nervousness. "I looked up the words you gave me."

"Did you choose a name?"

"No. Not exactly."

"Then what's the question?"

"Am I really a Kafele?"

"You mean: Are you Kafele?"

"Whatever." He didn't know her language well enough to defend his grammar.

She slid her arms around his waist and rested her head on his chest under his chin. He placed his lips on her hair and breathed in her mouth-watering smell. "Well?"

"That's why I didn't argue with Masou when I was forced to leave my home. I lost you once. I don't want to again."

"You won't." He closed his eyes and kissed the top of her head. When he reopened them he saw something he hadn't noticed before, "Hey, is that my old soccer jersey heaped on the floor?"

"Yeah, I slept in it the other night."

"Really? I bet that was adorable."

She smiled at him and blushed only slightly. She felt braver around him and didn't bother to hide her face or force herself out of these situations with anger. He brought one hand up to her face to brush some wet hair away. He didn't take his hand away after he tucked her hair behind her ear. She closed her eyes and he slowly brought his head down toward hers. The warmth of his breath brushed past her lips. Her heart skipped a beat and she could hear his pulse race.

"Dude, the monkey stole the remote!" Bailey stopped short and grunted Gabe's name in frustration.

Jailin dropped her head knowing that this wasn't the time to be getting caught up in her emotions. "I'll go take a shower. Be nice to Socrates. TV is new to him."

Bailey sighed. He didn't want to remove his arm from around her waist. He hated Gabe for being so careless. "Don't go anywhere." He tightened his hold once then slid his arm out from around her.

"Where am I going?" she asked playfully as he backed up to the open door.

"Nowhere," he stated as he closed the door to give her privacy.

"Dude, psycho monkey just took the remote from me. And he channel surfs like a coke fiend."

"He's a ring-tailed lemur." Bailey informed Gabe as he walked around him to sit on the empty couch cushion.

"Pfftt… monkey. Hey, you never said how work went this morning." Gabe swiveled his head away from the TV to look Bailey in the eye.

"I got that vacation you wanted."

"Sweet! Let's go out tonight." Gabe leaned forward, ready to run out the door at Bailey's acceptance of the idea.

"You go. I've got company." He glanced to the closed door.

"Right. Lovin' in the rain." Gabe slumped back against the couch. "Hmm, maybe I will go home."

Bailey's eyes flashed to the window. "Damn it, it's raining!" He ran to knock on the bathroom door. Had he misinterpreted what had been going on between himself and Jailin just a few minutes ago?

"Huh?" Gabe turned to watch Bailey run to the door.

17

Jailin heard the persistent knocking on the bathroom door. She disliked being interrupted during a bath. Taking a bath was always a tranquil time—enjoying the sounds of the jungle, the sweet smells of the surrounding flowers, and the rush of the cool crisp water running over her skin. This bath was nothing like that, but she still wanted her peace and quiet. "What is it?" she asked.

"It's raining!" he yelled back.

"You are very observant. Is this why GIA thinks you're a genius?"

"No, what?" He had heard Gabe joke often enough about how the Grundagon Intelligence Agency only accepted exceptional students from their elite boarding school, but he had never thought of himself as a genius. Unless, being able to infiltrate your enemies' secure databases without their realizing implied intelligence—then of course. "I mean… I just…"

"Can this wait until I'm done in here?" she asked, not bothering to let him finish what he was trying to say.

Bailey recalled her bathing next to her hut. The curves of her back danced in his mind. He shut his eyes to focus on the conversation. "Yeah, I guess." He sat down on the end of his bed and waited for her to come out.

"If only Dierno were here, then I could ask him what Ben's thinking," she thought as she wrapped a towel around herself and stepped out of the tub. Her hair was clipped up in a bun and she opened the door to see Bailey sitting on the bed, waiting for her. "Is it really that urgent?" she asked, as she stood in front of him. He didn't look up from the floor to meet her eyes.

"I need to know," he mumbled softly.

"Know what?"

"What happens when it rains?" His eyes shot up to finally meet hers.

"The ground soaks up the water and plant life feeds on it. I, in turn, usually eat that plant life and perhaps someday maybe I'll be eaten. Circle of life. Any other questions?" She smiled and hoped he would too.

"This is funny to you?"

"If I knew what you were so worked up about then maybe it wouldn't be."

"I almost kissed you…" he trailed off, wondering if they'd be having this conversation if he had.

Without knowing why, his statement hurt. She waited to hear what would come out next. Her stomach knotted. She couldn't recall ever being so nervous. Looking away from him, all she could bring herself to say after the long silence was, "But you didn't."

"Are your feelings real?"

"What kind of question is that?" Her temper was getting the best of her.

"Are you… using me?" he forced out.

She turned to look at him. She finally understood what he was so concerned about. He was staring at his hands and fumbling for the right way to hold them. It was as if he had never seen them before. He was nervous and afraid of rejection, or at least *her* rejection. She angled his chin up toward her and placed her forehead against his. He looked as if he would depart this life if she said "yes." Instead she replied, "Why would I do that? If you could hear what I hear, sense what I sense, and feel what I feel, you would know that I would never do anything to hurt you."

"What about the rainy season?"

"Ben, this isn't the rainy season… *yet*."

"Then what will happen when it does come?"

She dropped to her knees and interlaced her fingers with his. "I can't really say. So much has changed in the last few days that I don't know what will happen now."

"What used to happen?"

"I was out of control. Luckily, I was with Meovi. She would give me a sedative so I would sleep through the worst of it. I'd have horrible dreams. Mostly about my father being tortured or anything else that could put him in the state he's in now." Bailey winced knowing the truth about this, but felt now wasn't the time to tell her what he knew. "When Meovi wasn't there or strong enough, Masou would control me. That was hard for me because he's a man."

Bailey gulped, "Did you and he…"

"No, good lord, no. He's a gentle man. Brave and strong, but wouldn't hurt a woman, ever."

"Then why all the insinuations about… *it*?"

"Everyone figures I'll be too strong to stop someday and, if I can't control it, every man is in danger."

"So you've never..."

"No. Feel better now that you've embarrassed me?" Her tone sounded sarcastic.

"That wasn't my intention."

"Well, you succeeded anyway." She crossed her arms—tension was built up in her shoulders.

"This wasn't easy for me to ask, you know?"

"Right, sorry," she said shyly and relaxed her shoulders.

Bailey stood up to go and said, "I'll let you get dressed." She stopped him by grabbing his hand, stood up and pressed herself against his chest.

"Don't let my towel fall off," she whispered as she wrapped his arms around her waist and then placed her hands on either side of his face. He brought his lips to hers and she could feel the warmth of his mouth on hers with such need and desire. Her fingers laced into his hair and he gripped the towel tighter, causing it to creep up her thighs.

"O.M.G.! What the hell is this?" A squeaky voice came from the doorway. They turned their heads to see who it was.

"Tabitha?" Bailey was surprised to see her.

"How could you, Benji? I can't believe you'd do something like this behind my back!" Her arms were crossed and her right foot tapped on the carpet, making a deep thudding sound.

"Actually, he's doing this in front of you," Gabe deadpanned. He stood a full head length above her, which meant she was only a little shorter than Jailin.

"You knew about this?" Tabitha turned to Gabe.

"I told you he's distracted and to give him some space."

"Gabe, you told me you two slept together. I thought..." Bailey's eyes squinted as if it would help him to understand what was going on.

"You told him that?" Tabitha spun around to face Gabe. "Why would you do that?"

"I tell him everything," he shrugged.

Jailin slipped away from Bailey's embrace. She was very uncomfortable in this situation. Her stomach churned as she picked a shirt and jeans out of her bag and went back to the bathroom.

"Who is she?" Tabitha demanded to know. She pointed a condemning finger at Jailin.

"An old friend," Bailey answered. Socrates ran in from the living room and scratched at the bathroom door.

"This apartment has rats? Benji, you have rats!" Socrates turned to look at Tabitha in disgust.

"Ring-tailed lemur," Gabe said, feeling proud that he could correct someone else.

"You can't have pets in here!"

"Then you should leave," Bailey told Tabitha.

"Oh, ha, ha," she sounded out each word. "No! We have to settle this. You just have an infatuation. It'll pass. We'll still be together."

"No. I don't want this. I don't want you."

"I'm just another girl on your tally list? Is she the next mark?"

Jailin came out of the bathroom dressed in her light wash jeans and a black cotton T-shirt that was cut in a U-shape along the hem. It made her waist look even smaller. She scooped up Socrates and put him in her bag.

"What are you doing? You're not leaving, are you?" Bailey didn't know what to do. He looked at each girl, trying to decipher which one to address first.

"I've caused enough trouble for everyone. I'll find some place to stay."

"Damn right you will, honey." Tabitha put her hands on her hips and bent her right knee so that her left hip jutted out to the side.

"No, please stay," Bailey begged.

Jailin zipped up her bag and exhaled as she dropped her head. She didn't want to leave, but she knew when she was better off elsewhere.

"You can stay with me," Gabe offered.

"No, she's not staying with you!" Bailey stated. "Stay," he whispered into Jailin's hair as he came up behind her and lightly placed his hands on her hips. He put his lips closer to her ear. "Stay," he whispered again. Jailin's heart skipped a beat and an ache ran through her body. She wanted to kiss him again, but knew she shouldn't.

"I really should go," she exhaled.

"Let her go, Benji. You can hold me like you used to." Tabitha was hoping to anger the girl in her man's arms.

"You two should talk. Whatever happens, I'll still be your... *friend*." Jailin repeated the word he had used earlier to describe her to this whiney and annoying girl.

Friend. The word hurt more than she ever thought it could. There was no guarantee in life that people would always remain friends. She felt exceptionally worried that Bailey might disappear from her life so soon after being reacquainted—after losing him once already as a little girl. Jailin unzipped her bag and took Socrates out.

"Reassure him that I'm not far and will come back when the time is right. I know you don't want to be in the middle of this, but please do this for me," Jailin thought and Socrates jumped down from her arms and sauntered back into the living room. Jailin swung her bag onto her shoulder. "You know how to reach me." She looked into Bailey's eyes and hoped he understood Socrates' ability to talk to her.

As she passed through the doorway, she stopped only for a second to examine Tabitha. Her blonde wavy locks flowed over her shoulders. Her little white Queen-Anne collared, short-sleeve blouse fitted her curvy body perfectly. The red plaid mini skirt revealed her cascading legs. Obviously this is what got the guys the all-you-can-eat chicken wings. Jailin felt she was no match for this girl's beauty.

"She looked pissed," Gabe announced after Jailin had left the apartment.

Tabitha was looking pleased with herself. "Let's go out."

"You two go. I'm going to look for her."

"Sorry, dude." Gabe walked over and patted Bailey on the shoulder.

"You honestly thought we were over? Well, I'm not letting you go, baby." She stepped up to him and wrapped her scrawny arms around his bicep.

He shrugged her off. "We are over or whatever we were is over. I don't want anything to do with you. You blame me for such an innocent action compared to what you've done."

"What'd I do?" Tabitha asked in a childish tone.

"Gabe." He couldn't believe he had to remind her of this.

"Oh, that. It wasn't anything special. I didn't even enjoy it." She waived her hand in the air as if to dismiss the issue. Gabe's eyebrows raised and he was about to say something, but Tabitha elbowed him in the side in order to keep him quiet.

"Doesn't matter. Whatever we were is history. You considered me your boyfriend, but I never intended it to be that way. I never loved you. Sorry to be so harsh, but as far as I'm concerned, we never happened."

"Then you can't be mad about Gabe and me."

"I'm not. That's what's funny. When he told me, I was more concerned about your suicidal tendencies."

"Gee, thanks. Can't make someone jealous who doesn't care, I guess."

"Nope." He took his black light-weight jacket from the closet.

She turned out of the room. "Okay, Gabe, you're it. Let's go party."

18

Gabe was surrounded by loud music and flashing lights, and people dancing anywhere they happened to be standing kept bumping into him. Splashes of green, blue, yellow, and brown paint decorated the walls inbetween rough, untalented depictions of wild animals. He was trying to weave his way to the quiet side of the Dance Zoo night club to a room called The Pride. He could hardly hear his cell phone ringing in his ear.

When they finally picked up, he said, "Hello? Benji? Guess what? Well, rather who, just came through the door of Dance Zoo with the owner?" He paused to hear Bailey's reply. "No. Not me, Jailin." A muffled exclamation was heard, followed by a loud question and Gabe held the phone away from his ear. "I don't know, dude, but if she's hanging out with that guy you might have some competition. All girls want that rich asshole." Gabe was silent while he held his other hand to his ear to drown out the music. "So what if he's Vernore's son?" Gabe paused for a response. "Oh yeah, I forgot about that." Then he said, "Okay. I'll try to find out. Just get here as fast as you can." He slapped his phone closed and caught up to Jailin and Adrian as they started up the stairs to Adrian's loft. "Hey!"

"Hi, Gabe," Jailin said, looking emotionally drained.

"What'cha need?" Adrian turned to ask Gabe.

"Nothin'. I'm just seein' how Jailin's doin'." Gabe beamed a huge smile in Jailin's direction. She didn't return the gesture.

"You know him?" Adrian asked her, while placing a gentle hand on her shoulder.

"Yeah," she exhaled.

"Okay. I'll be right back. Gonna go get us something to drink and then we can talk upstairs." Adrian stepped back down the two steps and went toward the bar.

"No rufies, dude!" Gabe hoped someone would hear him over all the music.

"Haven't ever needed 'em." No one could embarrass this man.

"What do you want, Gabe?" Jailin was impatient.

"Please, don't go up there. Girls make the walk of shame after a night with Adrian. Don't do this to Benji, especially with his… you know. Plus, he's a Vernore."

"I know." She looked away so Gabe wouldn't notice the tears she held back.

"You do? Then why?"

"I think he's different from his father. I kind of enjoy his company and I might find out something I can use."

"Hey." Bailey showed up behind Gabe.

"Whoa, you got here fast." Gabe spun around.

"I was already out when you called."

"Where's your *girlfriend*?" Jailin asked him with disgust. She had gotten angrier while she walked the streets thinking. Running into Adrian provided a brief distraction.

"She's not my girlfriend. And she left my place with Gabe. Anyway, it doesn't matter." He came up the two steps to meet her eye to eye, but she didn't want to return the eye contact. She hated crying.

Adrian was coming back with a drink in each hand. He saw a man approach Jailin and place his hand around her wrist. He broke one glass as he thought to himself, "Doesn't he know better? No one stops a girl from ascending my stairs!" When he got to the stairway he addressed Jailin, "Is this guy bothering you?"

"No. Everything's fine." She looked up and met Bailey's gaze. His eyes were the same as Adrian's, but now for the first time she noticed a softness to his that Adrian's didn't have.

"Take your hand off her," he told Bailey.

"You have a really cool club. Something for everyone." Gabe tried to intercede.

"Get lost!" Adrian chided.

Gabe was unsure of how to react. He looked around trying to find some kind of escape, but didn't want to leave Bailey alone in this confrontation.

"Come with me," Bailey begged Jailin.

"She's not going anywhere with you!"

"I'm not talking to you. I'm talking to her. She can answer for herself."

"Fine. Tell him. Tell him he hurt you and you're hanging out with me tonight."

Bailey looked deeper into her eyes. He moved his hand from her wrist to her waist as he took another step closer to her. The other hand he placed to her cheek to run his thumb over her soft lips. "I didn't mean to hurt you." A single tear slowly fell down her cheek and his thumb moved to wipe it away. "God, I'm so sorry."

Adrian grabbed his arm to pull it off her. Bailey knew from his talk with Vernore that he couldn't overpower him so he took both arms away from her. "I don't want to lose you again. I'm scared I already have and we haven't had any real time together. You mean so much more to me now than when we were little. Please come with me?"

Jailin didn't know what she wanted. She enjoyed Adrian's company and thought he could understand her. Bailey she had history with. She had learned to trust him, understand him and she didn't want to give up on that. "I don't know."

"I'll make the choice for you. Come upstairs. We'll have fun and you won't have to think about this jerk."

"He's not a jerk..." She considered the times she had already called him one. "All the time," she added. Bailey smiled. He was glad she didn't think so now. His smile was like a drug to her. It pulled at her. *Why is he so addictive*? she thought to herself. She took one step down and extended her hand for Bailey to take.

"Hi, cutie pie," Tabitha squealed as she skipped up to Bailey, then she saw Jailin and Adrian. "Oh, wow, Mr. Vernore. How are you?" She blushed in his presence.

"Hello, adorable." Adrian was caught off guard and thought he might recapture Jailin's interest if she saw how desired he was.

"We should go now," Bailey whispered. Her heart always jumped when his breath tickled her ear and neck.

"You don't want more time with your brother?" she teased as quietly and seriously as she could. She knew Bailey wasn't happy about sharing a mother with Adrian—that was perfectly clear after

Bailey had met with Vernore a few nights ago. Adrian's eyes flashed in their direction, he didn't understand what Jailin had meant, but he promised himself to look into that another time. Quickly, he brought his attention back to Tabitha, as she blabbed on about how wonderful she thought he and his club were.

"Stop it," Bailey said and led Jailin toward the exit. With his arm around her waist he added, "Do you want to get something to eat?"

"Sure. Where?" No matter how much she tried, she couldn't stay mad at Bailey. Especially when those bright eyes and addictive smile pulled her into submission.

"I know a place you might like."

"Yeah? They serve vegetarian food, right?" she asked as they walked down the street, side by side.

"They'll make whatever you want," he said and smiled lightly at his private thought.

"You didn't drive here?" Jailin asked when she noticed they weren't headed to a parking lot. A lot of people were scurrying about at this late hour and Jailin wondered where they needed to be so badly.

"I did."

"Where's your truck?"

"In the parking garage of the old city hall. I'll get it later. I thought it might be nice to walk now that the rain has stopped. You can see the stars." He pointed up. The view was slightly restricted due to the towering buildings and street lights.

"That's strange." Jailin cocked her head to the side.

"What is?" Bailey looked up, expecting to see something abnormal. Everything was as he usually saw it.

"I've spent so many nights outdoors, sometimes sleeping in the trees, and the stars look so much prettier from the jungle."

"That's because the city lights mixed with the carbon monoxide from our polluting agents has formed a veil, causing your eyes to misinterpret the view of the sky."

"Now I see how you fooled GIA into thinking you're a genius. You're just like your father," she quipped.

"I'm not much of a scientist. Scientific terms never really enticed me. I prefer to interpret information into layman's terms. Not that I didn't do well in science in school. History was my poor subject."

"Your father would be proud no matter what."

"I wish I knew more about him."

"Would you like to meet my father sometime? I can't guarantee that it will be an exhilarating experience, but…"

"Yes. Yes, I would." He stopped walking, but she didn't notice at first and took two extra steps before she turned around. He took her by the hand and pulled her toward him. As she fell into his arms he lifted her chin with his free hand and kissed her. Her body relaxed in his arms and he held her up as he moved one hand to her cheek. She slid her palms down his chest to rest on his waist. He was incredibly warm pressed against her in the cool night breeze. She was perfectly content to never move from this spot.

He pulled back a little from her to speak but she moved with him. "No, don't," she worded between his lips.

"I wanted to finish what we started, but we're here." He said as he pulled back again.

"Where?" She looked up at the building and saw a beautiful roman architectural façade to a restaurant. "Are they even open now? It's past eleven."

"Luna Perfetta is always open for me."

"GIA privileges?"

"No, not exactly," he laughed. "Gabe assumed that too."

"Then what gives you special treatment?"

"A friend from military school had a passion. I think I was the only person he liked back then."

"Do you take all the girls here?" she joked.

"I've only ever come here with Gabe and he told me he never would again."

"Really? Why?"

"Let's just go in." He smiled and placed his hand on the small of her back. She'd know the answer to that soon enough.

19

Bailey led Jailin into the lavish restaurant. Ficus trees were lit with white lights, round tables were set with fine china on black tablecloths with lace runners. Large, tinted one-way mirrored windows lined the far wall to the left. An elaborate crystal chandelier hung in the foyer, underneath it was a beautiful ornate cherry-colored bar, with only the finest liquor selections.

"I'm sorry, but the kitchen is closed," the woman at the hostess table said seductively as she eyed Bailey from head to toe. There were still a few tables with people dining.

Bailey clutched Jailin around the waist and kissed her hair before saying, "Is Enrico here?"

The hostess smiled, picked up the phone and spoke in a fast language that sounded like gibberish to Jailin. "Beniamino," Bailey said as the hostess' eyes looked up at him.

Jailin raised an eyebrow at him, "Do you know this language?"

"The only one I don't know is yours." He spoke softly in her ear that was furthest from the hostess.

"Enrico says you know your way up," the hostess said.

"I do." Taking Jailin by the hand, he led her past the hostess, turned right and headed up the winding iron staircase. When they reached the top, a man in a perfectly tailored tux greeted them.

"Ah, Beniamino, it's been too long."

"Nice tux. You're not finally getting married, are you?" Bailey suppressed a smile.

"Such a kidder, this one." The man smoothed the shoulder of Bailey's jacket affectionately. "Is it a crime to look this fantastic? What's more, I'm expanding my restaurant, what do you think?" He turned from side to side, to display his grandeur.

"Perfect as always," Bailey teased.

"You two must be famished." Enrico swirled his finger in the air at them.

"Why else would we be here?"

"Such a silly bee." He placed a hand on Bailey's arm. "You never change. I've got the best seat in the house… mine."

Enrico led them past two closed doors. At the far end of the room a two-seater table was set with a cornflower blue tablecloth and sweet white violets. The large mirrored window from the floor below arched to meet the ceiling. Displayed before them was a beautiful scene of the cloudless starlit sky and Jailin could imagine seeing the jungle's tree line in the darkness.

"This is beautiful," Jailin said.

"Thank you, sweetheart." Enrico pulled a chair out for her at the little table. "The usual?" he asked Bailey, as he watched him take his seat.

"Not tonight. Vegetarian lasagna, if you would."

"Anything your heart desires, Beniamino." Enrico walked off toward the kitchen.

"He seems smitten," Jailin whispered after he left.

"He is." Bailey situated himself at the table.

"I was joking. Are you sure?"

Bailey shrugged. "He's a good friend, but plays for a different team. I stopped a couple of guys from jumping him at soccer practice when we were sixteen."

"Oh, his knight in shining armor, I see."

"It was nothing compared to what you can do."

"Me? What did I do?" Her eyes widened. No one had ever acknowledged her as more than just a simple girl. She always felt insignificant with the tribe until someone needed something.

"You're stronger than anyone I've ever met, including military, GIA, or whatever. I want to help you. I don't want to see you hurt again!"

"How do you expect to accomplish this?"

"Well, how about a new weapon, err…" Bailey stopped as he saw Enrico approaching. He figured that she wouldn't want a new weapon and that it wasn't the solution to keeping her safe.

Enrico placed their food down in front of them. He caught sight of his guests' body postures—slightly leaning toward one another—and left just as quickly as he had come.

"I like my bo staff," she continued their conversation after Enrico disappeared.

"I could get you titanium-lined gauntlets and a chest plate."

"Hmm." She was nodding as she chewed. It sounded like a good idea, but she wasn't interested in making any big changes. She swallowed and then added, "I like my patrol uniform, though. I made it with Masou's help."

"I hope you don't mind my asking, but what does his name mean?" Bailey didn't want to remind Jailin of why she wasn't at home in the jungle tonight, but he was curious about tribal customs.

"Fire God," she said between mouthfuls.

"Quite the name to live up to. Did Meovi name him that?"

"No, the yenena before her did. She was only learning the trade when Masou was born."

"What happened to the other yenena?"

"He passed away."

"So, are you to take Meovi's place?"

"She wants me to, but I don't care for all that. I can't prepare ointments like her and I let my emotions sway my actions too much. I'm not cut out for it."

"What would you like to do?"

"Due to my patrol stature I'm holding the place, or was holding the place as Masou's replacement."

"Really? The tribe's okay with that?"

"We need the strongest for the spot. No one minds, except the women." She pushed her food around on her plate.

"Why is that?" He watched her set down the fork and stare at her plate before she answered.

"Because our leaders are like polygamists, except they don't marry more than one woman. In fact, Masou isn't married at all."

"You're joking! You can't be serious?" He sat back in his chair and stared at her.

"Many men find it an honor to share their wives with a god."

"But he's not a god." Bailey leaned forward again. He couldn't believe what he was hearing.

"No. He represents one." She ran her finger in the leftover lasagna sauce on her plate and licked it off. She cherished the taste.

"Will the women find it an honor to share their husbands with a goddess?" Jailin saw his fists clench on the table. She toyed with the thought of him referring to her as a goddess and repressed a smile.

"No, that's part of the problem," she said as she pushed her cleaned plate away and set her elbows on the table. One hand supported her head and the other formed circles on the lush tablecloth.

"Well, I wouldn't share." He relaxed his hands.

"No one's asking you. And you don't have anyone to share anyway." The words rolled off her tongue as if she didn't need to think them through.

"I meant I wouldn't share you, with Masou or any deity for that matter."

"Oh..." His words made her blush and look down at the untouched food on his plate. Her hand went from forming circles on the table to playing with the pendant on her necklace.

"You're beautiful when you do that."

"Stop that!" She turned to look out at the trees.

"Why should I?"

"I'm not used to it," she whispered.

"Well, get used to it, because I won't stop." He leaned over the table to be closer to her. To study her face, memorize it.

"Why are you looking at me like that?"

Enrico overheard her question when he returned to check on them and said, "Why does anyone stop to smell a rose? Why does an artist paint a masterpiece? Why does the poet write a beautiful verse?"

"Sounds like you've got yourself a prompt," she smiled.

"If that were the case I don't think you'd still be sitting here."

"How do you know I'm not considering running off with this fantastic chef?" She winked up at Enrico.

"Funny girl. I like her," Enrico said, as he collected their plates to take them back to the kitchen.

"So do I," Bailey replied without taking his eyes off her. "Here that? He likes you," he added after Enrico left.

"More than you?" she whispered as she leaned forward. Bailey cupped the small flower-like pendant hanging from her neck and inspected every angle.

"I don't think it's the same thing." His brow angled with resentment. He suddenly felt the need to tell her what he had learned about their past from Vernore, but he couldn't. It would hurt her—cause her to leave.

Suddenly, the room began to shake. The table bounced on the hardwood floor and the sound of breaking dishes echoed from the kitchen. Bailey reached around the edge of the small table and pulled Jailin over to him. They heard people screaming downstairs and as the rumbling began to diminish, they saw a huge red cloud erupt in the distance, igniting the surrounding trees. "What is that?" Bailey pointed out the window to the cloud of smoke still rising from the fire lit trees.

"Dierno, what's happening out there?" Jailin thought, but there was no reply. "I'm not that far away. Why isn't he answering me?" she asked Bailey, knowing he couldn't know the answer.

"Did he fall asleep?" he attempted.

"He sleeps during the day."

"What about Socrates? Can't he hear you?"

"Socrates, where are you?" she thought.

"Under the table. During a worldquake, the safest place from falling objects is beneath a sturdy construction. I hope that is where you are."

"Can you hear Dierno? Do you know what just happened?"

"I have not bothered to converse with him. You cannot reach him, I presume?"

"No. Either he won't answer me, or he's out of my range."

"I will try."

During the mental silence, Jailin summed up for Bailey what she knew and said, "Socrates is trying to find Dierno."

"Any luck?"

"Nothing yet." She was shaking. She'd heard often enough about the Global Quake that had changed the world over 800 years ago. She could only imagine that this was what that one had been like. Bailey wrapped his arms around her for comfort—for her as well as himself. He too knew what worried her. News of the World Quake worried everyone—everything.

A few moments later Socrates was explaining to Jailin, "Dierno states that it was human error."

"What do you mean?"

"Construction workers at the dam were testing new equipment and it caused an increase in pressure to the water pipes. The main line ruptured, which is what you must have seen in the trees and felt in the building. Do not attempt to use the faucets right away. The pressure must decrease first."

"Enrico, don't..." Jailin didn't get to finish. A high-pitched scream interrupted her warning. Enrico came out of the kitchen, soaking wet.

"I guess you should have taken the tux off earlier. At least it's not food," Bailey pointed out, too late for any benefit.

"I'll be up all night pressing this for tomorrow's grand opening in East Central," Enrico pouted.

"I'm so sorry about you and your kitchen, Enrico. Thank you for the wonderful dinner. It was perfect," Jailin tried to console him.

"My life is my kitchen, honey. It's this damn wet smock of a tux I'm dreading to clean."

"We should go. Can we do anything for you before we leave?" Bailey asked.

"No, no. Enjoy the rest of your night, Beniamino. Don't stay away too long now, you hear me?"

"Sure thing, Enrico."

They descended the staircase into the dark room below. Only the track lighting illuminated the mess that had been thrown about the room by the bursting pipes.

"Thank you for dinner," Jailin said as they walked toward the parking garage where Bailey parked his truck.

"Did you enjoy it?"

"Oh yes, a very beautiful restaurant and Enrico is quite the cook."

"Good." He smiled and moved a little closer to slip his hand into hers.

They reached the garage and walked up the ramp to Bailey's truck. He opened the passenger door to let her in and when he was in the driver's seat next to her he asked, "So, where are you staying?"

"I have a room at the Starfield Inn. It's those one level buildings set up like cabanas where you don't have to set a checkout date or time. You know where it is? That's where my stuff is."

"Then that's where I'll take you." He started the truck, backed it out of the space and drove out of the garage. Jailin didn't know if she should say she wanted to go back to his place or not. It didn't feel right to push things too quickly, unless he offered first.

"How long do you think it will be before you can go home?"

"I don't know. Not until I'm past this phase."

"This *phase*? Ouch."

"Oh no, I didn't mean it like that. That was just what Masou called it." She turned sideways in her seat to look at him. She never really had taken into account what perfectly sculpted features he had. His hard jaw line and perfect nose were definitely his father's. Those gorgeous blue eyes, and those lips were from his mother. She realized he'd been talking to her the whole time she'd been staring at him and she had only caught the end of it.

"...so it's no big deal."

"What isn't?" she asked.

"That Masou thinks you're going through a phase."

"Oh, yeah, *that*."

"Are you all right?" He took his eyes off the road to quickly glance at her.

"Never better." She sat forward again as Bailey pulled into a series of one-story motel rooms.

"Which one is yours?"

"It's to the left, number twenty-one." Bailey parked in an empty spot at the front door. "Do you want to come in for a little while? I'm not used to being alone. I usually have Socrates with me."

"Do you want me to bring him over?"

"No! I mean, you don't have to go out of your way. I'm sure I'll see him tomorrow." She opened the door and got out. When she reached her room, she searched her pocket to find the key. She jumped when Bailey came up behind her and wrapped his arms around her waist.

"No goodnight?" he asked quietly into her ear.

She turned around in his arms but averted her eyes from his. "Goodnight," she said, straight-faced.

He didn't seem to notice the slight annoyance she had displayed with him after he had offered Socrates' company in place of his own. Smiling down at her, he placed his forehead against hers. She still didn't make eye contact; she knew if she did she wouldn't stay mad at his stupidity. When he brought her head up she closed her eyes so he couldn't win. Or so she thought. He kissed her lightly, not making full contact with her lips, only brushing over them in order to tease her. When she ran her hands through his hair, he kissed her harder. She stepped back into the room, pulling him with her by his shirt.

"What are you doing?" he asked.

"Keeping you here," she whispered and he closed the door as he kissed her again.

20

Metal scraped metal as Bailey pried open his mailbox. The usual bills and unwanted circulars overflowed the tiny rectangle in the wall. One thing that history had taught him was that postage ruined a source of communication. He disliked getting random unnecessary information, but since anyone could stick a piece of paper in a box without penalty, he wondered what life was like when you had to pay to get your "greetings" out there.

Heading toward his apartment from the foyer, he rounded the corner where, sitting slumped against his door, like a bum off the street, was Gabe. Bailey kicked his shoe to wake him so he could unlock the door.

"Dude, what took you so long? What time is it anyway?" His mouth was dry and he licked his lips as he awkwardly got to his feet.

"Six."

"In the morning?" He yawned.

"Yep."

"Where have you been?"

"Out."

"Thank you for the extremely descriptive story of your night. I'm sure it'll make headlines." He turned his back to the wall and pushed his hood back as he scratched his hair.

"Giving you details only causes havoc." Bailey turned the key in the latch.

"Come on, where were you?" He rolled toward Bailey to support the wall with his shoulder.

"I stayed at Jailin's motel."

"Liar! You didn't, did you?" He followed Bailey into the apartment.

"Yeah. And don't go getting over excited. We just talked about the last nineteen years we've missed."

"Uh-huh, sure that's all you did?"

"Mostly… She also wanted to know all about you." Bailey tried to hold back the smile creeping across his face.

"No, she didn't. Did she?"

"No." Bailey smirked and shook his head, which made Gabe feel like an idiot for being so gullible.

"Then what *did* you do… really?"

"I already told you. We caught up on the past."

"I don't believe you."

"I didn't expect you would." Bailey was flipping through the mail, adding to the already growing junk mail pile.

"So where is she?"

"Running. She'll be here later and I'm going to watch her spar. Oh, I also told her your idea of more defensive materials and she's willing to try it."

"Who's she sparring with?"

"A friend from another tribe who's been teaching here in the city." Bailey went over to the fridge. Gabe had already cleaned it out.

"Can I go too?"

"I guess so. You'll have to ask her when she gets here."

"Girl on girl action, sweet!" Gabe threw himself on the couch and put his hands behind his head, fantasizing about the upcoming event.

"Umm..." Bailey shut the fridge door, but didn't turn around to face Gabe.

"What?" Gabe searched the cushions to find the TV remote and sighed heavily when he saw Socrates asleep in the recliner with the remote sticking out from under him.

"Never mind." Bailey smiled. "I'm going to take a shower. Do whatever it is you do when you raid my place." He walked off toward his room.

Adrian's head was confined by pillows. The sheet was wrapped and twisted around his waist and knees. He began to stir, picked up a pillow and squinted into the bright morning light. "Did I get that drunk last night? I don't remember anything." He sat up and rubbed the heel of his hand into one eye.

"Good morning, handsome!" A familiar voice came from the kitchen.

Adrian swung his feet around to the floor and he threw on his red track pants. He scratched his head in hope of relieving the fogginess and went out to the kitchen. "Honovi? What are you doing here?"

"I think you know, sexy." She licked the rim of her glass of orange juice.

"Damn, my head hurts. I didn't think I drank that much last night."

"You had a couple of drinks with that little blonde slut. I didn't bother to catch her name."

Adrian squinted into the brightly lit kitchen. He blinked rapidly as if he couldn't quite focus on her. Honovi was leaning against the stainless steel fridge wearing only the black button up dress shirt he had worn the night before. "Honovi, no! You promised me."

"And you promised me, remember?"

"Before or after you whispered your little tune in my ear last night?"

"Now, now my little tiger, I'm not stupid. After, of course," she said and heard him grumble under his breath. He rubbed his head as she added, "Besides you're much more *attentive* when you're under my spell then when you're just plain agreeable."

"I agree so my head doesn't hurt the next morning." His aggression was escalating with each word out of her mouth.

Honovi could see that he was tense and ready to end this conversation. "You would have been agreeable *and* more attentive to that little blonde whore last night than to me if I hadn't stopped you," she spat.

"Can you blame me? You're not a mystery to be solved anymore. I already know every inch," he growled and turned to go back to his bedroom.

"Exactly why you need the persuasion!" she yelled to him.

"Screw you, Honovi!" he thought.

She slammed down her empty orange juice glass and a crack crept up the side. "Maybe Daddy needs to hear about your little secret."

"You can't pretend to know about that, Honovi. You can't break my block. You just know there is one. I'm stronger than you because I'm not engineered like you. So stop pretending and go back to your cage!" He turned the shower on as he finished his thought. Honovi picked up the glass with her tail and whipped it at the bedroom door. She grabbed her jeans and left the loft.

Bailey, Gabe, and Jailin came to a building that looked out of place for the city. They were in a ghostly alley. The tall surrounding buildings cast darkness all around them. The outside was enough to scare anyone away. Graffiti covered the walls like a New Age museum. Trash lined the streets and a couple of stray cats had obviously taken up residence.

When they entered the building, it was entirely different. Multiple weapons of various types, ranging over hundreds of years and from different cultures, hung on the walls. There were four rooms. Each room had a teacher with about a dozen kids. Some were learning cultural history, and others were learning self-defense moves and combat styles.

Jailin led Bailey and Gabe to the end of the hallway. They came to a wall, but she slid it sideways and a fifth room was revealed before them.

"Hello, Anaba." A man about the same age as Bailey rose to greet her. He was tall and had long dark hair pulled back into a pony tail. His chest looked like a bronzed replica of a god. Even his legs looked massive under his wide-leg linen pants. "You look amazing." He flashed his striking white teeth.

She was wearing white yoga pants and a matching sports bra stitched in navy blue. Her body exhibited no lack of regular exercise and routine.

"This is the sparring partner?" Gabe asked Bailey. "I thought you said we'd see some hot cat fight."

"I never said such a thing."

Gabe's mouth opened to reply but then he remembered that Bailey hadn't said a word about it.

"This is Ben and Gabe," Jailin said, "Guys, this is Contardo."

Gabe smiled from ear to ear, almost bursting into laughter. Bailey put out his hand to shake with the man. Contardo, straight-faced, only nodded in return.

"Shall we go out back and get started?" Contardo asked Jailin.

"Definitely."

"Dude, you're not going to let a tall, dark, and ripped guy like that touch your girl, are you?" Gabe leaned into Bailey.

"They've been doing this for a long time. It's no big deal."

"No big deal? Did you look at him? He's got a massive body that I couldn't muster up if I actually tried. His hair is shinier than silk and, shit, I bet they had something goin' on at some point."

"Why do you say that?"

"Didn't you see his hand on her waist?" He pointed to the door Jailin and Contardo had disappeared behind. "Are they starting this thing hand to hand or using weapons?"

"Does it matter? You'll find something to insinuate, either way."

"True, but dude, did you hear his name? Retardo, what kinda name is that?"

"Contardo. It means he who is daring and valiant."

"Like that's not a line to get into a girl's pants."

Bailey just shook his head and pushed Gabe out the door and onto the cement patio overlooking the field.

21

Jailin positioned herself at one end of the grass fighting field. She looked confident, and graceful. With her knees bent, arms raised, fists clenched, and a slight, taunting smile, she was ready for combat.

Contardo was stationed at the other end. His hands were clenched, ready to attack. His arms were more relaxed compared to Jailin's and he squared his body to her. One leg, bent at the knee, pointed to the enemy. Without any signal to begin, as if both just knew, they ran at each other.

Jailin lunged through the air like a cat and when her hands connected with Contardo's shoulders, he went down on his back. In a continuous motion he threw her over his body. As she landed on her back he raised his legs over his head and used the strength of his shoulders to push himself up so that he was straddling her waist.

"That's new," she said with a smirk.

"Dude, that's got to be an awesome move in the sack." Gabe inclined his elbow into Bailey.

"If you don't stop that, I'm taping your mouth shut," Bailey said. Gabe's eyebrows narrowed and he pouted out his bottom lip.

They watched as Jailin brought her legs up and wrapped them around Contardo's neck. She pulled him down and held him in place. "This round goes to me," she said, still smiling.

"Not yet." He grabbed one leg at the base of her knee and twisted it to the side. She yelled out in pain, causing Bailey to take one step forward.

"Where do you think you're going?" Gabe put a hand on Bailey's shoulder.

"He's hurting her," he said with a tight jaw.

"Like she's not used to it? How long did you say they've been sparring?"

"I think she said five or six years, but it's been almost a year since the last time."

"Then let her take care of herself." Gabe saw Jailin suddenly sit up and punch Contardo in the side of the neck. "See?"

Cantardo howled from the sting of the quick, illicit punch. Jailin used the moment his hand flew to his neck to hold his head down on the grass. She twisted his body so that he was lying on his hip, but his chest was flat on the ground.

"Dude, don't piss her off like you did yesterday. You don't want any of that," Gabe advised as if Bailey had never seen her fight before.

"I concede this round, m'lady." Contardo smiled as best he could.

Jailin stood up and let him regain himself. "Staffs?" she asked excitedly. It was her favorite.

"You're getting stronger," he said and then added, "You didn't use to fight like this. What's changed?"

"Nothing." She glanced involuntarily at Bailey.

"Ah, I see." He walked over to where Bailey and Gabe were standing to get the two bo staffs leaning against the wall. "She wasn't this motivated when we dated," he said to Bailey with a sly smile. Then he walked back to the circle and threw Jailin a staff.

"Told you. I can always tell these things." Gabe put his hands on his hips and jutted out his chin with pride.

Bailey glared at Contardo as they began their fight with the bo staffs. Jailin looked graceful and stealthy as she swung hers side to side intermittently. She got lower to the ground before she pushed her way up into the air. As she spun down, with one end of the staff locked in the crook of her elbow, she tried to hit Contardo.

"You're showing off. You shouldn't have brought him. It's making you sloppy," he advised as he jutted his bo vertically to stop the impact with a simple block at his side. Both his hands slid to one end and like a golfer, he swung at her legs. She jumped, but didn't have the height she wanted, due to the lack of time to adjust from the first jump. Contardo clipped her foot and clumsily she fell to the ground. He came back down with the staff over his head and just missed Jailin as she rolled out of the way.

"I still think you should try two small bo staffs," he said as she was getting back on her feet.

In a feat of strength, Jailin pushed her staff against Contardo's chest as she said, "I modified my staff. It can be one or two."

"And have you been practicing with heavier equipment? It will make you stronger and faster when you use a lighter weapon."

"I know," she grunted as she pushed him back. She ran the short distance she had created between them and then dropped down to the ground to roll once with the staff tucked into her stomach horizontally. When she was directly under Contardo, she pushed, thrusting the staff up into his stomach. He bent over to diminish the impact and pushed his bo out vertically to ease the force. As he blocked, she let go of one end of her staff. She slid the other hand down to where she had just let go, swinging up onto his back and pinning his arms down between herself and her bo.

He had no real injury to recover from and he grabbed one of her legs as she wrapped them around him. He spun her around his waist so that she was now pressed against him chest to chest. He slipped his arms under hers and wrapped his hands up over her shoulders. He did this so the impact of the ground would hit his arms instead of her back as they fell.

"Dude, if they were naked, I'd swear he just screwed her as they hit the ground like that."

Bailey was angry. He couldn't take anymore of Gabe's offensive commentary and couldn't bear to watch what should have looked more like a fight than a love scene. He turned to go to his car, but looked back one last time and saw Contardo kissing Jailin.

She pushed Contardo off her so that she could sit up. Her legs were still wrapped around him and Contardo continued to grip her knees. "What are you doing?"

"Sorry, I just realized how much I've missed you."

"You're my sparring partner. Nothing more!"

"I know. I know. I'm sorry," he said, but no remorse could be found in his dark eyes.

"I don't think you are."

"I'm not if you liked it." His smile was thin, not wanting to show how his offense had actually made him feel.

"Damn it, Contardo." She looked over to where Bailey should have been standing. "Oh, just perfect." She picked herself up and left Contardo squatting on the ground. "Where is he?" she asked Gabe.

"Umm… I think he went… to the truck." Gabe didn't know how to address her after what he had just seen.

"Will you wait here?" she sighed. "I need to talk to him, see if he's okay." She turned to walk back into the school.

"Sure, but I'll tell you now, he's not okay," he said as she walked through the door, down the hall, and out to the truck.

Contardo was wiping his face on a towel as he came up to Gabe. "Oops," he said as he pushed past him. Gabe was all talk and always too scared to confront anyone, so he sat down on the cement patio and waited.

Jailin tapped on the passenger side door. Without looking, Bailey hit the unlock button. She climbed in and sat staring out the windshield for a few seconds before she said, "I didn't know he was going to do that."

"He said you dated once."

"Well, he lied to you. He just wanted to piss you off. And apparently it worked."

"Then why were you climbing all over each other?"

"He's the only one, other than Masou, who can even come close to my strength. Who else am I going to spar with?" She let out a long breath and wiped the length of her arm across her forehead.

"How about someone who won't feel you up instead?" he rebuked.

"You mean someone like you?"

He flinched. "Me? What's that supposed to mean?"

"You hardly touched me last night. Contardo out there got further than you and you were actually welcome."

"I'm sorry. I…" Bailey trailed off.

"You what?" She felt her anger boiling over.

"I'm scared, okay? I've never felt like this before. I've never been so jealous in my whole life. I don't know if Gabe's comments had anything to do with it or not." He took a deep breath. "I'm afraid to lose you like I lost my parents. If I let myself fall in love with you and you leave, where am I then?"

"*If* you fall in love with me?" She leaned forward, trying to read the expression on his face. He hadn't looked at her since she had gotten in the truck.

"I don't want you to give up anything you have. You have a whole different world than what I have. We're so…"

"Diverse." She finished his sentence. He nodded in agreement. "Well, I can't change who I am," she said as she leaned back and faced forward.

"I don't want you to change a thing. I want you the way you are, but…"

"There's a but?" Her eyebrows creased with concern over what he might say next.

"I'm not good enough for you."

"Who says?" Her head jerked back to face him.

"Gabe said that since you…"

"Don't tell me you're listening to that smart ass," she interrupted.

"He just made me realize there are people better suited for you. You and Contardo look like you should be together. I can't compete with him."

"There is no competition. I don't care about him in that way. I care about you. Geez, I even chose you over your brother last night. Shouldn't that count for something?"

"He's a drunk, a man-whore, and a bastard. That's not a difficult choice."

"If you don't want me around anymore, then just say so." She crossed her arms.

"I want you around." His eyes flickered to her face in order to interpret the level of anger there. "I just wish *I* was a different person."

"Different how?"

"More like you. I could close this gap we have. I know someone at GIA who can alter me to be like you. I could help you. I could spar with you. Keep you from getting hurt."

Hurt? No physical pain she'd ever experienced compared to this kind of pain. "It takes years to find out what effects it'll have. You could die from it, for all you know. Why do things need to change? And I've been just fine without you for the past nineteen years, by the way."

"Because..."

"Because it makes you feel more adequate? More manly?" Her fury was explosive.

"No." He turned to finally face her and cup her small face in his hand. "Because I love you."

22

Bailey stared deep into her eyes. The sunlight heated the inside of the truck like a sauna. Sweat glistened on his forehead, whether it was from the heat or nerves he couldn't tell. He didn't really care either. "Did you hear me?" He waited anxiously for Jailin to reply but she appeared as if she was looking straight through him. "Jailin?"

"What? I'm sorry. I need to go." She looked down at her legs, rubbing the sweat on them before her hand went to open the door.

It didn't seem right to press her right now. He wanted so badly to ask again if she heard what he'd just confessed. The feeling of rejection slapped him across the face. Perhaps he'd said it wrong. Perhaps she didn't love him back and was sparing him the pain. Instead he only asked, "What's wrong?"

"Dierno says Sarana has found a wolf that's making its way toward the Maimugg tribe." There was no emotion behind her words. Her eyes were glassed over, like a tired child fighting to stay awake.

"Wolf? What kind of wolf?" He was relieved she had said anything other than words of aversion. The relief fought inside him with concern for the anguish she must have been feeling.

"Strong and powerful. There's no pack with it, which means it's got to be Vernore's wolf. I have to get home. Dierno and Sarana shouldn't do this alone."

"What can I do?" No matter how unwanted he felt, he didn't want to be away from her.

"Nothing." She jumped out of the truck, shutting the door behind her. Before she ran off she turned back to look at him. "I'm sorry you feel this way. I'm sorry I screwed up everything in your life. Don't follow me like last time. You really are Kafele." She shut the door and ran off into the mahogany trees behind Contardo's school.

Gabe came out and saw Bailey alone in the truck with his head on the steering wheel. He came around the side and got in the passenger seat. "Didn't go too well, huh?"

"I told her I loved her." His voice seeped with heartache.

"And she left? Cold-hearted bitch."

"Don't say that."

"Oh come on." Gabe was tired of always being the single friend who had to pick up the pieces of every broken heart he met. "She basically had a one afternoon stand right in front of you. And you, God only knows why, go tellin' her you love her, which is a mistake in the first place. Then she bails on you. Tell me where I'm getting this wrong."

"She didn't leave because she wanted to. She left because she had to. Something is after her people and she needs to protect them." Bailey knew Gabe was trying to help, but he wasn't about to let anyone speak of protection if they knew nothing about it.

"Her people? Dude, she's not really a tribal girl. She only hangs out with those characters because she's got no one else. I mean she has you, but in my opinion, she blew that."

"She has a family, unlike you and me, Gabe. No matter how well she fits in or not, they love her nonetheless. Besides, we were raised in GIA's boarding school. No one loved us."

"No one will. Love is for suckers who only think they're happy. Let's go home, drink ourselves silly, and then go pick up chicks at Dance Zoo."

Bailey started the truck. He had no intention of joining Gabe in his pursuit of an alternate reality. They drove back to the apartment while Gabe was still trying to convince him that girls were the devil in disguise.

Jailin had enough time to get back to her motel room and change into her patrol uniform. She was running through the tree tops faster than ever before to get back. Panic and adrenaline were forcing her legs to move. She was already physically tired from sparring with Contardo and emotionally tired from her conversation with Bailey.

"Dierno, can you read his thoughts?"

"He's got a much higher degree of intellect than that vulture did, but he's just repeating what he hears and smells. It's kind of odd in a way."

"Why is that?" A flock of crows flew out of a tree as she leaped into it. Leaves fell from each branch that she lunged from. She was glad she had taken the time to change into her patrol uniform. If it wasn't for her arm gauntlets and the protective cloth on her hands, the branches would have torn the skin from her palms.

"Well, he's talking in descriptions like he's blind. I can hear him mention smells, sounds, and tastes, but no sights. He seems to be repeating information like he's sending it to someone who can hear him. He's giving directions."

"To Honovi." Jailin figured that the only one who would want a second chance to fight her again would without a doubt be Honovi. Jailin knew they hadn't finished what they had started, and no one else had a grudge against the tribe like Honovi did.

"But she already knows how to find us. Why would directions benefit her?"

Jailin stopped briefly in a tree and looked out at the sun. A cloud, thick and puffy, slowly worked its way in front of it. No matter how dull the sun might be, the cloud would never be able to cover every ray, even if it tricked it into submission. "I don't know," she sighed. "Data collecting, perhaps?" She jumped into a neighboring teak tree and climbed to the top, overlooking the sea of green leaves.

"Doesn't seem right. Where's Socrates? He could figure this guy out," Dierno said. He knew she had stopped to ponder what might happen. She needed to prepare herself and get her mind off what was bothering her.

"Still watching TV. Little guy's going to rot his brain." The thought of where she'd left him gave her hope that she'd see Bailey again. Her heart sank as she reflected on how rude she had been to him.

"Hmm... are you sure you're ready for this? I heard your conversation."

"Nothing keeps me from protecting my people," she growled.

"You never answered him. You heard him and still didn't answer."

"Yeah, so?"

"Do you love him?"

She swallowed hard. "I don't know."

"You know."

"If you're so smart, why are you asking?" Her anger had never failed to deter people from prying into anything she preferred to keep to herself.

"You need to let yourself admit the truth."

"No. I need to concentrate on what lies ahead."

"Fine, but this isn't over. You still have to talk to Meovi."

"Damn it." She knew she'd lost this one. Dierno was a mind she was still getting used to. She couldn't impede his ability to make her feel guilty.

Jailin arrived at her hut. Everything appeared normal. Smoke was coming out of the chimney. She knew Meovi was inside because no one took better care of her home. Jailin didn't want to go inside and certainly didn't want to be pushed away again. Everyone would see what had changed in her in the last few days and she couldn't admit defeat yet.

"What are you waiting for?" Dierno asked from the tree below her. She looked down to see Sarana lying in the fallen leaves next to Dierno. His eyes twinkled. Jailin almost thought she saw happiness there. Had these two cats made some kind of connection while patrolling the jungle in her stead? She'd have to remember to ask him later.

"Dusk," she said. "The wolf won't make a move until then." She looked out to the surrounding trees and huts.

"No, I meant with Meovi. She knows you're here. I can hear her mock conversations with you in her head."

"Is it good or bad?"

"That depends on your reaction. She keeps playing it differently, depending on what answer she thinks you might give her."

"Does she miss me?"

"Of course she does. You're like a daughter to her."

Jailin came down the tree and walked through the door very slowly. Meovi didn't notice she had entered. She was busy at the stove making different ointments and teas. "Restocking your shelves?" Jailin asked quietly.

"Anaba!" Meovi grinned and threw her arms around Jailin. "I knew you'd come back. Are you all right? Hungry?"

"I'm fine, Meovi. How are you?"

"I've been tending a weak stomach while you've been gone. Sick with worry, I guess. Otherwise, I'm wonderful. I see you don't have your things with you. Why not?"

"Meovi, listen..." Jailin sat her in a chair at the little table in the kitchen. Seeing the sorrow within Jailin's eyes, Meovi knew what was going to be said.

"Sssso, you can talk... riiight? Gabe had a beer in each hand as he plopped down next to Socrates, who was still flipping channels. "Thiiis all you doo?" He pointed to the remote with one bottle. "Benjin...mmm," he licked his lips, "Hey, do we got any gin?"

Bailey exhaled with extreme force through his nose, "No. I think you've finished that already."

"Good. Whazit they say? Beer for liquor, in the… kicker? You dunt ook hap." He hiccupped once before continuing. "Happy. Aren't you?"

"It's: liquor before beer, you're in the clear. And I'm not drunk, Gabe."

"But you wiilll beee!" He stood up, wobbled over to the table where Bailey was sitting with his laptop. "Wha-cha doin'?" The sour smell of alcohol wafted through the air.

"I'm trying to figure out the components of Jailin's bo staff. I want to improve it by finding the lightest and strongest metal for defense."

"You… don't wanna dooo… any a that. That's boooriing. Dink this." His words slurred more with every passing moment. He shoved the untouched beer in Bailey's face. Bailey took it and put it on the other side of the table away from Gabe. "I'm gonna call Tabby cat," he stated as if he had given the world the answer to all their problems. "Maybe she'll bing a kitty wither." He got down on his hands and knees. "Here, kitty, kitty," he repeated as he fumbled around for the phone.

"Gabe. Don't." Bailey was trying desperately to hide his annoyance. He knew that Gabe wanted to make him feel better but he swore that the man was the biggest idiot ever to walk on Grundagon soil.

"It's already ringing already. It go Raahhnngg! Raahhnngg!... Oh she said hello! Hello, Tabby cat. Want to bring a kitty over? No. I'm not dunk. No, this not Gabe either. Okay ha-ha you got me. I am Gabe and yes I am dunk. Come join the fun." Then he attempted to say quietly but failed, "Benjin. He's drumped. So we gots 'em dunked." He handed Bailey the phone. "She wants to jam wit you."

Rolling his eyes, Bailey took the phone out of Gabe's hand and hung it up. He placed it next to the untouched beer and went back to his work.

"Ooh, no! Poor kitty tab. She not be a happy tabby. Scratch your eyes out, she will."

Socrates had found Gabe slightly more amusing than TV all of a sudden. He jumped up on the table, looked at Gabe who smiled back at him, and then looked at Bailey's computer.

URMISNGSPLTKAP. He wrote to Bailey.

"O.M.G.," Gabe mimicked Tabitha the best he could in a shrill voice and then began laughing so hard that he fell on the floor. "He. Can. Write."

"I don't know what this says," Bailey said to Socrates.

Socrates looked as if he had sighed as his shoulders rose and fell. He tried to write it again. UR. MISNG. SPLT. KAP. This time he pointed to the center of the drawing on the pad of paper.

"I'm missing… something. I got that much." Socrates looked around the room. Nothing on the table could help him describe the staff. He jumped down, went over to the far end of the kitchen nook and from on top of the counter opened a drawer. From the drawer, he took out a small, straight object. When he was back on the table with Bailey, he showed him the pen he had taken from the drawer. With an end in each paw, he popped it open and then slid it back together. The sound of the pen snapping together echoed through the room. "Oh, that says cap. Split cap. I forgot about that, didn't I?"

Socrates was proud of himself, but was now bored because Gabe had fallen asleep on the floor. He turned back toward the couch and Bailey asked quietly, as if he was afraid to hear the answer, "Do you know what she's doing right now?"

Socrates felt bad for Bailey after having overheared Jailin's conversation with Dierno and Meovi. He wrote: TELNG MEOVI Y SHE HOM.

"You mean about the wolf?"

YES.

"Is she going to be staying there?" Each word was difficult for Bailey to say. He didn't know if he wanted to hear the answers, but the questions had been distracting him all day.

NO.

"Why not?"

Socrates deliberated on how best to answer Bailey. It wasn't his place to tell anyone what Jailin's thoughts were, but he decided this was an exception to the rule. SHE RATR B WIT U.

"But I don't want her to give up anything for me."

TEL ER NO ME.

Bailey nodded his head to signify that he understood. He got up from the table to drag Gabe over to the couch. Then he grabbed his laptop and the drawings before heading out the door.

23

"Quiet. Slow breathing… many asleep. Smell smoke. No heat. Food prepared hours ago. Low murmurs heard from the west. Smell rain coming." A wheezing voice spoke in slow gasping words.

"Did you find her?" A restless voice sounded back.

"No. None of smells… match."

Adrian paced back and forth across the holding container on the top floor of the Vernore Building. He was dressed from head to toe in black. Red stripes stood out down his arms from neck line to wrist. His black hair with gold spikes popped out from under his hood. "Tell me when you find her. Don't let father know you're out there."

The deep crackling of emphysema responded, "Understood."

Adrian ran up the metal staircase, went through the dark doorway at the top and then turned one corner to emerge from a heavy metal door into what looked like an office with a sea of cubicles. He went straight to the elevator at the right and hit the button marked with a seven.

When the elevator doors opened, he saw that his father had come out of his office and was locking the large wooden doors.

"Father… err, I mean, Sir?"

"What is it?" Vernore was displeased about being interrupted. His long face looked forlorn and hollow, as if he hadn't slept in days over a lost love.

"Can I ask you a question?"

"I don't have time right now. Can it wait?" Vernore adjusted his collar and straightened his red silk tie.

"No, it can't." Adrian's eyes narrowed.

"If this is about Honovi, I don't want to hear it."

"It's not." Adrian's eyes shifted to the side. That was a topic for another day.

"Well, make it quick." He loomed in a sinister way over his son. Vernore wasn't much taller than Adrian, but he held himself with more power and finesse than Adrian ever would.

"Well… um…" he trailed off, unsure how to ask his question even though he asked it to himself a million times.

"If you can't hurry this up, it'll have to wait." Vernore looked at his watch.

"It's about…" Adrian cleared his throat. "…mom, err, Johanna."

"This again? I hope you're not reminiscing about your childhood or lack thereof with her?"

"No," he lied. The thought of what his life would have been like had he had a mother occurred to him quite frequently.

"What is it then?" Vernore ticked off the seconds with his finger against his watch. Nothing was ever subtle.

"How did this," he pointed to his chest, "kill her?"

"It's very complicated. I don't believe now is the right time." Vernore sidestepped Adrian.

"When is the right time?" He turned with his father.

"Check with my secretary," Vernore said over his shoulder while he walked over to the elevator and hit the down button.

"Is it true that I have a brother?" The question surprised Adrian as much as it did his father.

Vernore rubbed his forehead. It appeared as if the question gave him a sudden pain. He never wanted to discuss this. "Yes," he sighed, and turned back to Adrian. "And that's all you need to know right now." He stepped into the open elevator doors, letting them close as Adrian stared and watched him go.

"I found her. The smell. From the west." The crackling was back in Adrian's head.

"Track any move she makes. I'm on my way."

Bailey rang the door bell three times before Contardo answered. It was opened so that only the width of Contardo's face was visible. "Can I help you, Ben… is it?"

"Uh, yeah. Listen… I need a favor."

"Depends on what it is." Contardo was always full of himself. He enjoyed making others feel out of place and insignificant around him.

"You seem to know a lot about fighting and weapons. So, I was wondering…"

"You want to spar?" Contardo cut Bailey off with eyebrows raised in amusement. He'd love to test this guy's abilities. What it was that Anaba saw in him, he would never understand.

"No." Bailey was direct. He had a lot to do and only a short time to do it in.

"Then what do you want?" Contardo's eyebrows lowered into a slant. It wouldn't be a first to have another man hate him.

"I want to enhance Jailin's bo staff."

"Ah, so here you are asking for my help," he stated with a slight smile. "And where is Anaba, anyway?"

"With Meovi." Bailey wasn't about to confide in this jerk. What Jailin did was her own business. It also would have been a huge kick in the gut if Contardo ran off to help her, leaving Bailey feeling even worse about his abilities or lack thereof.

"She still mad at me?" The question was indifferent to either answer it would receive.

"I think so, but I really can't say." He wanted to say, "She should be."

Contardo didn't reply to this. He just smiled and opened the door so Bailey could enter.

"Do you live here?" Bailey asked when he saw no one else around. The peaceful environment gave no indication that Contardo taught about weapons and fighting styles.

"I have a small living space upstairs. Although, it's better if we talk in the room from before." Bailey didn't understand how this could possibly matter. Contardo opened the wall to the fifth room and they sat at a low table on the floor with cushions for chairs.

"This is different. I never knew people sat so low to the floor."

"Don't know your planet's history very well, do you?"

"Only subject I couldn't grasp in school. It's all just a lot of dates and events. Big deal."

"Weapons and fighting techniques have changed, blossomed, grown, and faded over the years. You'd be surprised." Contardo sounded like he was recruiting new students.

Bailey didn't care for the history lesson so he took out the drawings of the bo staff and the transparent layers of the changes he had made and handed them to Contardo.

"Very interesting. Whose idea was it to split the staff into a modified nunchaku?"

"A what?" Bailey was unfamiliar with this term.

"It's an ancient weapon. Apparently it's making a comeback, in an improved way, of course."

"Jailin made this. I only want to change the materials out for something lighter and stronger."

"Uh-huh."

"My problem is that I don't want to make her change her fighting style if she's comfortable with it."

"If changes are needed, she'll adjust. She always does." Contardo could see how Bailey felt about her. It pissed him off. "She's a handful, just so you know."

Bailey didn't say anything at first. He decided against an argument about who had known Jailin longer and went back to the reason he had come in the first place. "She prefers the staff to be short, but would it work if it were longer? For a better reach, I mean."

"That should be her decision. You'll need to be prepared with multiple types in various sizes. She won't know without the practice. And you may still have to make adjustments again."

"Makes sense." Bailey nodded with every word out of Contardo's mouth.

"What are you changing other than the material?"

"What makes you think I am?"

The left side of Contardo's lip curled up into a half smile. "You can't purely be doing this for her defense. She's going to have to strike back at some point. Otherwise, what's the point in the first place?"

"I really hadn't thought it that far through. I only know how to keep out of sight. Besides, she already has an edge with her strength and speed."

"Against a *normal* man, yes." Contardo crossed his arms and jutted out his chin as if to accuse Bailey of being the last normal man alive. He watched Bailey squirm under the pressure. It only fed Contardo's arrogance.

"If I could protect her then I wouldn't be here, so tell me what this needs." Bailey was getting short-tempered with Contardo. The normal man quip had drawn the line and he decided he didn't want to stay any longer than he had to.

The night had stolen away the blue of the sky. Not a single star could twinkle through the solid clouds. "You see anything from up there?" Dierno thought.

"Just the same old blackness," Jailin answered. She was sitting on her roof with one leg hanging off and the other knee up so she could rest her chin on it. "I take it he isn't planning to make a big show of this? And where's Sarana?"

"I asked her to case the tree line for me tonight. As for the wolf, I can still hear him going over directions. He keeps mentioning the wind from the west."

"He's downwind of us!" Her head shot up. She turned around to look into the trees behind her. A feeling of prying eyes washed over her.

"So?"

"That's why he can smell our whole camp. If he's not mentioning visuals how can we know how close he is?"

"I can," Dierno replied in a whisper even though it was a thought. Jailin pulled up her dangling leg and crouched at the edge of her roof. "He just moved from behind Masou's hut."

"Where are you?" she whispered aloud as she squinted toward Masou's hut.

"*I'm* right here," a voice whispered from behind her. She spun around and glowing eyes shrouded in total blackness peered back at her.

The fragrance in the air seemed familiar. Masculine. It didn't scare her. Nothing much ever did. Jailin peered back at the eyes, trying to figure out who they belonged to. The color seemed off in the darkness. Almost unnatural.

"Yes, you know who I am," the familiar voice said. She couldn't see it, but she heard the grin in his voice.

"You can hear my thoughts? Who are you?" She squinted as if it would help to lift the darkness. Even her night vision was blurred, but she could tell it was due to the hood he wore.

"I can hear his thoughts," his head jerked toward Dierno. "You're tricky. Like a locked door, but I can pick locks in time."

"Vernore?" she hissed through clenched teeth.

"Close enough. I hunted you down with the help of one of Honovi's creations."

"The wolf was a trick?" She had figured as much, but couldn't allow herself to let something happen if the wolf really wasn't just a decoy. Plus, her curiosity had just plain gotten the best of her.

"Sorta. He could do harm, if needed. As of now, he won't." He slid his hood back and the moonlight caught the gold of his hair. With the help of her night vision, Jailin now saw Adrian's entire face for the first time tonight.

"Adrian!" She inhaled with shock. "What do you want?" Her mind was spinning. She knew he was Vernore's son. She had always felt so comfortable around him, but it never dawned on her until now in the dark, that his eyes were like an animal's. That he was strong and aggressive. He was just like her. "I'm so stupid," she thought.

"I'd like to ask you something." He walked to the edge of the roof to look down on the huts. His feet were light and didn't make a single sound against the roof. No wonder she had never heard him come up behind her.

"You had to trick me into believing someone was out to destroy my jungle and all you have is questions?" Anger simmered insider her. It wanted out, but she held back as long as she could.

"We could destroy it." He turned to look at her. His face portrayed a hint of sympathy. "Would that make anything easier for you?"

"What's your question?" She balled her hands into fists.

"Who was that guy you left my club with?" It came out of his mouth like he'd been wrestling to hold it in all this time.

"Why?" She straightened her back slightly, but remained down low on the roof.

"I heard you say something to him when you were leaving." He looked back out at the sea of roofs as if it would console him. "Is that wimp really my brother?"

"What if he is? And he isn't a wimp!"

"He's bad news. You should stay away from him." He sounded like an overprotective father after her first date. He sounded just like Contardo. She hated that.

"You don't know him. What makes you think you can make any demands of me, anyway?"

"My father…"

"No!" Jailin cut him off. She was standing now and had her staff pointing toward him like a sword. "You will not involve your father with this. He's a devil and anything he says is a lie to benefit himself."

"Some of his lies benefit more than himself." His head gestured in a mixture of nods and shakes as if he wanted to agree with her but couldn't.

"He's still included with the benefactors."

"True, but it doesn't change the fact that that guy is GIA."

"That *guy* is your brother. You should be happy about that." She heard the resentment in her voice. Sudden hatred for Adrian and herself overflowed in her for the treatment Bailey had gone through as of late. No matter how angry anyone seemed to get with him he never took it personally. In fact he had told her he loved her and all she had done was leave him.

"Happy? I should be happy that some bitch left my father to have that traitor?"

"Johanna wasn't a bitch, Adrian, and you're the traitor!" Jailin sprang at him and they both fell to the roof with a loud thud. With her staff she pinned him across the chest.

"I'm not going to fight you." He felt her push the staff against him harder. He grunted as the air escaped him, but didn't resist her strength.

"Then you're going home with your ass kicked!"

"Perhaps, but that won't hold Ronin back from destroying your camp."

Their heads were close to the edge when they fell. She looked down from the roof and saw the wolf, who Adrian had just referred to as Ronin, pull a small child out of another hut. The parents followed slowly and cautiously, while crying and begging the wolf to let the child go. Dierno was stalking the side of the hut, out of view, waiting for the right moment to intercede.

"Leave them out of this!" She turned her head back to Adrian. He enjoyed how close she was. This was the kind of closeness he had only dreamed of the night she walked out of his club.

"*I* will. I only came to talk. You jumped on me, pretty." Adrian smiled up at her. She wasn't amused by him as she had been in the past, but she let him up anyway. "I didn't expect you to get that disturbed." He dusted off his jacket and pants.

"I'm not disturbed. You pissed me off." Her arm stretched up the length of her bo staff. It supported her weight as she leaned on it and rested her other fist on her hip.

"Same thing. Besides, he can't be better than me." Adrian looked her up and down and only wished he was his brother.

Jailin laughed. "So many assumptions about someone you don't even know."

"I know some pretty big secrets." He wiped some more dirt off his pant leg.

"You think he doesn't? He's GIA, remember? For all you know, he knows your secrets and has some of his own."

"You're bluffing." He looked up at her from his crouched position on the roof. A smile crept up one side of his face.

"Am I?" She stood up taller. Trying to look confident.

"Yes." He watched her fidget, hoping her statement could hold some truth. "Have you ever noticed the change in the heartbeat of the person whom you speak with? Ever notice how a body posture becomes uneasy when a person lies?"

"What's your point?"

"I could show you how to understand these things." He stood to take a step closer to her. "Hear the difference in the heartbeat. Understand the adrenaline due to anger, all the way to nervousness due to lust." He heard her heartbeat. He was surprised that it remained fairly consistent. "You're engineered, beautiful, not born with the Vernore gene. I could help you." He was only a few short steps away from her. With every step he took, he wished she wouldn't take one backward.

"Born with the Vernore gene? What do you mean?" She stepped back.

"I'm the only one born with my mother and father already possessing this." He laid his palm against his chest slowly. "I admit, I was a little uncontrollable at first, but the engineered part keeps me stable. We're all engineered on some level, and until those manipulated have perfect children it will continue this way."

"All of us?" Her fingers touched her lips in thought.

"We are my father's perfect race." His hand went from his chest out to her, beckoning her closer to him.

"That means…" Jailin trailed off as her eyes searched the roof, as if the answer would jump out at her. As if she could escape.

"Yep." His hand dropped back down to his side. "Eventually, everyone will be a carrier of the Vernore gene. We're a minuscule population now, but growing."

"Hmm." Something had occurred to her.

"What?"

Jailin's head turned to the side and she looked down the rooftop toward Dierno. "If I reproduce, then..." Dierno shot a worried look up toward Jailin.

"Hey, yeah, we could reproduce super Vernores! Sounds like fun, sweetness."

"We?" She couldn't believe he thought she was talking about the two of them.

"Well, yes. You were the perfection of the serum. After my father took my blood and analyzed the defects, you drank the perfect drug."

"Must go. Father in head. Looking." Ronin thought with a deep wheeze.

"Sorry, beautiful, I gotta run. We should do this again some time." Adrian jumped down from her roof and disappeared as quickly as he had come.

"Dierno, do you know what this means?"

"You have a little more light on our dark journey."

"No, well, yes, but if Adrian was born with this..." Jailin trailed off, staring at her open hands. For the first time they looked foreign to her. Weapons that she didn't know she had and didn't necessarily ask for.

"There is an additional one who is a probable candidate for a dormant strand of this *gene* in his DNA structure."

"Socrates!" Jailin and Dierno yelled in their heads together.

“I could not refrain from eavesdropping. Have you been enjoying this escapade without me, Jailin?”

“TV has done nothing to rot his brain in the slightest,” Dierno deadpanned.

“Should I come get you?” Jailin asked.

“Your arrival will undoubtedly reveal a new succession of events.”

“Well, fill me in.” She took off with Dierno toward the North.

25

The girl and her white shadow kept to the darkness of the surrounding buildings as they made their way to get Socrates. When they arrived at the patio of Bailey's apartment, he and Socrates were already sitting there and waiting. A long slender duffle bag was cradled between Bailey's feet. Jailin figured Socrates had told Bailey they were coming.

Socrates popped up from a meditating position when he heard Jailin's footsteps and ran to her. She dropped one arm and Socrates used it to climb up onto her shoulder.

"Hi," she said softly as she approached Bailey.

"Glad to see you're okay." He remained sitting and looked up at her face. The rising sun cast an orange glow out from the horizon behind her.

Jailin noticed the bag between Bailey's feet and kicked it lightly as she said, "What's this for?"

"I'll show you, if you'll go for a walk with me?" His right hand rubbed his elbow and he looked around. It was awkward knowing he had put himself out there and had no idea how she felt in return.

She hesitated on her answer, "All right." Her thoughts were directed to Dierno as she nervously asked, "Is he planning to continue our conversation from the truck?"

"He's thinking about it, but also hoping that maybe you'll bring it up," Dierno replied, as he sat on his haunches next to Jailin's feet.

"Me?" Jailin thought, then exhaled and dropped her shoulders.

"Everything all right?" Bailey asked, in regard to her change in posture.

"Yeah. So, where are you taking me?" Her head tilted to the side.

"You'll see. It's not far." He smiled and stood up. He liked the way she had asked him where they were headed. It made him feel a little better somehow.

Quickly, Jailin changed out of her patrol uniform before she and Bailey set out back the way she and Dierno had come. She surveyed the quiet streets. There were only a few people stirring about in the city while the early morning sun peaked its glistening gaze over the horizon.

"What have you been up to for the past twenty-four hours?" she asked. Looking at the long bag she now realized it wasn't a normal duffle bag. It rolled up instead of zippered and looked like a five-foot long painter's brush bag.

"Catching up with some old friends."

"You mean Tabitha?" She looked off into the distance where the sun was now over the horizon. She grabbed her necklace for comfort. She didn't want to see the emotion on his face when he answered her.

"No, I have no reason to talk to her. Ever."

"She must've been important to you. You don't have any memories worth holding onto?" She kicked a pebble and watched it bounce into the street.

He drew in his lips and bit the bottom one while he thought about this. "Yeah, some things were fun."

"See?" She didn't enjoy being the one to bring these memories back for him and couldn't believe she had initiated this.

"Only because of Gabe, though." A small chuckle escaped as if he remembered a particular time that Gabe was more amusing than annoying.

"You're just mad right now. Eventually, you'll remember the good times. I just hope you don't regret any of this."

"I won't."

She didn't reply. She glanced at him out of the corner of her eye and saw that he had a slight smile hinting across his lips.

"Here we are," he said once they reached a tall building with large heavy glass doors. The gold paint on them spelled out GIA: Grundagon Intelligence Agency.

"What are we doing here?"

"I want you to meet some people I work with." His hand slid his GIA key chain over the sensor plate. As he grabbed the handle, Jailin slammed her open palm against the door frame.

"Do they know who I am?" she asked in a rushed voice.

"What do you mean?"

"That I'm… like *this*."

"You'll need to elaborate on the term *this*." He smiled, thinking she was overreacting. He enjoyed it when she expressed herself. A strong-willed girl with an opinion was always welcome. Especially this one.

"Are you turning me in as your great discovery? Are they running tests on me?"

"Only if you tell them to," he joked.

"So they don't know who I am?" She relaxed. His carefree nature made it easier for her to accept this.

"No. I didn't say I was bringing anyone with me. You decide who you want to be. I would never put you in harm's way. You can trust me. Besides, Jim's a nice guy. I think you'll like him." The knuckles of his hand ran quickly over her soft cheek.

"Jim? Who's Jim?" His touch was distracting. She wanted it to last longer, but also knew she had to focus. He smiled and placed his hand on the small of her back to nudge her into the building.

Once inside the maze that was the Grundagon Intelligence Agency, she followed Bailey down the long white corridor. Every door they came to, Bailey placed his hand on a sensor plate. The last set of doors opened up and on one side of the large room was an old man looking into a microscope. At a computer next to him was a short stout man with jet black hair and round glasses, in black pants and a white overcoat. The opposite side of the room was set up like a gymnasium for gifted athletes. Machines that monitored vitals lined up against the far wall. Unused exercised equipment collected dust in the corner. A portion of the floor was padded and tape divided the mats into sections. Jailin recognized this as a sparring mat. One she never had the privilege of using since nature always served as her arena.

"Good morning, Dr. Simon. How are you?" Bailey walked up to the little old man with white hair whose wrinkles smiled back.

"Good, Good, Agent Bailey. You're here early, what do you have for me?"

"Nothing. I've been on vacation. I still am as far as I know, but I came by to see if you might be able to tell me what you've found out about all those other blood samples. Mind filling me in?"

"By all means. Pull up a chair, young man."

"Oh, Kishi." The little man at the computer turned around. "Check out the bag. You'll find it very interesting." Bailey pulled a stool around and sat with Dr. Simon. Jailin felt left out and unsure of what to do.

"Ooohh." An expression of enthusiasm came from the robust man. He had rolled out the black bag and seen five bo staffs. Each was a different size, design, and weight. He pulled out the longest one. "This is very light," he said as he held it next to him to gauge the height difference. It was a foot taller than he.

Jailin's mouth dropped slightly and then she clenched back up in anger that this chubby man who reminded her of a rat with an accent she'd never heard before was getting a gift she could only dream of.

Without realizing it Bailey's voice whispered in her ear and her anger melted away at the warmth of his breath on her neck, "Go look. They all belong to you anyway. He's just my critic."

She whirled around. "Seriously? But how?"

"I talked to Contardo." Jailin's eyebrows raised in disbelief. Was Contardo one of the "old friends" he had mentioned on their walk here? "He gave me his supplier and I got them for you. If adjustments are needed, I'll see that they get done." His fingers slid down her spine and she shivered from the pleasant sensation.

She kissed his cheek and went over to the bag. This short chubby man didn't seem like much of a rat anymore to her—not since her jealousy proved unnecessary. He had taken the bag over to the padded floor and was testing the long silver bo staff he had picked out of the bag earlier. She eyed those that were left. There was a four-foot green one with black vine work scrolled on it, and black tape for a grip at either end. The second one was white, plain, with no design or personal appeal. White tape was also used for grips. This one was about two inches shorter than the green one. The third was black. Already it was more appealing to Jailin than the others. It had a design on it so she withdrew it from the sheath to take a better look at it. The design was raised and she ran her hand over it. It was a simple random tribal design that held no specific meaning to her. The tape grip was a beautiful blue with a hint of gray to it. When she checked the height it stopped exactly at her nose.

"You want to test it?" the little man next to her asked.

"Yes." She was smiling and very excited to try it out.

"Let's go over here. I want to see what this silver bullet can do." He led her over to the platform.

"Excuse me, Dr. Simon." Bailey said as he caught Jailin walking off with Kishi. "Hey, Jailin?"

"Yes?" She turned to face him.

He was mesmerized by her eyes. When she was happy, he couldn't help but stare at her. It took a moment before he could say, "They don't split yet."

"Oh… okay. Thanks." She walked off with Kishi with a bounce in her step.

As he sat back down he heard Jailin and Kishi smash their staffs in a cross.

"Interesting girl," Dr. Simon said.

"You have no idea."

26

Another crack was heard echoing through the room. Jailin blocked the downward swing of Kishi's blow by holding the black and blue staff above her head. She was down on one knee after the impact. This man knew how to use all his weight—which was a lot considering his short stature.

"Wow! You're strong," she exclaimed and put her fists, still gripping the staff, down on the mat before her. The little man was panting through his smile. "But I have a lot more endurance," she pointed out with full composure.

"I've had many sensei in my time. Perhaps I could teach you the ancient ways."

"I'm familiar with your technique, but if I have any questions, you'll be the first one I ask."

He nodded once and together they walked back to where Bailey was sitting with Dr. Simon.

"Looks like Mr. Moirota has made a new friend," Dr. Simon whispered to Bailey. "Good to see him away from that computer. He needs a girlfriend."

"Hey, Doc, that's not nice," Bailey whispered back.

Dr. Simon smiled, knowing he might have offended Bailey, but he turned back to his microscope and slid a new slide under the lens. "Ah, here it is, look at this one." He pushed back his rolling chair so Bailey could see.

"I see mitochondria. What's your point?"

"Silly boy," the doctor shook his head. "They're huge! The Power House is what mitochondria are also known as."

"Yeah, I remember that from your class. So, if they're huge is that a bad thing?"

"What are you two doing?" Jailin interrupted.

"Young lady, we are working!" Dr. Simon swung around in the chair to face her. "Haven't your parents taught you any manners?"

"I'm sorry, sir." Jailin dropped her head. "My mother died when I was five and my father is sick in the hospital."

"My deepest sympathies," he sighed and looked at the chart marked confidential on the desk. He quickly glanced at Bailey and saw him nod his approval before turning back to the microscope. "I am going over blood samples with Agent Bailey from the Munrow crime scene nineteen years ago."

"Oh really? Whose blood is that, if you don't mind my asking?"

Dr. Simon didn't say anything as he continued to stare at the bright red letters stamped out on the chart. When Bailey pulled away from the microscope he looked up at her and said, "Johanna's."

"Oh, I'm so sorry, Ben." She suddenly felt as if she was intruding. "I'll just be over there." She went back to the bag containing the staffs and looked over the last one that Kishi had referred to as the silver bullet. She realized they were all made of the same material—metal, but of what kind she didn't know. She knew it felt lighter and still bowed with movement like her old wooden bo staff, but these seemed indestructible. She juggled it in her hand, then balanced it at the center between her thumb and index finger.

She heard footsteps stop behind her. "Is this hollow? Is that why they're so light and yet so strong?"

"Well, they are hollow," Bailey sat down beside her, "but they're made of tungsten and titanium. Long ago, titanium couldn't be re-sized or manipulated once forged. Then the two metals' best properties were combined and this new metal was created."

"You made these for me?"

"Not exactly, but I can have them adjusted for you." He pointed to the four staffs. "I bought these."

"The silver one is a little..."

"Flashy?" He smiled.

"Mmm... high maintenance?" She pushed one strand of her hair behind her ear.

"That too." He watched her hand glide over her ear.

"I agree with you that it draws attention. In the dark with stray light from a fire or the moon, it could give me away before I intend. It also captures every finger print like a photograph. I'd have a difficult time cleaning it and if it got lost, well, I don't want to think about the consequences."

"That's true. I hadn't thought about all that. I can return it... I think."

She hesitated before she asked, "Can I give it to Kishi?" It seemed impolite to give away a gift, even if there were three others.

"It belongs to you. You can do whatever you want with it."

Jailin got up and walked over to the stout man at the computer. He looked at her, pushed his glasses up, and then smiled.

"Kishi, thanks for testing out the bo staffs with me. Though, I don't know much about your… history, I'd like you to keep the silver bullet."

"Oh, thank you, miss," he said and kept bobbing his head up and down. Jailin returned the smile and for some reason she felt compelled to bob her head also.

"You made his day. Ready to go?" Bailey asked, when she returned.

"Sure. Where are we going next?"

"Depends. Are you hungry or tired?"

"Both, but that can wait." She watched him roll up the remaining staffs in the bag and throw it over his head and one shoulder so it hung freely off his back. "Did you learn a lot from Dr. Simon?"

"Yes. Very enlightening."

"What did he say about Jo… your mother's blood?"

"It's abnormal. He hasn't seen those traits in any other samples I've found."

"He knows that she was your mother, right?"

"Yeah, why?"

"Well, didn't he want to test your blood too?"

"GIA drew my blood to run for routine diagnostics and screenings when my grandparents enrolled me in school. I guess nothing showed up, otherwise I wouldn't be working here."

"You never looked at it?" She was surprised.

"No. Should I?"

"I'd just be curious if something unexplainable showed up in my mother's blood. That's all." She hoped he didn't hear an implication of the secret her words concealed. Withholding information about how he might possess the Vernore gene was difficult.

Bailey turned to walk out the lab and they wound their way through the halls of GIA. "Let's get something to eat."

Jailin shook her head with cynicism at Bailey's attempt to change the subject. She followed him and decided to ease her way into the topic she had been avoiding since she had left him in his truck at the Starfield Inn.

She took a deep breath and slowly exhaled. "You said you talked to Contardo."

"Yeah..." He stopped but didn't turn around.

"Does that mean you're not mad at him anymore?"

"He's still an ass."

"I'm sorry."

He turned around to face her. They were standing in the middle of the empty parking lot. The sun burned high in the sky. Not a single cloud shaded Grundagon. "You don't have anything to be sorry for. He shouldn't have kissed you and I should have done something... anything, other than walk away."

"I meant I'm sorry for leaving you in the truck."

"Hey, no big deal. You have more important things in your life."

"No. Not *more* important." She stepped closer to him, resting both her palms on his chest, and stared at her hands as she said, "I didn't know how to tell you then..."

"Tell me what?"

“I didn’t know what I felt. But I do now.”

“Hey.” He held her chin in his hand and his eyes met hers. “It’s okay. You don’t have to.”

“But I do. I love you,” she whispered just before he wrapped his free arm around her waist and drew her in as he kissed her softly.

27

Shining relentlessly in the sky, the sun bore down on Adrian's face. He watched the bustle of people on the city streets from the roof of his father's building. It was as if he were the only one left to care about where their lives were leading them—but Adrian didn't care about the people below. Adrian cared about Adrian. And a girl he hardly knew.

The metal door of the roof clicked open. "What are you doing up here?" Honovi asked.

"Have you ever followed me? Without my knowledge, I mean."

"Why would I waste my time trying to figure out what you do all day long?"

"I saw… a girl, who looked so in love with a man. A nobody. He's as immaterial to *our* new world as the poor are to the wealthy. And I want to be that man. I want her to look at me that way. To love me!" He sat with his feet hanging over the edge of the roof and scratched Ronin behind the ear.

"This is what's got you in such a bad mood?"

"It's numerous things, actually."

"Talk to your Honovi, sugar. She'll make everything better," Honovi said.

"You can't help me, so back off!"

"Don't bark at me!" She drilled a hole through Adrian's back with her eyes. "You shouldn't hold all these things inside you. You'll have a heart attack before you're fifty."

"Thank you, *Doctor* Littlecreek," he deadpanned.

"Fine. I'm going back to work." She walked over to the door and said "Ronin" only once. The wolf slipped through the crack before the door closed behind her.

"Wish she'd mind her own business," he thought.

"Who would that be?" A voice he'd never heard before entered his head.

"Who is this?" Adrian swung his feet back over the side and regained his footing on the roof.

"Don't know."

"You don't know who you are?"

"Don't remember."

"Where are you?"

"It's dark, but warm. Plenty of bamboo. Yuck, I just put my paw in…" Adrian heard a sniffing sound. "Oh, it's just water."

"You're not human?"

"Not if humans have large claws and a gigantic appetite."

"What do you see around you?"

"There is a label on the lock. It says A-6."

"You're experiment A-6," Adrian whispered.

"Is that bad?"

"Depends on who you are." A devious smile came across Adrian's face.

"I told you I don't remember who I am."

"I meant what perspective one would take to you being an experiment. PAAL would be out for blood knowing you're here."

"Can you get me out?"

"Most likely, but perhaps you should have asked *if* I will get you out? Some don't trust me, especially your trainer."

"The girl who feeds me and pokes me with needles? I don't trust her either." The new voice was growing on Adrian's good side. This new experiment might come in handy—solely for Adrian's benefit. "Will you get me out? I don't think I have anything left to lose," the voice continued.

"Why are we back here?" Jailin asked Bailey as she looked up at the Luna Perfetta sign. "They don't make lunch." The sign in the window read CLOSED.

"I've got a surprise for you." Bailey pushed the unlocked door open and entered the restaurant.

"I think the bo staffs are enough."

"Don't be ridiculous. I worked hard on this."

"Beniamino! Oh goodie, you brought our flower," Enrico exclaimed as he held the second set of glass doors open for them and locked it after they entered. "Everything is complete. You'll be pleasantly surprised. I know I am." Jailin peered back at Enrico, confused.

They ascended the spiral staircase and entered a doorway to the left of the landing. A desk was placed against the side wall and a sketch book was open on top of it. Pencils, pens, paper, markers, and fabric samples were thrown around the room. In one corner there was a white clothing bag hanging from a closet door.

"Miss Munrow, Beniamino has told me a little about you. No need to worry, dear, nothing offensive." He winked at Bailey. "He wants to do his part to keep you safe and I agree with him."

"Enrico has a flare in the arts for more than just cooking." Bailey explained to Jailin. "I asked him to make your patrol uniform more…"

"Durable," Enrico finished for Bailey.

"But, I like it the way it is."

"Uh-huh, yes, he told me that, sweetheart." Enrico sounded disgusted with Jailin's present patrol uniform. "I also promised him I wouldn't make any drastic changes." He swept the air with his hand before resting his fingers on his chest. "Now, you should know I'm not exactly a man of my word, although not a single client of mine has ever been disappointed with my masterpieces."

"It does what I need. I don't see where this is going." Jailin crossed her arms.

"Jailin." Bailey squared his shoulder to hers and looked into her eyes. "Just look at it. I only want to keep you from getting hurt."

"Fine, I'll look at it. But I don't have to accept it."

"I paid for it, so you have to take it home. But you don't have to wear it, if it's not to your liking."

Enrico didn't like what he had heard. He let out a loud disapproving grunt at Bailey and pouted a tiny bit, but revealed the new suit anyway.

"Oh my, it's not what I expected at all." Jailin stepped toward the closet.

"Me neither. Enrico?" Bailey didn't sound enthusiastic for Enrico's flare for fashion or for his idea of attractive yet, protective clothes—at least not when Jailin would be wearing it.

Jailin walked up to the uniform. It was still the same black and blue color scheme. The black body suit looked like spandex. "Looks a little restrictive," she said under her breath. The shorts she was used to, but they were connected to the sides of the bodice that stretched up to the chest. Hanging on the door the way it was, it looked like Enrico had cut a triangle in the bodice. From the top of her rib cage the point of the triangle looked as if it would create a subtle curve to the top of her hip bones. A blue belt wrapped around the lowest part of her waist. There were two extra belts on the suit as well, one hooked around the top of her waist, just under her breasts and the other hooked over her chest and under the arms. The cross the two chest belts made on the back held a sheath for her bo staff. Her same gauntlets for her arms and legs draped over one shoulder of the hanger.

"What's this made of?" She traced the fabric's edge with her fingers.

"It's a lightweight, metal microgrip fabric. Soft, yet impenetrable to any known material. It's revolutionary." Enrico cupped his hands and brought them up to his chest.

Jailin noticed another belt hanging with her gauntlets. It held three small daggers. "Wow, what are these for?"

"Try it on and then I'll show you the accessories!" Enrico was overly excited.

She took the uniform into the small walk-in closet and changed into the uniform. When she came back out, Enrico had the belt in his hand.

"This one," he held up the belt, "is a dagger holster. It holds three small knives in the side for throwing, cutting, and *persuasion*." He glanced over at Bailey. "I hope you have good aim." He clipped it around her right thigh for easy access.

"How do I look? Am I a super hero now?" She smirked at the absurd thought of it.

"You're missing one thing," Bailey's voice broke. He was amazed at the transformation Enrico had made to her and he couldn't stop staring at how the suit formed to every angle of her body.

"What's that?" Jailin and Enrico asked together.

"Where does the staff go?"

"Oh, yes. I didn't forget." Enrico shook one pointed finger at Bailey for doubting him. "Deary, if you'll just turn around." He moved a full-length mirror from behind the door and angled it so Jailin could see her back. "You may have noticed when you put it on that there was a blue sheath on the back where the two belts connect from across your chest and the empire waist. The staff should slide into that perfectly."

Bailey picked up an old wooden bo staff he had borrowed from Contardo to give to Enrico for reference. This one popped in two just as Jailin's did and slid it into the pocket on her back.

"Almost perfect," Enrico said.

"Almost?" Jailin asked, a little self-conscious. "What's wrong?"

"That dreadful necklace of yours. Must you always wear that?"

"It's important to me. A reminder." She placed her hand over it and realized it had been awhile since she was anxious enough to have to rely on it for strength. "But I suppose I can keep it safe elsewhere." She lifted it over her head.

“Jailin you don’t have to take it off.” Bailey was worried that Enrico might have hurt her feelings.

“Will you wear it for me? Keep it safe?” She placed it in his hand and cupped both of hers over it.

Bailey stared at their hands. She was parting with it and still didn’t know that this necklace was actually more sentimental to him than it should be for her. “I will. I promise.” His free hand cradled her cheek. She closed her eyes and felt warm and safe from his simple touch.

28

Adrian was sitting on the edge of his father's secretary's desk. She hadn't arrived yet and Adrian didn't expect her to. She had a habit of notifying her boss at the last minute before her absences. He was waiting for his father this morning and spinning the brass name plate that read: Megan Stahl. Knowing how punctual Vernore liked to be and that there was going to be a meeting with city planners at nine, there was no way he'd miss him this morning.

At quarter to nine the giant wooden doors opened. Adrian stood up trying to look as if he had just arrived, but the door never opened any further than a mouse's width.

"You've been out there awhile. Why didn't you knock?" His father's voice sounded in his head.

"You don't like to be disturbed."

"Since when have you been concerned about what disturbs me?"

"I'm not. I just want to know something."

"Why don't you come in then?"

Adrian pushed the ornate wooden door and stepped inside. "Don't you have a meeting at nine?"

"My meetings begin when I say they do. And since you've been waiting awhile, I thought I could give you a few moments of my time."

"Gee, thanks. Glad I'm so high on your priority list."

"What do you want with A-6?"

"I really wish you wouldn't do that." Adrian hated having his mind read. He only wanted access to others' thoughts.

"Honovi tells me you've been keeping secrets. I have to search your thoughts when you least expect it."

"Honovi's a bitch," Adrian mumbled. His father cracked a crooked smile. "I want to be involved more with A-6."

"What for?"

"He seems loyal… to the right person. I just want to see what I can do with him."

"You're holding out on me, but I suppose that's reason enough." Vernore slid a paper across the desk. "Sign this."

"What is it?" Adrian picked it up and skimmed it over.

"Responsibility," he said as he handed Adrian a pen to sign the guardianship form.

Socrates was sitting on the couch with the remote, as usual. Jailin was sitting on the floor with her back to the couch. She was tweaking the drawings Bailey had made of her new bo staff and clarifying how it should pop apart. The black and blue one was perfect and she wanted to make sure that when Contardo's supplier implemented the retractable cord, it was done right.

"Wait. Go back," Jailin said as Socrates passed a news release.

Bailey had just come out of the shower. All he had on was a dark pair of jeans that hung slightly below the elastic of his pale blue boxers. He was vigorously rubbing a towel through his honey blonde hair. "What's this?" he said as he plopped himself in his recliner. Jailin glanced toward him as he sat down. She noticed how perfectly toned his abs were. And was thankful he didn't look like one of those over-bulked wrestlers. She was dying to touch what she knew would feel smooth and firm against her skin. She caught Bailey looking at her as she stared at him. Quickly she looked back to the TV.

"Dr. Adolph Vernore," the news woman had initiated, "of Vernore Biotech and Pharmaceuticals, met with North Central, South Central, East and West Central City planners today. The purpose was to find a faster mode of transportation between the four cities."

"What's he expect to accomplish with this?" Jailin asked. She wasn't entirely distracted by the luscious bare-chested man sitting not more than three feet away from her—even if she couldn't get rid of the mental picture of his mouth-watering body. Not that she wanted to. Suddenly, the phone rang. Bailey recognized the caller ID and took the phone to the bedroom.

Jailin turned back to the TV. "The outcome today was a complete success for Vernore Biotech and Pharmaceuticals. The plan is to create a monorail that will be able to quickly get travelers to their destinations. Construction is to begin in a few days and will start at the vacation resort on Ecnamor Isle. It will then continue through Grundagon Jungle." The camera panned to some protesters outside of the meeting house. "Members of PAAL or Prevention of Animal Abuse League feel this is unnecessary.

"Excuse me, sir. Why do you think this new monorail will be more of a problem than a help?"

A scruffy man, unshaven, and looking as if he'd been sleeping on the streets for months, answered, "Everyone deserves a safe home—a place where nothing can harm them. Vernore has taken that away from too many already. Now he's destroying the homes of animals and the tribes who live there. Couldn't he just make a giant circle around Grundagon? Why cut through the jungle?"

"We asked Vernore that very same question," the reporter said looking back into the camera. "And he told us that the shortest distance between two points is a straight line. Back to you, Mike."

The anchorman introduced the weather man and Jailin got up to turn off the TV. She went to find Bailey in his room and overheard the end of his conversation.

"When do I have to leave? All right, I'm heading over to Northpost and I'll meet the chopper there. Thank you, sir." Bailey opened the door fully dressed and unexpectedly found Jailin standing there. "Hi." His smile was as inviting as usual.

"He's going to destroy the jungle." She looked down, trying to hide her emotion.

"You're joking! When?"

"It's starting in a couple of days in Ecnamor Isle and extending from there. I don't really know how long it will be before..." She couldn't find the words to finish. He pulled her against his chest and rested his lips on her hair.

"I'll see what I can do," he whispered.

"What can you do?"

"I just got a call from GIA's commissioner at Westpost. I have a job in Ecnamor Isle. I have to leave now, but I'll find out what I can and we'll try to stop this."

"How long will you be gone?"

"Hard to say. Stay out of trouble for me. I'll be back as soon as I can." He grabbed his black duffel bag and the messenger bag with his communication units and tools. They were always packed for short notice. "Oh, I almost forgot."

"What?" Jailin was very unenthusiastic about Bailey running off on such short notice. He put his bags down and came back over to her. He wrapped himself around her and parted her lips with his as if to imply he'd never see her again. His hands slid slowly down her back until he caught her by the waist. As he released her he wiped a single tear away from her cheek. "Don't be upset. This is my life. I can't help it. I promise I won't be gone long." She nodded and looked down, although there was no gap between their bodies for her to see anything else but his chest which was now clothed in his gray GIA T-shirt. "You're welcome to stay here, although you may have uninvited visits from Gabe. There's an extra key in the silverware drawer."

"Thanks." She half smiled at his concern but was torn between a feeling of sadness over a home she didn't fit in and his leaving.

He was already out the door when she thought to herself, "I'm gonna have to get used to this, I suppose."

29

"You've been briefed?" Dr. Simon was scanning the pages of one of his medical books. He didn't have to look up. He knew Bailey had just entered his lab.

"Yup. I'm here to get your sequence number, in case I have anything for you."

"Oh, yes, of course." Dr. Simon slid a bar code across his desk that had no written numbers on it and Bailey took out a small black rectangle and popped the top off. A blue light scanned the bar code and a feminine voice came from the tiny scanner, "Dr. James Simon, level five, restricted."

"Do you have a moment?" Dr. Simon asked.

"Depends, is it interesting? The chopper's ready, so if it's going to make me late, then no, I don't."

"It's about Johanna's blood sample. I took a closer look and with the help of her medical records, I found some interesting information."

"If you can walk with me, by all means, tell me."

"I said the other day that the mitochondria of her cells had been abnormally large. Past studies have shown this could be common for a poor woman who didn't have adequate nutrition, but according to her medical records she ate perfectly and exercised a lot."

"So what are you saying, Dr. Simon?"

"I'd like to get a sample of your blood."

"What for? GIA has it on file."

"No. They have written labs on file of what routine tests show. There are no samples of your actual blood in this facility. And what I do is not routine."

"What do you expect to find?"

"Well, mitochondria produce ATP energy. If your mother's were increased in size, the rate of ATP may be exceptionally higher. I only have a written complaint of an increased heart rate and documentation of a fever, but no other symptoms. You may have this in your blood and I'd like to study it, with your permission, of course."

"Uh, okay. I'm not sure I completely understand, though."

"ATP is incorporated in DNA replication and transportation. If it's dormant in your DNA, I might be able to find it."

"Why wouldn't I have the same symptoms?"

"Well, I'm not sure. I can't find the cause of an increased heart rate and temperature. It seems the usual explanation for having a fever, which is to break down the bacteria causing an infection, was not the case for Johanna. The increased temperature could have caused the heart rate to increase in order to circulate the blood for white blood cells to fight off the foreign contaminant. Unfortunately, I can't ask Johanna any of this, so you're next on the list."

"I see." They had reached the helicopter platform and Bailey had to yell to Dr. Simon, "I'll be in touch!"

"Safe trip, Agent Bailey. As always."

Honovi picked up a paperweight off the desk in Vernore's office and threw it at Adrian. The glass flower shattered against the wall. "How dare you!"

"How are things going with the M.S.s?" Adrian prodded, inquiring about a more complex experiment than A-6.

"Don't ask *me* that. I'm not the geneticist." She squinted toward Vernore.

"If you both don't calm down, I'll replace both of you. Now get out of my office. I have more important lives to ruin."

"But Anubis isn't ready!" Honovi protested.

"That's none of your concern anymore, Honovi. Concentrate on what you have."

Adrian and Honovi left Vernore's office and, after the doors closed, she said, "He is beyond anything you've ever seen or imagined. You'll be begging me for help before the week is through."

Jailin sauntered up to the door of Contardo's school. Her fist paused a few inches from the door before knocking. "Is this the right thing to do?" She looked at Socrates on her shoulder.

"You are not here to forgive and forget. You are looking for another with a common goal. Do not disregard yourself."

She looked back at the door, exhaled as if she were exhausted, and knocked.

"Good evening, Anaba." Contardo opened the door with a wide grin.

"Contardo," she said straight-faced.

"Aw, still mad at me?"

"You were stupid, but that's not why I'm here."

"No? Where's that crybaby boyfriend of yours?"

"This is serious." Her jaw was set hard and she raised her head higher. She was not weaker than Contardo. She could hold her own. She wouldn't forget her purpose just because of some childish bantering.

"All right, come on in." She entered and Contardo took her up to his loft above the school.

In appearance his minimal belongs resembled the inside of her hut. Nothing fancy like the rooms below. Books were piled up next to his bed. An armoire was in the corner for his clothes and a small table with one chair sat under a window.

"Sorry I don't have a seat to offer you. Why don't you sit over here on the bed with me and you can tell me what's bothering you?"

"I'll stand, thanks." She looked around the room and it made her think of Meovi. Even though Contardo had a fascination with other cultures, his tribal roots showed through in this room. The walls were plain and painted beige. The window had no curtains and the small kitchen had only a sink, stove, and a two-foot high fridge.

"Oh, Anaba. You can't be mad at me forever, can you?"

"I can try," she growled.

"But we've got so much in common." He sat on the end of his single bed and watched her gaze around the room.

"Not according to tribal ancestry." She knew she was an outcast. There was no tribal blood anywhere in her veins.

"That was a barbaric civilization. Those tribes don't exist anymore." He misinterpreted her statement and realized what she meant when he saw Socrates cock his head to the side. He thought she had meant the customs and traditions of civilizations past—not actual blood relation.

"Did you watch the news?" she asked.

"You're changing the subject."

"Yes, but it's the reason I'm here."

"No. I don't watch TV. I'm surprised you do."

"I don't. Socrates has discovered a new liking." She scratched him behind the ear as he looked around the room from her shoulder.

"I see. And what fairy tale did you hear from our incredible Grundagon newscasters?"

"Vernore is going to destroy the jungle," she said softly as she approached the one window that overlooked the jungle, "to put up a monorail."

"Really?" Contardo couldn't believe what he had heard.

"Yes."

"Hmm." He hunched his shoulders over his legs and his hands clutched his knees. With his head hanging low, he stared at his feet. Long, dark, and silky hair, which wasn't pulled back as usual, draped like a curtain from his head and around his shoulders.

Jailin couldn't remember ever seeing Contardo wear a shirt. She remembered the way Bailey had looked this morning. Both men had broad shoulders and sculpted biceps. Contardo was much bigger though—more defined. She realized this was the kind of man who was overly muscled, which she believed was his way to compensate for his lack of self-confidence. Bailey, on the other hand, was sculpted with such precision, such splendor. He was perfect.

"I think we should call a tribunal." Contardo's words invaded her thoughts and her fantasy was lost.

"Tribunal? You mean have our two tribes meet at the clearing together?" She'd only been to one tribunal in her lifetime with the Maimugg and Taimugg tribes. That was the last time Contardo had been home. His father, the two tribe's Primary, Darwishi, needed to decide if the cause of a young boy's drowning was indeed Contardo's fault. Even though both tribes had ultimately found Contardo not-guilty, Contardo's guilt had caused him to search out solitude.

"Yes. I'll head my tribe and you yours. Since you know more about this you'll have to talk to them both."

"Me? I don't know enough. This is too fast."

"Find out everything you can. And I'll do the same. We'll meet tomorrow night." He rose from the bed and stood by Jailin, closer than she liked. "Do you want to stick around… for a bite?"

"Are you implying food, or something else?" She furrowed her eyebrows and put more space between them.

"Food first." He winked. "Besides, you might as well wait for the rain to stop." He pointed to the window as the first few drops tapped the window in the darkness.

Ecnamor Isle was paradise. There was no place in Grundagon more beautiful than the small island off the coast of West Central City. The founder and the one who had designed the luxurious resort was Ronald Sterling. He was almost as well known in Grundagon as Adolph Vernore, but Mr. Sterling was a simple man and kept clear of the media as best he could. As important as the man was, nothing prided him more than his personal habitat.

No climate had as a much color and life as this one did. Mr. Sterling populated the grounds with exotic animals such as the Raggiana Bird of Paradise. The males had beautiful red and orange feathers with a yellow head, green neck, and powder blue bill. Second in beauty was the Blue Bird of Paradise. Many guests raved about this bird purely because it hung upside down. Mr. Sterling's favorites, which were also pets of his, were his Scarlet and Blue and Yellow Macaws. Their cage was the vast borders of Ecnamor.

Some tourists believed that Mr. Sterling loved his Giant Moa above all else, due to the *Grundagon Globe* newspaper that printed pictures of him with his arm around the nine-foot bird. It was reasonable to assume this since he was the one to bring the bird back from almost total extinction.

Birds were not his only choice of exotics. The Cotton-top Tamarin was adorable and loved to follow tourists who happened to drop food as they walked the winding trails. It's cute little black face always seemed happy. People desired to touch its fluffy white fur and the brownish-black coat which ran down the center of its back to the tip of its long tail. A few Iguanas were also seen resting on warm rocks or sometimes hiding in the shade.

The buildings on Ecnamor Isle were a marble cast of ancient Rome. The Ionic columns supported arches to every entryway on the island. Vacationing here was like finding the lost city of Atlantis, or living through death in order to see heaven and return home. The weather was always perfect. It never rained, it never snowed, and the heat never reached over one hundred and ten degrees. In Grundagon, the jungle alone could surpass one hundred and twenty-five degrees and the rain on any given night could drop the temperature down to seventy. Such quick and drastic changes in temperature would leave anyone feeling frozen and ill.

It wasn't long after the sun peeked over the horizon that the helicopter landed on the platform of GIA's Westside headquarters called Westpost. Bailey stepped out and a tall, stocky, but not well-muscled man walked up to meet him.

"Afternoon, Commissioner Reilly!" Bailey shouted over the rhythmic pounding of the helicopter's propeller as he shook the man's hand.

"Agent Bailey." He looked past Bailey and saw one duffle bag thrown onto the platform. "Is that all you brought?"

"I'm only one man," Bailey smirked.

"Funny. You've been briefed already so you can go ahead and check into The Grand." The man's eyes shifted around every possible angle. Bailey had heard that Commissioner Reilly was paranoid, but he didn't know what to expect. They headed off the platform and into the building.

"Who's my partner for this mission?" Bailey had been told he wouldn't be working alone, but he didn't yet know who his partner would be.

"Agent Stern." Reilly wiped his forehead with a cloth. Ecnamor was even warmer than his old station at Eastpost. He hated the heat and East Central had a much milder climate.

"Not familiar. New?" Bailey could see that the man wanted back inside the building with the air conditioning. They started walking toward the doors.

"Newer than we'd like." Reilly followed him. He didn't know how this kid could handle such a high temperature. It was baffling.

"Any field experience?"

"Simulators mostly. This is her second mission and she does her job well." Bailey had joked around in the past with other agents about training ops, but he never actually had done one. "No need to worry. She won't need guiding." Reilly saw the slight concern cross Bailey's face. "Think of it as a quick assignment."

"Commissioner Levin hasn't returned yet. I didn't expect to get a call from you, sir." He held the door while Reilly entered the building.

"Yes, I expected as much. Your file listed you as on hiatus, but you're the best, Agent Bailey. No snoop can get more information than you."

"When's the rendezvous time?" Bailey looked at his watch. He wanted an idea of what kind of time frame meant a quick assignment to this man.

"0300."

"See you then." Bailey headed toward the exit on the opposite side of the building. The landing pad they had come from was on the outskirts of Ecnamor Isle. Bailey still hadn't seen the real beauty of the place he only knew from pictures.

"One more thing, Agent Bailey."

"Yes, sir?" He turned before crossing the threshold.

"Which identity did you bring?" Reilly handed him a manila envelope.

"Who else could afford to come here?" He smiled back, knowing that Reilly already knew. "Thank you, sir." Bailey waved the envelope as he walked out the door.

It had been raining all afternoon. Jailin was fiddling with Bailey's spare keys as she approached the apartment door. Suddenly she knocked into something on the floor. It was Gabe. He woke up and slid his hood off. He hadn't been there for long. His hair was still damp.

"Oh, hey, Jailin." He looked up through squinted eyes. This boy could sleep. Hard.

"Gabe, Ben isn't here." She was perplexed as to why this guy was always waiting around. Even to the point of sleeping at the door step. Gabe was certainly a bizarre guy in Jailin's mind.

"I know."

She sighed and rolled her eyes. "Did he send you, of all people, to keep an eye on me?"

"Benji? No, he wouldn't do that." Gabe scratched his damp hair. "I came due to my own concern."

"Concern for what?" Jailin looked less enthused than usual with Gabe.

"I saw the news." He looked down the hall as if embarrassed that he cared about what might worry her.

"Oh, that. Well, you needn't be concerned. I can handle this just fine." She unlocked the door and turned the handle. It opened quickly due to Gabe's weight against it. He fell backward on the floor.

"Wow." Gabe flipped over and got to his feet. "This is amazing."

"Yeah." Jailin stepped inside and closed the door behind them. She was astonished. Stepping over the threshold was a complete transformation into another world. One she knew all too well.

Ivy and clematis climbed over white lattice that covered every inch of wall space. Ficus trees were scattered around the room like an obstacle course. Gutted logs with wild flowers growing out of them were elegantly placed at the bases of some of the trees. Jailin found herself weaving through the room. She was in awe of the miniature indoor jungle. Every room was like this. The bathtub was laid with river rock like the pond by her hut and ivy lined the curtain rod. Lattice work was against the walls in here as well. The bedroom was covered with more flowers than a greenery.

"So when did you have time to turn this place into a greenhouse?" Gabe asked from the bedroom doorway.

"I didn't. It wasn't like this yesterday."

"Yesterday? Where have you been?"

"Errands. Setting up a meeting to save the jungle and doing research isn't as easy as it sounds, you know." She had a habit of casting important deeds as if they were nothing at all.

"A meeting is going to stop Vernore and four city planners?" He looked at her as if to judge whether or not she was still sane.

"The outcome of the meeting could solve this. We'll see." She rubbed a petal between her fingers. It was so soft and fragile in her hand. It made her miss Bailey even more.

"We?"

"Contardo and I are organizing a tribunal."

"You and *Contardo*?" Gabe's eyebrows went up.

"Don't start. I can't do this alone."

"Then ask someone else!" His implication was obvious. He wasn't going to let his best friend's heart get broken like his had. Not if he could help it.

"You don't understand." She shook her head.

"Obviously not, but do you know who did this to *Ben's* apartment? Remember Ben?" Gabe was doing all he could to provoke some kind of emotion out of her besides this subdued happiness. He couldn't understand how she loved one man and while he was away planned things with another.

"I thought Ben did." She smiled and looked around again. She hugged herself and wished her arms were his.

"I didn't see a note. Usually when someone sends you flowers, or in this case, a huge damn jungle, they include a romantic card or something." His arms were crossed, but he didn't intend to make it sound like this was beneath Bailey to do.

"Oh." She looked at each flower arrangement in the room for a card. Nothing.

"If you could think of anyone else who might send you this, who would it be?"

"Well," Jailin considered. "Contardo would send something to my place, not Ben's." Again Gabe raised his eyebrows. "What?" she directed at his shaking head in disgust with the ideas that milled around in it.

"I don't know. You tell me." He put his hand out to gesture that she should know the answer to her own question.

"I can't think of anyone else… except maybe…"

"Who?" Gabe thought that she was becoming more trouble than she was worth for Bailey all of a sudden.

"Adrian."

"*Who*?" Gabe's head shook once to clarify the question further.

"Good lord, Gabe. Don't you remember anything? Dance Zoo?" she prompted.

"Oh yeah." He felt a little idiotic. "Really? Why?"

"Why? He says I'm the perfect race and should," she cleared her throat, "reproduce with him."

"Gross." His eyebrows angled down. Jailin took this as a comment against her. "Oh no, not you. You're not gross. It's just that with his *habits*, he probably has some new, undiscovered STD."

"Oh, stop. You're just jealous of his popularity with the girls." She threw a small balled-up paper that was on the dresser at him and laughed.

"Am not! Why are you defending him?"

"He's been nothing but nice to me… considering." She rethought her statement.

"Considering?"

“The last time we ran into each other was... stressful.” She walked over to lie on the bed. Her hands slid up under the pillows. She liked to feel the cold between the sheets. “Hey, there’s something under here.” She drew her hand out and held a receipt. “Who’s Bryce Flynn?”

Gabe stared at her blankly. “You don’t know, do you?”

“Know what?”

Gabe grabbed his sides and keeled over. He was laughing too hard to stand up anymore. Bailey didn’t talk as much as Gabe thought he did in regard to a secret life that only a select few knew about.

31

The restaurant at The Grand Hotel on Ecnamor Isle was the fanciest place to eat or even have a drink. It was also the most romantic. The ambiance was set by flameless candles in the chandeliers as well as on every table as a centerpiece. The dimly lit room was full of people enjoying the exquisite atmosphere. Slow, beautiful music drifted through the room. Tucked into the shadows next to the bar were three men in tuxedos. Each was playing a different stringed instrument—a violin, a cello, and a harp.

Bailey sat at the bar drinking a scotch. Of all three of his secret identities, being Bryce Flynn was his least favorite. He hated scotch, suit jackets annoyed the hell out of him, and he detested wigs.

Bryce was a clean-cut man and stinking rich. He wore tailored clothes, drove expensive cars, and was attracted to high-maintenance women. He was also quite serious and very vain. Bailey did his best to channel Enrico when it came to being vain, but polite. Bryce was married, but supposedly seeing another woman. Bailey also hated that about Bryce, but reminded himself the man didn't really exist. He guessed that Agent Stern was going to be playing the role of his mistress tonight.

His wig itched at his scalp and to soothe it he made a habit of running his palm over his head and then down the short black pony tail that brushed the inside of his collar.

"Everyone must be excited about the new transportation system starting at the resort?" he coaxed the bartender into conversation.

"Yeah, but tourists don't like to see or hear construction on their vacations, especially romantic ones. Some of the shareholders are worried that they'll lose money."

"I am." Bryce smiled over the rim of his glass, finishing off the last swallow of scotch.

"Hello, sweetheart. Miss me?" Agent Stern walked up beside Bailey. She wore a slim-fitting black dress that stopped just below her knees. The v-neck plummeted almost down to her tiny waist. Her whiskey-red hair was pulled up into a tight twist on top of her head. A few strands fell gently around her face.

Bailey's face gave away his first impression. He raised his eyebrows as he thought, *She's a dignified over-achiever.* Agent Stern, as inexperienced as she was, interpreted his expression as lust, which she believed she saw frequently in men. She draped her arm around his shoulders.

"Lydia, you're late as usual," he said to her. This was their first meeting, but Bailey had to act as if it wasn't. All the information he had concerning her was based on the manila envelope Commissioner Reilly had handed him when he arrived.

"You know me so well," she giggled. "Shall we get our usual table?"

"Of course. You won't sit anywhere else." He stood and walked over to the hostess. They were seated immediately due to Mr. Flynn's shares in The Grand. The corner booth was veiled in darkness. It was the most romantic seat in the house. They were able to see and hear everything. Once they were seated, he began to look over the menu, even though he didn't intend to order anything. "This is your second job?"

"Yes." She straightened her dress over her knees as she sat down next to him. She propped her chin up with her hand and gazed at him as if they hadn't seen each other in years.

"You're doing well so far." Bailey tried not to lean away from her. Their cover was to look like a couple, but it didn't feel right. For the first time he really felt like a cheater. He really felt like Bryce Flynn.

"You make it easy." She smiled and batted her eyes at him as she leaned closer.

"Why is that?" He thought she was overacting as he leaned back. He rested his arm on the back of the booth behind her. It gave him the intimate distance that he needed.

"Ever since I started the simulators, I always chose to work with your identities. I like the way you look, err work." She averted her gaze and searched the table. When her eyes rested on the napkin she opened it up and began to spread out the wrinkles.

"The reason I'm so successful at my job is because I don't confuse business and pleasure." He looked over at the entrance and

Mr. Sterling, whom they were there to interrogate, walked in. "He's here. Ready?"

"I'm always ready." She had her confidence back and looked determined to get their job done. Their eyes followed Mr. Sterling and, just as planned, he was given the booth next to them.

Ronald Sterling was an older gentleman with great influence on the Grundagon Commerce Board. He also owned The Grand, which was as lavish as the entire isle. GIA was mainly concerned for the well-being of import and export trades with other countries. The Grundagon Commerce Board seemed to be heading all foreign business and it was a huge bargaining chip to have them reestablish the economy and diffuse the monopoly that was Vernore Biotech and Pharmaceuticals.

Bailey got up with Agent Stern and walked over to Mr. Sterling's table.

"Mr. Sterling? I'm Bryce Flynn and this is Lydia Roberston. I'm a shareholder for The Grand. Mind if I speak with you?"

Mr. Sterling looked up from his menu. "Mr. Flynn, is it? I'm sorry, but I'll tell you the same thing I've told everyone else. The monorail, as old a concept as it is—though since the Gobal Quake, our century has never actually seen a working model—but it is sure to provide more access for everyone to Ecnamor Isle. By which, sales will increase and bring a greater profit over time."

"What Mr. Flynn is asking about is the connection you have with Vernore Biotech and Pharmaceuticals. He simply wants to know that the economy will not bear the force of this monopoly and that it will not overpower G.C.B.'s foreign investments." Agent Stern flashed her pearly whites and nodded her head when he took notice of her.

"Well, miss. You certainly are as smart as you are beautiful. Please, sit with me. Both of you." His hand swept through the air as an invitation to the booth.

Agent Stern was first as they slid into the offered seat. "Thank you," Lydia batted her eyes at Mr. Sterling.

"Now." Mr. Sterling straightened his silverware on the table. "I do understand the concern with Vernore. He is a bit… overzealous. But I assure you the economy will be safe. He does seem to have a great hold on North Central City and some current residents are still fighting to keep their small businesses. I expect the natives of the jungle to give us a hassle with the recent developments, but Vernore has reassured me that he will take care of them." Mr. Sterling parted his lips as he exhaled. He could care less about that group of people. Bailey's jaw tightened and he narrowed his eyes. "Mr. Flynn, if I remember right, you live in North Central, correct?"

"Yes," Bailey said between clenched teeth.

"I hear there is going to be quite a thunderstorm tonight." His attempt at small talk was not warming Bailey over. The gentleman saw the anger in the young man's eyes, but decided not to comment on it.

"I haven't heard that." Bailey looked away to calm himself so he could refocus.

"That's what's so nice about a vacation. Wouldn't you say?" Mr. Sterling didn't know what he had said to anger the man, but he tried to correct it.

"I don't mean to be rude, but won't the monorail increase Vernore's power? I mean, as you said he's a big deal in North Central. Is it wise to let that spread?" Bailey knew his focus was not solely the monorail, but all of G.C.B.

"Excuse him, Mr. Sterling. He doesn't really care about the monorail." Agent Stern shot a look at Bailey.

"Why destroy the jungle?" Bailey couldn't help but ask the one question burning in his mind.

"I'm sorry, we've kept you from your dinner. We should get back to our room," Agent Stern cut the conversation short. This was nothing like working with his simulation personalities. She wanted to believe it was she who was distracting his thoughts. She pushed at Bailey's elbow to get him out of the booth.

"Not a problem at all. I enjoyed the company. Have a pleasant stay." Mr. Sterling raised his hand in goodbye and laid it back down on the table.

"Thank you," she flashed her most seductive smile.

Neither Bailey nor Agent Stern said anything to each other until they reached Bailey's room. "We're supposed to have concrete information for Commissioner Reilly at 0300. You've got trains on the mind. What's wrong with you?"

"Sorry," the word escaped his mouth like a boy trying to keep his mother off his back.

She grunted and leaned against the wall. "Something is obviously bothering you. You want to talk about it?"

"It wouldn't help anyway. I've left my mind at home this time." Bailey sat down on the bed and took off the wig so he could scratch his head. *And my heart*, he thought as it ached for the girl at home.

"Oh," she caught her breath.

"What?" He looked up at her and saw the astonishment on her face. Water welled in her eyes, but she closed them to keep it back.

"I've never actually seen *you* before. I mean I've had to memorize your identities, but never you." When she opened them, the water was gone. She almost looked relieved.

"Why does it matter?" He was confused. She didn't look or carry herself like an agent, but she knew how to act like one.

"I thought Sam Connell was gorgeous." She looked away. Bailey second-guessed her knowledge of his identities.

"What? That's gross. You need to work on your memorization. Sam is a lawyer in his mid-fifties. I wear a lot of prosthetics to become that jerk."

"Who am I thinking of?" She pressed her finger to her lips.

"Only one left is Colin Duque." He rubbed the back of his neck like a weight had been relieved.

"Oh, yes. Now I remember." Her eyes glassed over as thoughts of her simulation training ran through her mind. She took a few steps closer to Bailey, and standing next to him she ran her fingers through his matted hair that the wig had caused.

"Stop that." He jerked his head around. She slid her hand down his neck and stopped between his shoulder blades.

"Why? Is it bothering you? Am I making you nervous or…"

He grabbed her hand and put it back down at her side. "No. I'm already committed."

"Humph." She made a face of displeasure. "What's your real name, Agent Bailey?"

"We're not supposed to discuss personal topics unless we're from the same command post."

"I won't tell anyone. I'm Molly. See? That was easy, now it's your turn." She caught him smiling at the floor. "What? You don't trust me?"

"No, I don't. But I've just thought of a perfect person for you to date. How do you feel about tall, dark-haired assholes?" He looked at her sitting next to him to gauge the reaction on her face.

She shifted her weight from side to side to push her heels off her feet. Her posture admitted defeat. "Maybe I'll see if I can get anything important out of Mr. Sterling. See you at 0300, Agent Bailey." She stood, picked up her shoes and left the room.

"Good lord." He exhaled and let himself fall back on the bed. The chain of Jailin's necklace slipped up his chest to his throat. Pulling the pendant out from under his shirt—anger mixed with passion as he squeezed it in his hand. This symbol represented all that was Vernore's—North Central City, dozens of companies and small businesses, the truth about his mother, and Jailin. No. Not Jailin. He owned what she had become—a life-altering gene, and he wasn't going to stop "fixing" people. After deliberation, he rolled over to the phone and dialed the operator. "Could you get me connected to a Mr. Benjamin Bailey in North Central City?"

"Certainly, Mr. Flynn," the operator replied.

The phone rang three times before he heard Gabe's voice. "What are you doing there?" There was a pause for Gabe's summary of the previous twenty-four hours. "Is she there?" And then, "Meeting with the tribes? Oh, I see." Bailey smiled. "Good. I'm glad she likes it. Tell her I'll be back late tomorrow." Then Gabe hung up and Bailey added into the dead receiver, "And I miss her."

Jailin met Contardo at the rain tree in the clearing. The night air was damp, but the sky was cloudless for the time being. The real girth of the storm wasn't expected until just before dawn. Jailin could smell the clean, crisp blue-eyed grass, sweet white violet and springcress in the air. She could see from her spot up in the tree that some tribal members had already arrived for the tribunal.

Contardo was leaning against the trunk of her tree. "Is everyone here?"

"I see Masou. Although, I don't see Darwishi yet."

"He's getting older and slower with every passing moment. I'm not surprised he's not here yet." A soft breeze blew through the trees. She peered down at Contardo. He looked tranquil standing in the jungle. He had never told her why he left, but she knew it was because of Darwishi.

"Don't say things like that about your father," she reprimanded and he shrugged in return. "Dierno," she thought, "Have you finished sweeping the border?"

"Taking one more lap around. So far, so good."

"There he is." Contardo pointed to an old man hunched over a Markhor horn which he used as a cane. His arms were longer than a normal man's. His jaw was square and his skin was nicely tanned from many years in the sun. He wore the various pelts of all the kills he had made in his lifetime. Jailin was amazed he could hold it all up.

"I guess it's time." She jumped down and Contardo handed her her new black-and-blue bo staff. The adjustments she needed had been completed by his weapons supplier. The staff could now split and then retract on its own with the push of a small button. The end of the staff held a small silver spear that could be popped out like an army knife. She fiddled with it for a second, even though she knew Contardo would have checked that everything worked properly before giving it to her.

Contardo followed her through the mass of men and women and up the incline of the boulder. At the top, Jailin began her speech to the tribes, while Contardo translated for those who didn't know the universal language of Grundagon.

"Thank you all for coming," she paused while the tribes quieted down and settled into their places. She locked eyes with Meovi once and smiled. The smile was returned, but it was somber. "I don't know how much you already know, but we are here tonight to speak of the impending destruction to our homes and the way of life for so many species." She paused to let Contardo catch up. "Those who have not adapted to our way of life have no compassion for the surrounding beauty. I speak of Adolph Vernore, who has gathered the four great cities and passed a proposal to build between them." A lot of commotion began to ensue in the crowd. Jailin tried to speak louder. "In only a short time, our way of life will be destroyed. People will come to build a transportation system; the center focal point being our jungle. And I can assure you it won't stop there!"

"How do you know this?" someone shouted.

"Why are they making a cross between the cities instead of a circle?" Another voice sounded out of the crowd.

"Everyone, please, one at a time!" Jailin begged. The crowd got quieter and Jailin began to answer what she could.

"I found out about all this two days ago. There really isn't any logic to this construction proposal. They seem to rely on the statement that says the quickest way between two points is a straight line. But I found out more. We all know our weather is unstable. It could change drastically at any time. Each season never lasts the same amount of time twice. The monorail needs protection from the unstable environment. The housing containment is to go where our jungle is. This is why we are being eradicated."

"They won't move us!"

"They won't even notice. They'll plow right through."

"So what do we do?" The first voice was heard again.

Jailin spoke over the two voices. "That's why Contardo and I called this tribunal. We need to come up with ideas. We need a way to stop this."

"Kill Vernore!" A woman with a crying child was heard.

"If that was possible, we would have done it already." Contardo chimed in with enthusiasm for this woman's comment.

"Well, we can't petition this. We don't have enough people to contradict the cities." A deep, grumbled voice rang out above the others.

"Then we fight it." Jailin stepped closer to the edge of the rock. "We still have some time before construction starts. We should set posts around the border. Let no one in. I'll take the fight into the cities."

"What?" Contardo asked. "You can't do that!"

"Yes, I can," she said to him. "I'll be the eyes and ears of North Central City. If I can stop it first—I will."

Contardo grabbed her elbow, "Anaba, no!" His face was drawn with fear. The thought of her fighting against a man of such stature and abilities only spelled death to his ears.

She hardly heard his disapproval. The crowd was happy that there was a plan—even if it was a rough plan. She turned back to Contardo to see the concern still lined in the curves on his face. "I have resources," she smiled. "And connections."

He let her go, but wasn't happy. "He's going to get us all killed."

Jailin knew Contardo's "he" meant Bailey, but she didn't agree. She looked around the clearing. The crowd was talking amongst themselves about what they could do and who would take shifts when and where around the jungle. She was proud of herself.

Masou approached her and rested one hand on her shoulder. "Very nice speech, but do you think you can handle this?"

"Time will tell," she said as she watched small children run, chasing each other and yelling about fighting off the impending doom.

"Yes, it will. It always does. And our tribe will know if you are capable of taking my place in this tribe." He turned to watch the children as Jailin did. One day, they would be looking to her for guidance as their parents now looked to Masou.

"Seriously? You're top patrol guard?" Contardo was shocked, even though he knew he shouldn't be.

"I was." Jailin looked down at her feet. She didn't want to assume that Masou had just reinstated her.

"She's the best," Masou called over his shoulder as he walked down the flat side of the boulder. He stopped once to look at Jailin again. His eyes darted to Contardo, "Nice to see you again too, young Primary." Contardo nodded in return.

"Going back to the city?" Contardo asked Jailin.

"Yes." She smiled, thinking about sleeping in her new pseudo-jungle surrounding.

"Why do you look so happy? You may have just doomed two tribes and yourself."

"This is where we met." She looked around the clearing. Almost everyone was gone home and she watched the blue-eyed grass sit back up after lying under everyone's feet. Soon there would be no trace of the person who had just been standing there.

"We who?" Contardo sounded annoyed and then regretted asking.

"Ben and I. I mean on the nineteenth anniversary of our parents' death. It's kinda strange now that I think about it."

"Yeah, well, I don't want to hear about it. You want a ride back or not?"

"Nah, I'll walk." She certainly didn't want to be around this downer any longer.

"Nice patrol uniform, by the way." He looked her up and down slowly. She didn't like the longing in his eyes. No one was able to control their attraction to another, but Contardo only wanted to remember how beautiful she was, in case he never saw her again.

33

She took her time, walking and half running back to Bailey's apartment. The rain had started coming down lightly as she arrived in the city. When she reached the apartment complex, she ran inside to Bailey's door. It was unlocked and she expected to see Gabe watching TV or eating. But Gabe wasn't there. A black duffle bag was lying by the door.

"Ben?" she called, peering through the ficus trees.

She made her way to the bedroom door and Bailey was sitting on the bed. A blanket was spread out on the floor and he had an expensive bottle of Sauvignon Blanc. The finest wine from Ecnamor Isle.

"Hi." He smiled at her and stood up. Her heart raced. "I thought you might like a picnic, but since it's raining, I brought the picnic inside."

She smiled and threw her arms around his neck—recalling a time when they were young and eating peanut butter sandwiches in her backyard. "You're back early!"

"I couldn't stay away any longer. You've been busy, I hear." He wrapped his arms around her waist and skimmed her neck with his nose to breathe in her scent. As he exhaled, he pulled her back to sit on the bed. A pleasurable shiver ran down Jailin's spine.

She laid down next to him, propping her head up with her hand. "Aren't you hungry?" she asked, jutting her chin to the blanket on the floor.

"Not anymore." He rolled onto his side so that he was facing her. With his free hand, he ran one finger down the side of her face, contouring its shape, and then over her lips. She closed her eyes. He moved his hand to her waist as he kissed her. Her hand came up to hold his jaw and then slid into his hair, and he brought his hand down over her leg until it met the back of her knee. Hitching her leg up over his waist, she was even closer to him. "There isn't an ounce of space between us, and yet I still want to be closer to you," he whispered.

"One of us might crush the other, then where would we be?" she answered, her smile pressed against his lips.

He withdrew his head from hers slightly. She hated when he did that. "I need to ask you something." The panic in his voice didn't go unnoticed.

"Okay." She felt her heartbeat quicken and wondered if he could feel it with his chest pressed to hers the way it was. She could feel the fast rhythm of his.

"I gave Dr. Simon a sample of my blood."

"When?" She traced the nape of his neck with her lips—trying her best to allure his attention back to her.

"Today." He squeezed his eyes tight, trying to focus on what he needed to say.

"What for?" She rested her cheek against his shoulder and looked at him through her lashes.

"He found some interesting things," he took another moment to concentrate before continuing, "about my mother, that he can't explain." His thoughts swirled every time he breathed her in. "And he wants to see if I am the same way."

"What was wrong with her?" she whispered in his ear.

"She had complained of a rapid resting heart rate and a fever." Bailey tried desperately to stay focused.

"Well, you have a fast pulse right now. I can feel it." She tilted her head to look at his chest pressed against hers. Then she ran her hand along his shoulder and down his chest to stop over his heart. "And I always have a fever by human doctor standards. My temperature is always one hundred and four—a normal temperature for a cat." She kissed his bottom lip lightly and then brushed her nose over his ear. "I think you're warm, but in a very tempting way." Her breath warmed his ear as she spoke.

With longing, he brought her face to his so he could kiss her deeper and longer. Then he stopped and looked at her hand as if to study it like a work of art. "Please don't be mad." His eyes met hers, looking solemn. "This is something that I really want."

"So do I." She rolled to her back and pulled him with her. She felt his heart skip and then race even faster.

"Oh!" He looked surprised by her advancement. "No… I mean, not *no*, but I meant… Shit." Dropping his forehead onto the bed next to her head, he felt like a complete idiot for having brought this up now.

"What is it? Did I do something wrong?" She was concerned. Without realizing it, she was holding her breath.

His head shot up and he held her face in his hands. "No! Oh, God, no. You're perfect, absolutely gorgeous. I'm stupid. Only an imbecile wouldn't..." He couldn't find the right words. "It's just that... It's something else entirely."

"Okay." She searched his face. "So, let's talk about it. It's obviously very important to you."

He paused and hoped he could take it all back. No, there was no going back now. "If Dr. Simon can figure out your DNA..." Panic had crossed her face. He rolled to the side as she shot straight up. He sat up to meet her and placed one hand on the side of her face so he could look into her eyes. "Please, don't worry. GIA doesn't know we're doing this. They still don't know about you. This is only a hypothetical situation."

"Maybe you should have mentioned that first!" Her hand pushed his away from her face. She was angry and he could see that.

"You're right. I should have. I just want you to say that you agree with me. That you're..." He searched her face for the emotion he had seen before she got so angry. The same love-struck girl was now just too angry to let him see that part of her now. "I don't know if I could handle your resentment," he spoke softly, feeling guilty for causing her panic and fear.

"Just say it already!" She knew she wasn't going to like what he wanted. What he was asking of her was going to be hard enough.

He sighed lightly before saying, "I want what you have. For all I know, I could have the same blood disease or whatever *gift* my mother had that got her killed. I want to know that you're behind me on this. I want Dr. Simon to make me strong and gifted like you."

"He could kill you! He doesn't know what he's dealing with." She stood up. Every distance she placed between them hurt him more and more. Now, with her standing over him, he wished he could go back in time and never bring it up.

"Vernore offered to make me like you. He said the vial you drank was meant for me." He didn't meet her sour face. He played with his hands like a child reprimanded by his teacher.

"And now you're just going to go to him and get it? I don't understand. Have you lost your mind? You don't know how this will change you. You don't know anything." He winced at her contempt.

"That's why I need your help. Help me. Please?" He glanced up at her.

"That's what you wanted to ask me? To help you achieve this? Why?" Her anger cracked. The way he looked sitting there in front of her made her feel guilty. He looked helpless and so fragile. She wondered if he felt that way too.

"It would be something we can share. We'd be the same, closer even. I could protect you and understand everything you go through."

"The Vernore gene. The perfect race," she mumbled as she dropped her head. Vernore was going to win after all. She couldn't stop the madness of this murderer or his convoluted ideas.

"Okay, sure. If that's what you want to call it."

She looked into his eyes. A single tear streamed down her face. "I have to tell you something. Before Dr. Simon finds out what I already know." He swallowed hard in response. He was going to have to tell her a secret he had been holding onto as well.

Lightning flashed outside the window and the rain came down hard, as they told each other their deepest secrets.

34

Jailin walked up and down the city streets. She didn't care that the sky was crying a river and that she was soaked because of it. She needed to be alone to think. Bailey had told her about her father. She didn't know who she was angrier at: Bailey, for keeping this from her for so long, or Vernore, who was forcing her father to keep secrets by drugging him, which caused an extremely early and advanced dementia.

She placed her hand on the small messenger bag that bumped against her hip as she walked. Enrico had given it to her so that the new patrol uniform could be easily accessible. Alternatively, she used the bag to hold her clothes, depending on the situation. She had met with Enrico about designing a mask before she met with Contardo to form the tribunal. To take her mind off the disagreement with Bailey, she considered seeing if the mask was finished. With the mask, she could spy on Vernore without being easily recognized. Recognized? She thought that sounded absurd because who else would be spying on him, but the girl he'd mistakenly altered?

Her thoughts inadvertently went back to Bailey. He understood her demand to be alone. He also wanted to help her through this, but she wasn't asking for help. He wasn't mad at her for telling him that he very likely had the Vernore gene in him. He had almost appeared relieved. This confused Jailin. She had spent so many years alone. Years of being ridiculed by other kids in the tribe, and the adults, who only saw her as an outcast. The only exceptions to this were Meovi and Masou. She was treated as a threat to them, which she never saw in herself.

She knew Bailey wasn't childish, but would his personality change if he went through with this? Would he still love her? Would she still love him? She kept asking herself all these questions about how their lives would change. She didn't want to seem selfish by making him keep a promise not to pursue this, but wasn't he being selfish by wanting it?

"Why aren't you saying anything? You always listen to my thoughts. Now, of all times, you keep quiet?"

"A thousand apologies. I misinterpreted your request to be alone. Does being alone not also exclude me?" Socrates was following at her heels.

"You've never considered yourself separate from me."

"You must figure this out on your own. I cannot persuade you."

"No, maybe not, but I *would* like another opinion."

"My opinion is this. If anyone should do this for him, it should be your father."

"You're joking, right? That's your opinion?"

"Yes."

Jailin arrived at Luna Perfetta and knocked on the door. It was early in the morning, but the darkly clouded sky gave no indication that it was dawn.

Enrico showed up at the door after what seemed like forever. He smiled and opened it once he recognized Jailin's soaked face. "Aw, a poor wet kitten. Come in, love."

"Thank you. I came to see about the mask. Is it finished yet? If not, that's okay. I know it hasn't been long."

"Actually, it's almost ready."

"Really?"

"Come on up. I'll show you what I have so far."

"Great." Jailin beamed.

Enrico took her into the same room as the one in which he'd unveiled her uniform. It was even messier than before. A small armature of a tiger head sat in the middle of the floor.

"What do you think?"

"This is done? It's just wire and sheets of metal soldered together." She looked it over, trying to understand how this was going to serve as a mask instead of a sculpture.

"That's not the final piece."

"Oh. How much longer will it take?"

"Not long. Go take a nap. You could use it."

"Excuse me?" She was taken aback.

"Your eyes are puffy. You're tired and you've been crying. Go rest. I'll wake you when I'm done."

"But I'm soaked."

"Clean clothes are in the dresser, my dear. Pick for yourself. I don't own anything scandalous."

Jailin narrowed her eyes at Enrico. When he worked, he had a purpose and that purpose drove him to curt, direct demands.

Jailin cleaned up in the bathroom and chose a simple shirt. She was surprised Enrico would keep this plain, unflattering shirt in his home, let alone wear it. The shirt was long enough that she figured she wouldn't bother to find anything more. When she pulled the shirt over her head there was a familiar smell to it. "Ben," Jailin sighed. No wonder it was kept here. Enrico would never get rid of this.

The bed looked like a giant cloud. Inviting, warm, and white. She carefully got in as if she would tear the fragile bedding. Enrico was right. She was exhausted. Her eyes were heavy and she fell asleep, but not before she saw a picture next to the bed. It was a photograph of Enrico wearing a military uniform and shaking hands with a tall, dark and handsome, yet familiar, stranger. The engraving read: *Thank you for everything. – C.D.*

The sun was setting in the distance and an airy voice was heard calling for dinner, but there was no house visible for miles. Between the roots of a giant sycamore fig, a boy was kicking at piles of sand and roaring like a monster. The little girl laughed and dug her stubby little hands deep into the sand.

"Look. I foun dis." She pulled a chain out of the sand slowly.

"Watch out! That's quicksand, Jay-Jay. It will pull you in!"

"How?" The round, chubby-cheeked little face scrunched up in confusion. She was squinting into the light behind the boy's head. His light blonde hair only seemed to make it harder for her to see him clearly.

"Sand steals people. If you get sucked in, you'll never return."

"I don't want to disappear." She dropped the chain.

When she looked back up it was dark. She was all alone. Not a single light shone from the sky and no sounds could be heard, not even a cricket. Suddenly she felt as if she was being carried away from the Sycamore Fig. It kept getting smaller and smaller until she couldn't see anything but the surrounding teak trees.

"Daddy?" No voice was heard in return. "Mommy?" Still no replies.

The little girl began to cry. She heard a familiar voice, but she couldn't put a face to it. She whirled around and a dark figure stood in front of her.

"Don't be afraid, little one. The sand has taken your family, but you will not be harmed. Follow the correct path and good fortune will always be on your side."

"Who are you?" she asked.

The dark figure said nothing. The little girl stood, and when she was upright, she was the same height as the mystery figure. She stretched out her hand to touch the darkness before her, but she couldn't reach. No matter how many steps she took, the distance to the figure was always the same.

"What have you done to my father?" she yelled. It was Jailin's own voice she recognized now—her own adult voice. Her hand was thin and her fingers were long. She tried to reach the figure again, but as it faded, it turned red and then was gone.

"Wake up!"

Jailin opened her eyes and saw the same picture she had fallen asleep next to. She was still drowsy and didn't realize where she was. "Ben?" She rolled over, and standing in front of her was

Enrico holding a petite tiger mask in front of her. "Oh." She held out her hand to take it.

Turning it over and under, inspecting every side and angle, Jailin's smile grew. The tiger mask was black. The markings were powder blue where a normal tiger would have black stripes. It matched her uniform perfectly. The ears stood out to the sides and angled back as if to be dominating its prey. The nose jutted out into a muzzle to create a perfect tiger profile over Jailin's face. The mask's eyes were cut perfectly to the size of Jailin's own.

"Put it on. I want to make sure it fits."

"How will it stay on? There's no string."

"It's the same material as your suit. The micro grip will cling to your skin."

Jailin looked skeptical. She put the mask to her face, and just as Enrico said, it clung to every curve and facial muscle.

She looked around and swung her head violently to check to see if it would slip. "How will it come off?"

"Just like the suit."

"That seems to interlock with my skin. I always have to pull it up before folding it down to get it off."

"It will get easier. Like an adhesive bandage."

"But won't hurt," she quipped.

"Right." Enrico smiled at her and saw a tiger smile back in return. "You will have the same protection on your face as the rest of your body."

She looked out the window. It was still raining, and the sky was even darker now. "I'll be a shadow in the rain," she said, captivated by the fingers of water gliding down the window.

"A shadow reign that protects us all," Enrico said, looking out the window with her.

“Would you call Ben for me, Enrico? Tell him to meet me at Vernore Community Mental Hospital.”

“Of course, love. Your clothes are cleaned and on that chair.”

“Who’s that?” She pointed to the picture when Enrico pointed to the clothes next to it. “Do you know Adrian?”

“I don’t know any Adrians. That’s Colin Duque.” He smiled at her and winked before turning toward the kitchen. “It’s quarter to six. Almost time to open.”

35

Anxiety gripped Jailin's stomach as she waited outside the hospital. She had decided to wear her cleaned clothes over her uniform, just in case. The messenger bag held her staff, which was unsnapped and folded into two two-and-a-half foot sections. She also had kept her arm gauntlets in the bag because her shirt was short sleeved and she didn't want to draw attention to them. She made sure that Socrates stayed in the bushes, out of sight.

Bailey parked the Ridgeline in the visitors' lot. It was late enough that most visitors were long gone, doing personal things or seeing other family and friends. Bailey got out of the truck and walked slowly over to Jailin. She glanced to her left once out of nervousness before advancing to meet him.

"I'm sorry." One hand gripped her elbow at her side. "I might be able to support your decision with time," she confessed.

"I'm sorry, too, I should have told you all this sooner."

"Me too." She took his hand and led him into the hospital.

"Here's your passes." Through the opening in the glass window the nurse slid two laminated cards with V.C.M.H. VISITOR written on them.

They walked down the long, sterile corridor and came to a door with a small window. The glass was lined with safety wire. When the nurse hit the button, the door buzzed and Jailin pushed it open.

Elderly men were scattered around the room. Most of them were older with gray hair, wrinkles, and either a cane or a wheelchair. Jailin's father stood out. He was the youngest man in a geriatric mental ward. Normally, those of his age with a mental illness were treated as outpatients, but Dr. Ted Munrow required special attention. Attention that was specialized in V.C.M.H.'s geriatric ward. Jailin pointed Ted out and Bailey nodded. Together they walked up to the man in the straight-backed chair.

Ted was slumped over. His appearance from afar suggested that he was in a deep slumber. When Jailin reached out a hand to place on his shoulder, only his eyes shifted in her direction.

"Daddy?" she asked, "Are you all right?"

He looked up at her and squinted as if it would help him recognize who was addressing him. His eyes shifted to Bailey and they went wide. "Dad, this is…"

"Nick!" He leaned forward and grabbed Bailey's arm, "Nicky! Kathy, get me my notebooks. I have to discuss some important matters with him."

"Sir, I'm not…"

"No. Don't." Jailin stopped Bailey's next words. "Be who he thinks you are. This is the biggest reaction I've ever seen."

"I'll try."

"Kathy! Get me my notebooks!" Ted glared at Jailin.

"All right, hold on a second!" She disappeared in the direction of the sleeping quarters.

"Nick. You won't believe what I found on our last night out."

"Our last night?"

"Yes. After you left me in the jungle to be with your wife so she wouldn't leave you."

"Oh." Bailey was shocked to hear that his parents had had marital problems. "Right. So, what'd you find?"

"A ghost."

"Ghost?" Bailey was skeptical.

"You heard me."

Jailin came back with two notebooks. One was filled with scribbles she didn't understand and the other was blank. She handed both to her father and he set them on the floor by his feet.

"Tell me more about this ghost," Bailey pushed Dr. Munrow to continue.

"Hmm? Oh yes, the ghost. I collected fecal samples right after you left, although I can't find them now." Ted patted his pockets and looked around the room. "Nothing in my lab is the way I remember it. Anyway, a small ghost cat with red eyes was glaring at me. I could have sworn it was a tiger or a leopard, or some kind of felidae, but something was off. It was the opposite of any feral cat I had studied. Other than it being all white, I mean."

"Dr. Munrow, it's time for your medicine." A nurse walked up with a small paper cup with two purple pills in it.

"Oh boy, grapey goodness!" Dr. Munrow held out his hands like a child allowed candy after throwing a temper tantrum for the past hour.

"May I give him his pills?" Jailin stood up and held out her hand to the nurse.

"As long as you make sure he swallows." The nurse smiled and handed her the cup.

"Not a problem." After the nurse walked away, Jailin dumped the two pills into her hand and put them in her pocket. From the other pocket she pulled out two grape-flavored children's vitamins. She had heard her father in past visits get excited over these purple pills the nurses always brought him.

"What was different about this cat other than it was white?" Bailey asked, after Dr. Munrow had chewed up the vitamins.

"Evil."

"How do you know that?" Jailin sat on the edge of her chair.

"The eyes, Kathy. Aren't you listening?"

"Sorry." Jailin rolled her eyes toward Bailey.

"So, Nicky." Ted inclined toward Bailey. "You know how we've been trying to spy on that odd character renting my extra lab?"

"Uh..." Bailey's eyes flickered to Jailin, "Yes."

"I know who he is."

"Who is he?" Bailey prompted.

"Augustus Vernore's son."

"Augustus?" Jailin leaned forward even more.

"Kathy! Do I have to ask you to leave us? This is no information for a woman to overhear."

"Fine." She slumped back.

"Augustus was my mentor for zoology. I learned a lot from him."

"What does any of this have to do with your lab tenant?"

"Augustus is his father. I'm not going to keep talking if you interrupt me all the time, Nick."

"All right, please continue."

"As I was saying. Augie was a good man. Very knowledgeable. His son, as smart as he was, was power hungry. Just like Marianne."

"Marianne?"

"Augie's wife. Mean lady. Selfish and arrogant."

"Do you know this son's name?"

"No. I think it's Andrew or something." Bailey looked toward Jailin quickly. They knew Ted was talking about Adolph Vernore.

"What's he been doing in your lab?"

"Making ghost cats. Evidently, giant ghost cats."

"And you know all of this because of one white cat?"

"No. He left a bag of them in the jungle. Dead, of course. Except…"

"Except?" Bailey and Jailin asked simultaneously.

"One. A male. Such beautiful eyes. Like the grass after the rain, and the other like the sky on a cloudless day."

"What did you do with him?" Bailey asked.

"Ran." Ted looked up at Bailey like there could be no other answer to his question.

"Where did you take him?"

"Nowhere."

Bailey looked at Jailin as if to ask, "How do you run nowhere?" Jailin only shrugged. She knew it had been another three years before he was found starving and on the verge of death in Cluce, just outside South Central City. "What happened to the cat?"

"I cared for it until it got too big. Strange thing is he knew when I was hungry, tired, or cold. Then he knew when it was time to leave me. I always felt like he could read my mind."

Jailin smiled. This made her feel relieved and thankful. Almost serene. She loved this feeling. She knew how Bailey made her feel and that was the greatest feeling ever, but Dierno was now even more important to her than ever.

"Dierno," she thought with a tear in her eye. "Thank you so much."

"For?" His voice sounded back in her mind. He was within range and Jailin was glad of it.

"My father. You kept him alive for three years."

"Who's your father?"

"Ted Munrow, the one who hid with you in the jungle for three years."

"He's your father?"

"Yes." Even in her mind, Dierno could hear her expression of joy. She wiped at her eyes before the first tear could fall.

"Glad to be of service." Jailin couldn't tell if he was glad he serviced her or her father, but it didn't matter.

"Jailin?" Bailey whispered.

"Huh?" She came back out of her personal conversation.

"Did you hear what Dr. Munrow just said?"

"Please, Nick. Just Ted. You know I hate that."

"Can you repeat what you just told me for Kathy?"

"I suppose so. I said I named him Dierno. A tribe called him that when I told them our story. The translation is White Shadow, if I remember correctly."

"White Shadow? That's from an old Maimugg legend. I completely forgot about that bedtime story." Jailin stared deep into her father's eyes. She smiled and wrapped her arms around his neck.

"Kathy?" Ted was mystified and apprehensive. "No." His voice wavered slightly and Jailin pulled back to look at him. When their eyes met all he said, with recognition and love, was, "My little girl."

After a few moments of holding the daughter he had thought was gone forever, he let his grip loosen. "And who are you?" He looked at Bailey as if he'd never seen the young man in his entire life.

36

The windshield wipers desperately tried to clear the sheets of water while Bailey attempted to view the road between the gaps. He wasn't concentrating on the road the way he should have been. He wanted to be home reassuring Jailin that he could get her father out of that hospital. He also wanted to meet with Dr. Simon to find out what he could on Ted's condition.

"There's got to be some way of getting him out of there." Bailey's hand moved from the wheel to caress Jailin's palm.

"No. I've tried to transfer him. Nothing is allowed without Vernore's approval in North Central City." She took the pills out of her pocket. "These things are killing him slowly."

"Wait. Give me those." Bailey put out his hand.

"Why? We should destroy them. No one should have to deal with that. He's not crazy. You saw him. He recognized me. I'm going back tonight and stealing all of those meds."

"Now wait, some of those people really are ill. The second floor alone houses young adults who are in need of special arrangements."

"Maybe the bottles are labeled."

"Jailin, promise me you won't do anything dangerous."

She smiled. This was child's play compared to what she'd done before. "Okay."

"Give me the pills. I'll take them to Dr. Simon." His hand was still out, waiting for the pills and she placed them in it. Hope for Dr. Simon's analysis of the pills was all she had left to reassure her that her father's health wouldn't be depleted forever and that the pills' effects weren't permanent.

Bailey dropped her off at his apartment and told her he'd return after meeting with Dr. Simon. The rain, still falling in buckets, caused the quick departure. She stood under the overhang of the apartment building and watched the truck go. Socrates was clinging to her back, begging to go inside.

The hospital was dark. Dim lights glowed from the windows, but hardly displayed any movement within. Some murmurs could be heard from patients talking in their sleep. Others were snoring. The windows were reinforced with bars and Jailin knew this was more for keeping people in than keeping others out. Tonight she was an uninvited guest who wanted in without a visitors' pass.

She heard the footsteps of the security guard making his rounds while the nurses at their stations played easy listening music. The smells were different on every floor. She could differentiate between the young kids, the middle-aged, and the elderly.

She had come in through the roof and clung to the shadows while moving through the halls. When a stock boy walked by she slipped into a patient's room to keep out of sight.

This room was dark, but Jailin could see pictures on the wall by her head. The pictures displayed a happy family. One was of a man and a woman holding a small girl. The little girl had pale strawberry blonde hair. She was skinny, but still very pretty. Jailin felt sorry that this little girl's family member was stuck in this place.

She heard a stirring coming from the bed. "Who's there?" a faint sing-song voice asked.

Jailin stayed very still. The voice wasn't heard again. Instead Jailin heard the heartbeat slow and the breathing become light and even. She crept closer to the bed.

"She's so young," Jailin whispered. She walked out of the room and checked the name card before she slipped down to the next ward. "M.S.-3?" Jailin was running out of time. She repeated the name card in her head and quickly went down to the next floor.

Only one young nurse sat at the nurse's station. Jailin figured she wouldn't be keeping her job after tonight. Jill, as her name tag read, was slouched in her chair with headphones on. She was asleep. Jailin reached her hand through the glass hole and hit the button to unlock the nurse's station.

She slipped behind the door, and with a quick light touch to the nurse's neck, without waking her, she rendered her unconscious. Jailin laid the young nurse down as if she had fallen asleep on the desk and turned up her music. Jailin hit the release button to the door at the end of the hall. With her speed, the thirty seconds allowed for walking though the door was more than enough. She pushed the door just as the buzzer stopped. No normal person could have done all this alone.

Immediately Jailin went to the supply cabinet. The padlock was easy. She had watched the nurse open it earlier and knew the combination. She sifted through the bottles. Some were labeled with the drug names and a couple others had patients' names on them. None of them were labeled for Theodore Munrow.

"Curiosity killed the cat, you know," a voice came from behind her.

Jailin whirled around to see Honovi standing in front of her. Honovi had to know who was rummaging through the supply cabinet at this late hour. Jailin was sure she was caught.

"What do you think you're doing? Stealing to support a drug habit isn't a good idea. Not from Vernore, sweet thing."

Jailin put her hand to her back to pull out her bo staff. Then she hesitated.

"Oh? You want to play?" Honovi's nails slowly grew. She turned her hand and beckoned Jailin closer with one long nail.

Jailin gracefully strode over and in one continuous move she slid down to the floor. With one leg extended she swiped at Honovi's feet. Honovi jumped and Jailin caught her with her other hand. Honovi fell to the floor, landing on her back. Jailin grabbed her by the hair and was about to punch her in the jaw, but she suddenly had a weak feeling crawl down her spine and snuggle into her gut. Her heart palpitated and she dropped Honovi's head.

Honovi saw the weakness in her. "Another dose needed, M.S.-2?"

Jailin didn't speak. She only looked up and saw Honovi's foot driving toward her. It stunned Jailin, but Honovi hopped up and down. The impact had hurt her foot more.

Jailin pulled herself up. She was still too weak to make any advance on Honovi. Stepping closer, her heart skipped again and she caught herself on a chair. Honovi pushed her and she fell backward onto the floor.

"You're not that tough. Where'd you get that mask anyway?"

Jailin backed up across the floor until she knocked into the supply cabinet. Honovi reached for Jailin's mask. It took great effort, but she was able to peel the edge of the forehead away.

Jailin couldn't overpower Honovi. Not right now. She smelled the drugs in the cabinet behind her. The scent of passion flower caught Jailin's attention. It was the sedative that Meovi used in its leaf form for Jailin when she was uncontrollable during the rainy season. This would stop Honovi, and protect others from herself in a few hours.

Honovi was still prying at the mask. She didn't know it was interlaced with Jailin's skin and would be difficult to get off. It didn't hurt Jailin. Her head was tugged in different directions while she felt around for the right syringe.

Jailin popped the cap of the syringe when she found the right one and pushed it into Honovi's leg. She didn't bother to take the needle out. She needed her strength for more important things right now. Honovi shifted herself back against the far wall and then slumped down. Within seconds she was out cold.

Jailin felt her heart jump again, but the palpitations were getting closer together. Her senses were heightened tenfold. She could smell everyone and everything in the building better than before. She heard the security guard on the phone. People were either crying, yelling, or snoring. Everything was louder than it usually was. She clutched her ears. Every year this made her head pound. One more hour was all she had left.

She got up and ran to the small locked drawer at the nurse's desk. With her abilities increased she could smell her father's pills.

She yanked the drawer and the lock broke off. She dumped the pills in her bag. Then she replaced her father's pills with a bottle filled with purple children's vitamins. She headed for the exit, but remembered she had wanted to take extra sedatives with her. She threw two in her bag.

As she left the building a small delivery truck backed into the loading dock. She could smell more drugs inside the truck. The diesel engine overwhelmed her senses, but as soon as the driver stepped out she was consumed by the masculine draw of his scent. She approached the man and the tiger's face staring at him made him drop a case of drugs. His hand went to his hip that was hidden from Jailin's view. The tiger smiled at the rain soaked man.

37

Gabe was pacing back and forth in front of Bailey's apartment door. He looked worried, confused, and tired. Continuously running his hands through his hair had made him look like a slob. Unintelligible words tumbled out of his mouth.

"Where have you been?" Gabe shouted as soon as he saw that Bailey had rounded the corner.

As Bailey looked closer, he saw that Gabe's shirt was torn at the seam. His hair was messier than normal and he'd never seen Gabe so agitated in his entire life. "Sorry. Got held up. What happened to you?"

"Me? Where do I start?" Gabe was shaking. Bailey was waiting for him to collect himself and continue. "I got here earlier, but you already know that."

"Why don't we talk about this inside?"

"No! Not inside." Gabe grabbed the doorknob before Bailey could.

"Why not?"

"We stay out here. That's an order!" Gabe tried to be forceful to insure that Bailey would take him seriously.

Bailey raised his eyebrows. "An order from who?"

"Jailin." Gabe looked to the floor. The time to tell Bailey the information he had had finally arrived. Gabe could feel himself shaking from worry and fear.

"What? Now you're just confusing me."

"When I got here she was already inside. She has blood on her and…"

"Is she okay?" Bailey interrupted. Panic pained his chest and he found it difficult to breathe. He held his breath instead.

"She's fine. Sort of."

"Let me by!" Bailey exhaled and asserted himself toward the door.

"No. It's to protect you." Gabe put his hand on Bailey's chest to stop him.

"Me? Look at you. Did she do this?"

Gabe put is hands in his pockets and dropped his head with a sigh. Bailey noticed that Gabe's jeans were torn. The belt buckle was broken and a button was missing. "I tried to help."

"I'm supposed to believe that? What did you do to her?" Bailey was furious with confusion.

"I didn't do anything. She did this to me. I saw her with a needle. She was going to inject herself with some drug. She said if it didn't work I was to give her the second one on the table and then stay out of here."

"And?"

"And what?" Gabe rubbed his eyes and yawned. The depletion of adrenaline was causing him to crash.

Bailey rubbed his forehead. "Did you give her the second shot?"

"I had to. She looked obsessed, crazed. I didn't know what she had drugged herself with, and then she sprang on me."

"Sprang on you?" Bailey was questioning Gabe's usage of the word instead of the validity of his story.

"Jumped me. I think she could have… she almost… Dude, she's strong."

"What happened after the second injection?"

"She fell on the floor. Muttered something I couldn't understand. It sounded like a strange language. Now, I hope, she's knocked out."

"I have to go get Meovi. Where's Socrates?"

"Inside. Sitting on her. Unless he's moved by now."

Bailey opened the door a tiny crack. Jailin was laying half on the couch. It appeared like she had fallen asleep while praying. Bailey called softly for Socrates.

The little ring-tailed lemur scurried out into the hall. He had a piece of paper in his mouth. Bailey took it and unrolled it.

PASSON FLOUR. TWNTY FOR HORS. B OK.

Bailey rolled up the paper, stuck it in his pocket and turned away from the door to head down the hallway. Gabe let Socrates back inside and ran after Bailey.

"Where are we going?" Gabe asked as he got in the truck.

"For help."

They drove deep into the jungle. Gabe felt like they had been driving in circles. Now that the adrenaline was worn off, he found it hard to keep his eyes open.

“We’re here.” Bailey shook Gabe awake.

Together they got out of the truck and walked up to Jailin’s hut. Bailey knew the tribe had no locks on the front doors so he gently opened the door. Meovi was sitting at the table with a man Bailey didn’t recognize. The man made eye contact with him and Meovi swung around in her chair.

She came up quickly and grabbed Bailey’s arm. “Where is she?” Then she saw Gabe and the condition of his clothes. “Too late?”

“I don’t know what’s wrong with her. I need your help.”

“Where is she?”

“Back at my apartment with Socrates.”

“Asleep or unconscious?”

“Does it matter?”

“Yes. Sleep she can be awakened from easily. Unconsciousness takes more work.”

“Gabe said she injected some drug into herself. Socrates gave me this.” He handed the note to Meovi.

“Passion flower. When did she do this to herself?”

“Maybe an hour ago. I don’t know.”

“Well, according to this she’ll be out for twenty-four hours. That’s too long.”

“Why? What will happen to her? She’s not dying, is she?”

“No, she’ll be fine when she wakes up. Masou and I have been talking. Something has been seen checking our borders. Our men are tired. If anything gets through, we will have a huge problem.”

“What’s been seen? Do you know?”

“Looks like a silhouette of a man and a woman with a dog and a bear. Or that could just be the delirious ramblings of the tired night watchers.”

"We need her help." Masou stood up and walked over to Bailey. "I understand you are very close to her and the only connection to her past."

"That's right, but she doesn't seem to remember all that much from back then."

"My point is that you may be able to control her so she doesn't hurt the wrong people. Has she been in contact with anyone else tonight?"

"I don't know. I don't understand. What's wrong with her?"

"This is the height of the rainy season. For one day her animal instincts take over. She can't control it. Her small body can't keep up with the fast rate of hormone production. We've always sedated her since she was fourteen," Meovi explained.

"We need her extra strength during this time to fight off what's coming," Masou summarized.

"Can we do that? Is it safe for her to be awake?" Bailey asked.

"She won't hurt anyone. Not intentionally. Her body can withstand the torture it causes itself once the first half is over," Meovi added.

"Will I be safe?" Gabe asked from behind Bailey.

"That's happened before to others. Her mind fights with the animal inside and she usually wins. I believe she'll have to fight harder to stop herself when Ben wakes her up. Of course, that also depends on whether he *wants* to stop her." Meovi's eyes shifted quickly from Gabe to Bailey.

"There was blood on her before she did this to me," Gabe added.

"Well, she'll have to explain that later," Meovi looked concerned, but there was nothing she could have done and her face turned solemn.

Suddenly a young boy with tears streaming down his face ran into the hut. "They're coming!"

"Who's coming?" Masou peered down at the weeping boy.

"The, the, sh, sh, shadows, but th, there's more of them," he stammered.

"How many?"

"Um, a woman wit, with a dog, a, a, man ride, riding a bear, a gi, giant bird in the air, and a, a, lar, large white cat are leading an ar, army."

"Tell Contardo to ready his men. We only have about an hour now." The child ran back out the door at Masou's command. "You two wake up Anaba and get her here. We'll stop what we can," he said to Bailey and Gabe, then walked out the door after the boy.

"Here, take these with you." Meovi handed Bailey three tea leaves.

"You want me to brew these?"

"No. Put the blue leaf in her mouth. It'll wake her enough for you to explain everything. Hand her the green ones. She'll know what to do with them. Do this after you get her in the car. Tell her to be ready to fight."

"Let's go, Gabe." Bailey grabbed his friend's shoulder and walked him out of the room.

38

Jailin couldn't tell if it was night or if it was just dark. It was too cold for her to be standing in the jungle. She could see her breath in the air. It was getting late and she had been waiting for hours.

"Where are you?" She considered walking, but the darkness didn't reveal any paths.

In the distance, she could hear footsteps coming up behind her. She turned around, but total darkness surrounded her. A hand rested on her shoulder.

"Took you long enough." She turned around again. Standing in front of her was someone she'd never seen before, with a drawn and regretful expression. "What's wrong?"

"I'm too late."

"Only a little." She smiled.

"What will we do with all of them?"

"All of whom?"

The figure before her spread out an arm as if to shed light into the darkness. It was difficult for Jailin to understand what she was seeing. The view was blurred, like the horizon of pavement on a hot summer day. The sky was glowing with fire and the trees were charred black.

Jailin saw a man and a woman standing on top of a hill. They were embracing and viewing the carnage below them. People were scattered around the jungle floor. Some were screaming for mercy, others lacked the breath to cry out. Jailin saw the rain tree she had loved to sit under and pick wildflowers as a child. Those she loved were piled up at the feet of the embracing couple. She saw Dierno first. His eyes were open and the blue and green were faded. She saw Gabe, with his hair and face splattered with blood. Socrates was slumped over Contardo, as if he had tried to save him. Then she saw her father, still so thin, now so lifeless. Lastly, her eyes rested on Bailey. He was lying on top of everyone else. He looked as if he had begged, not for himself, but for the dead one he embraced in his arms.

Jailin stepped closer. She wanted to know who was lying in his arms. She made a wide circle around them, not wanting to get too close. She gasped. She was in his arms. They had died together. She looked up at the embracing couple. She saw the woman with reddish blonde hair pressed against a man in dark clothing. He lifted her head and Jailin saw her face.

"No. This can't be." Jailin dodged to the side again to see the face of the man. Suddenly, red eyes showed up in front of her. She saw nothing else, but the black, flower-shaped V angling off of the right eye.

"Jailin!" Gabe shook her knee against the seat. "Wake up!"

"Why didn't you drive, like I told you to?" Bailey was driving as fast as possible back to the jungle.

"Cuz when she wakes up, I don't want to die by hitting some stupid tree. Besides, I don't know where we're going."

"GPS, dumb ass."

Jailin moaned again from the back seat. "I think she's waking up," Gabe stated.

"So go back there and make sure the tea leaf is still in her mouth."

"Oh no, I ain't that stupid."

"Gabe!"

"All right, all right." Gabe swung his torso around to face the back seat better. He wasn't going back there in case she did wake up. "Jailin, wake up!" He shook her knee again. "We have a cup of water I can throw in her face?"

Bailey was fed up. He knew they were short on time. He could see that Socrates wasn't happy and knew that his glazed expression meant he was updating Dierno and finding out how late they were. Bailey considered all the negative factors of stopping, but pulled over anyway.

"What are you doing? We can't stop!"

"You drive. I'll take care of getting her awake, *properly*."

"Properly? I didn't know there was…"

"*Drive*!"

"*All right*!"

Bailey climbed in the back seat. It was a tight fit.

Never before had he sat in the back of his own truck. He rested her head on his lap and tucked her hair behind her ear. "She's having a nightmare."

"Oh yeah? Probably about me fighting back from earlier."

"Stop it. You're not funny."

"Sometimes I am." Gabe was sadly defensive.

"Jailin?" Bailey whispered in her ear. "Wake up. We need you." He hugged her as tightly and as comfortably as possible in the cramped space. Jailin let out a slight whimper and he turned her face towards him. Her eyes fluttered under her eyelids.

"I think we're here," Gabe said.

Bailey turned to look out the front window. "Let's get her inside. Meovi said she'd be awake by now. I don't know what's wrong."

"What happened to waking her *properly*?" Gabe deadpanned. He pointed out the window when he looked forward again. "Is that bad?"

"Him? No, that's just Dierno. He's here to help."

"Creepy." Gabe opened the door and was wary of his movements around Dierno. He helped Bailey take Jailin inside. They laid her down on her bed. Bailey asked Socrates to find Meovi and Gabe reluctantly sat outside with Dierno.

Bailey sat down on the bed and watched Jailin restlessly sleep. "Ben," her breath escaped her sleeping lips.

Bailey pulled her up into his arms. Her eyes weren't open and he couldn't help but kiss her lightly. Before he knew it, she was kissing him back and he pulled away enough to ask, "Are you all right?"

Her eyes opened slowly. "I am now," her voice was sultry.

His own voice caught in his throat, "Good."

She turned in his arms and pushed Bailey back against her pillow. She swung a leg over both of his and straddled his lap. Her lips pressed against his and she ran her hands down his chest to his waist. Two fingers slid into the elastic of his boxers above his jeans and she traced the soft skin from hip bone to hip bone. She pulled him up by his belt so that he was sitting up with her. His mouth traced her neck and her head fell back willingly. The warmth of his hands caressed her back. As she ran her hands up his chest under his shirt, he exhaled with desire. She quickly took her hands out to push his jacket off his shoulders. His shirt was stretched taut against his broad chest.

"What's this?" She pulled back when her hand rested on the leather holster.

"That would be my gun." His hands clutched her hips, holding her close while his lips spoke against her collar bone.

"Okay. Let me be more specific." She pulled back. "What are you doing with it?"

"I am one hundred percent accurate with it because of GIA training." His breathing was slightly labored.

"That doesn't tell me why you have it with you *tonight*."

He heard her temper begin to rise. "I think you should talk to Dierno and Socrates." He tried to ease his excitement.

"Why? I'd rather be alone with you right now." She traced her hands up his chest while leaning forward until she reached his shoulders to steady her.

He held her back. "We actually have a big problem. Meovi's on her way. I'm supposed to give you these." He reached into his pocket to hand her the two remaining tea leaves.

"Why do you have these?" She appeared concerned.

"Ask Dierno and Socrates."

Jailin's eyes glazed over and Bailey could see that she was being briefed. "Oh, no. Please, no."

"Yeah. That's why I brought my gun. I'm good. I have to be. I'm the good guy, right?"

"Attempting funny, Benji? I didn't know you had to reassure the ladies about your abilities in the sack," Gabe roared with laughter as he came in behind Meovi.

Jailin quickly jumped off Bailey's lap. He hiked his jacket back up on his shoulders. Jailin glanced at him, but found she couldn't look away. The cut of the black jacket with the short erect collar lining his jaw emphasized his wide shoulders and tapered down to his waist. His dark jeans, faded at the thighs, gave his body a strong, slender look.

"Jailin, mind on the matter," Socrates interrupted her thoughts.

She looked back at Meovi. "How did this happen?"

Meovi looked to the left and hesitated to say anything at first. "Word got out that our tribes would rather fight than be homeless."

"Who declared the war?" There was no reply from Meovi. "Answer me!"

"I don't know. It's only a rumor, but some are saying Contardo started it."

"How many men does Contardo have?"

"The numbers are falling. We need to stop the fires. They're destroying homes."

"How many?"

"Maybe thirty."

"Any women?"

"I doubt it. Why?"

"Honovi's out there!" She didn't need to remind Meovi of the Minowa.

"I'll talk to Masou's head priestess and see if she knows anyone willing."

"Thank you." Jailin headed to the door.

"I'm coming too." Bailey followed her.

"No. You stay here. Protect the women and children. I won't have you dead."

"Who says I'd die?"

Jailin remembered her dream. A picture of the embracing couple with Bailey lifelessly holding her at their feet flashed into her mind. Dierno growled at the picture he could see as well. "All those people fighting out there would say that."

"All right. If that's what you want, I'll keep watch."

"Thank you." She inclined her head up to him and intended to quickly kiss him goodbye. Instead, it was more like their first kiss in his apartment. She didn't want to let go. She forgot all about the horror on the other side of the door. Unknowingly, her hands glided along the edge of his belt and she found herself sliding it out of the buckle. His hands met hers to stop them. He blushed as he pulled away from her lips. He was more aware of the eyes around the room than she was as he re-buckled himself.

"You have the tea leaves?" Meovi asked.

"Yes." Jailin held up the last two.

"Seems as if you need another one now."

Jailin blushed, popped a leaf in her mouth and headed out into the jungle with Dierno at her heels.

Jailin was crouched up in the limbs of a tree. She looked out over the masses of people falling to their deaths. The vulture swooped, picking his targets. Then she spotted Contardo. He was dominating the field. Death was nothing but a game to him. A game he thought he couldn't lose. He certainly was the most likely candidate for having brought this chaos on the tribes.

Jailin jumped down from the tree and ran up behind him. "Everything going as planned?"

"Where have you been?" he grunted out, between clenched teeth.

"I got caught up with another problem. Sorry I'm late."

"Glad to know you have your priorities in the correct order." He landed a punch into the face of a man wielding a torch.

As Jailin stretched through the air, she landed on the back of another man. She quickly snapped his neck and with the force of her feet pushed on his back. He landed face down on the ground.

"Nice move."

"We've still got a lot of work ahead of us. And I have to warn you." She ran her hand along the dead man's ear.

"About what?"

"There's a Minowa out here." She held up the ear plug from the dead man.

"Seriously? Who?" Suddenly, a log flew through the air. It hit Contardo and he fell to the ground. She knew he was fine and that he hated to be coddled like an injured child.

Jailin saw Honovi standing on higher ground, so she took off after her. "Watch out!" she heard Dierno yell. As she glanced backward, another log came flying at her.

"This is new," Jailin thought, as she dropped to her hands and knees.

"It's Anubis. He's Adrian's new toy. And he's telekinetic."

"*New* toy? What the hell is he?" She slammed her elbow into a man who tried to stop her advance on Honovi.

"A panda."

"So much for being cute."

"Pandas?"

"Yup." Jailin swung herself up into a tree to get higher than Honovi. She paused only for a second to put her mask on and slide her bo staff out of the loops on her back. She snapped it together, popped out the spear and then threw it into a teak tree. It missed Honovi's face by centimeters and kept her from attacking Masou from behind.

Honovi swore under her breath. Before she could turn her head to see where it had came from, Jailin had landed her fist into Honovi's face. Honovi fell back against the tree and rubbed her jaw.

When Honovi looked up she kicked at the masked girl and then lost a bit of balance. Jailin took her bo from the tree and advanced on Honovi again, swinging it on alternating sides.

"You're not an M.S.!"

"Nope." The tiger smiled at Honovi.

Nails grew out long from Honovi's hands and she spun around to get momentum to land a harder hit on Jailin. Jailin blocked it with her bo and brought its other end up to slam against Honovi's ear. Honovi's hand went up to ease the pain. It felt warm and wet. She looked at the blood on her hand. She swung her free hand at Jailin, but wasn't close enough. Jailin stabbed her bo into the ground and used it to support herself as she swung her feet around, landing a heavy blow into Honovi's stomach.

Jailin regained her balance from the impact and kneed Honovi in the face quickly before Honovi could right herself. Honovi was on the ground, but she wasn't giving up that easily. Quickly she regained her footing and as Jailin advanced again, Honovi bent herself backward. With hands on the ground, she lifted her feet and struck Jailin in the jaw. Honovi's feet hit Jailin under the chin, where the mask didn't cover. She rubbed her throat and Honovi was already bringing her long claws down onto Jailin's head.

"No you don't!" Jailin put her bo staff above her head to block the downward motion.

"You only block what you see." Honovi kicked out one leg as she came down. It slammed into the center of Jailin's abdomen.

She buckled forward and somersaulted toward Honovi. Springing up out of the roll, she extended the bo into Honovi's jaw. "And you need more reinforcement."

Dierno had run into Digna on his way up the hill to help Jailin. They circled each other before they extended their paws at each other's faces. Dierno went for Digna's throat but she moved away just in time. She jumped on Dierno's back and bit into his shoulder. He roared and bucked, sending her to the ground. She didn't give up. They continued to circle and chase each other through the trees.

At the bottom of the hill, Contardo had woken up after only a few seconds. He could see Jailin dominating the fight with another woman. He saw the two white cats batting and biting each other. He looked around for anyone or anything that could have thrown a log at him. Suddenly, he heard feet land on the ground behind him.

Contardo looked up and said, "Did you dye your hair?"

"No," the man said as he kicked him in the shoulder and he fell back on the ground. His foot was pressing down hard on the center of Contardo's chest. "You have mistaken me for someone else."

Contardo grabbed his foot and twisted it so that the man fell down on his stomach.

"Then who are you?" Contardo put all his weight onto the man's back to keep him down.

"I'm sure you can figure that out on your own." He pushed himself up. Contardo weighed the same as a five year old compared to this man's strength. Contardo slid off the man's back. The man grabbed him by the hair to lift him up. Contardo thrashed and punched the man, but he was too solid and every blow only hurt himself.

"You're Adrian, aren't you?"

"And you're Contardo. We've been looking for you."

"Me? Why?" Contardo dragged his feet as he was pulled away. He didn't intend on making it easy for Adrian to haul him off to who knows where.

"Dude, there's a wolf outside. He just ran off with a baby hanging out of his mouth. At least I think it was a baby," Gabe yelled as he rounded the corner of Jailin's hut to find Bailey already consoling the parents.

"I'll get her back for you," Bailey said. He didn't know if they understood him, but he thought he saw the father nod once. "Gabe, stay with them. I'm going after that wolf."

"Good luck," Gabe said as Bailey ran by.

He chased the wolf to the tribunal clearing. The wolf set down the bundle and if Bailey hadn't known better, he would have sworn the wolf had just winked at him.

There was no baby in the blankets. He didn't know if he had been tricked or if the wolf still had the baby. He continued the chase. When he arrived at the hill, Jailin was fighting with Honovi, and Adrian was dragging Contardo up the hill. Bailey ran toward them, but he wasn't fast enough. It made him wish he wasn't so normal.

"Hurry up, Honovi. This guy is a real pain in the ass," Bailey heard Adrian complain.

A sweet three-note melody rang through the trees and Bailey watched Contardo fall to the ground at Honovi's feet. He looked infatuated all of a sudden. Bailey continued his run up the hill.

"No, Ben!" Jailin yelled. She was kneeling on the ground. Honovi was standing over Jailin whose hair was knotted tightly in her fist.

"Ah, my little brother has decided to show his face. Do you have a fancy for Honovi too?" He took the plugs out of his ears.

"This stops right now!" Bailey aimed his gun at Honovi's head. "Let her go!"

"Oh, someone impervious to your charm, Honovi. I wish I had that, but no, I have to wear ear plugs and babble to myself," Adrian whined.

A quick, high-pitched whistle came through the air. Bailey's vision blurred and he felt a stinging sensation in his thigh. He looked down and saw a tranquilizer in his leg. Weakness overtook him and he slowly collapsed to the ground. He saw Jailin hit the ground too and before his eyes shut he saw two big black paws in his line of sight.

"Do we have what we need?" a gruff monotone voice asked.

"Yes. Take the boys while I dispose of Jungle Kitty here," Honovi smiled down at the sleeping girl at her feet.

Adrian draped Bailey across the panda's back and Contardo, who didn't want to leave Honovi's side, reluctantly followed the panda.

Digna was on the run back to base once she heard they had what they wanted. Dierno wasn't about to let anyone dispose of his family again. He quickly went to Jailin's side. No one was going to harm his family again.

40

Jailin heard the comforting sounds of mourning doves. She could hear the crisp babble of the creek. The smells of early morning dew on the grass and leaves filled her senses. She didn't have to open her eyes. The red she saw behind her eyelids confirmed the rain had stopped, the sky was clear, and the sun was warm on her face.

When she did open her eyes, she saw Socrates sunbathing on his usual rock next to the pond. Dierno was lying on his back with his feet sprawled up into the air. He was snoring heavily.

"Maybe last night was all just a bad dream." She picked herself up off the ground. "Nope." She hurt all over.

Then it hit her. "Oh no. Please, no." She ran over to Dierno. "Wake up." She pushed him over onto his side.

"I don't get much sleep anymore." He yawned and stretched his arms out in front of him. His back curved as he raised his hips off the ground.

"What happened to Ben? Where is he?" She was panicked and looked around as if being watched.

"Vernore has him." Dierno stood and licked his paw to wipe his face.

"Where? We have to get him back." Jailin paced back and forth. She couldn't wait. They needed to get him back now. Who knew what they were doing to him?

"I don't know. After I brought you back here I scanned the border for any clues, but got nothing within the two-mile radius."

"I have to find him." A door slammed behind Jailin and she jumped. Too many things sounded like the mayhem they had endured last night.

"Oh, good, you're awake. Meovi and I made breakfast." Gabe had come out of her hut with a dish towel in his hands. He threw it over one shoulder and crossed his arms.

"Ben's gone. We need to get him back." Jailin's intensity almost knocked Gabe to the ground with surprise.

"Yeah, I know." He sounded upset, but he didn't show any other signs of distress. She figured that was the influence of the military school.

"You know? Why aren't you doing anything? Why isn't anyone notifying GIA? Is everyone stupid?" Jailin was losing control.

"Yes, to some of that. Why don't you come inside?" He turned to head back to the hut.

"Going inside isn't going to bring Ben back."

"It's a first step. Breakfast is brain power." Gabe tried to sound cheerful but Jailin only crossed her arms. She wasn't budging from her spot. "You're not well enough to go after them right now anyway. In broad daylight, no less." Gabe was beginning to sound just like Meovi.

"I'm fine."

He frowned. "You were crying in your sleep. Did you have another nightmare?"

"My life is a nightmare!"

"What did you dream about?" Gabe inquired, as if he could heal her grief with a simple act of listening.

"I relived last night, over and over." She gritted her teeth. There was no way to get him to back down from his interrogation. She considered walking away.

"What about the nightmare before that? Meovi says you always have nightmares during the first few days of the rainy season."

"I don't want to talk about it."

"Why not? It might help." He thought he had finally gotten through to her when she turned back to him. Then he saw the fury on her face and thought otherwise.

"Everyone was dead. Vernore and Johanna stood right over there with everyone dead at their feet. See? No better. Only worse!"

"Sorry. I didn't know." He tried to defend himself.

"Of course you didn't. Now that you know you know nothing, are we going to get Ben and Contardo back?"

"*We*?" Gabe was worried that he had just gotten himself into something he would never have asked for.

"You're such a coward."

"That I do know," he tried to joke. She didn't laugh or break the slightest smile. He felt like an exotic bird stuck in a cage for all to gape at.

"Then *I'm* going after them." She picked her staff and mask up off the ground and walked deeper into the trees.

"I'll help you track them." Dierno was up and following closely.

"Thanks," she whispered and kept on walking. There was no indication of which way to go, but she figured she would walk forever until she found some kind of clue.

"I saw the dream," Dierno said reluctantly.

"Which dream?" She sniffed a leaf hanging low from a tree. It only smelled of fear and death.

"The one everyone was dead in." Dierno didn't like to remember it anymore than Jailin did.

"Yeah, well at least it didn't happen." And she hoped it wouldn't still come true either.

"Why was Johanna there?"

"It's a dream, Dierno. It's not supposed to make sense." He didn't answer. He walked behind her, waiting for her to cool down. She wasn't going to be able to fight if she wasted all her energy on anger and lack of food. "I've been thinking."

"About?" Dierno heard something from behind him and his ear angled back against his head.

"Leaving," she thought nonchalantly.

"Leaving? What do you mean?"

"If I can get my father out of that hospital, maybe he can fix me."

"Can't fix what's not broken."

"Is that a compliment? Wait, don't answer that." She knelt down and traced the dried mud imprint of an animal. It was bigger than normal, but not any deeper. The size and weight held no indication of its carrying anything or anyone. She still wanted to head in the direction it went because it wasn't Dierno's print or the wolf's. It was bear-like.

"You just want to take your father and run?"

"I'll come back when things are normal." She stood to follow the tracks.

"What's normal these days?"

"Stop that. You've spent too much time with Socrates." She motioned for him to continue following.

"And what about Ben?"

"You could use some more time with him." She glanced back quickly, trying to hide the smile creeping up.

"Glad you're feeling better, but you know what I meant. You can just pack up and leave him? Without saying a word?"

"He wants these abilities because he thinks that it will make him closer to me. I want to lose them. I just want to be normal and that will bring me closer to him."

"You think he'll agree with that?"

"You already know he won't. That's why I'm not telling him." She stopped. The tracks had disappeared. Looking over the ground, it didn't make any sense. The thing couldn't have just evaporated into nothing. That would be preposterous.

"You do see the problem with that, don't you?"

"He may be dead by now." She shook the thought out of her head. "We don't know what the future holds."

"I mean if he ends up with abilities and you end up without. It's putting you both in the same situation as right now." Dierno looked at her and cocked his head. She didn't look like she was listening to anything he was saying. And if she was listening, she certainly wasn't retaining it.

"Hey, wait." Her nose went up in the air. She inhaled long and hard.

"Yeah, I smell it too." Dierno opened his mouth slightly to pick up the scent better.

"Why would they go south?" She turned to her left. There wasn't a leaf out of place, no trodden path, and no broken branches. The only hint was the subtle smell of expensive cologne. Adrian.

"I don't know. Only one way to find out." Dierno looked toward her and she nodded once.

"Let's go." They started to run off toward the south, led only by their noses.

"Sir, this man is moving." Anubis was walking slower, trying to evenly distribute Bailey's weight on his back.

"Let him fall. We can drag him." Adrian smiled. He liked the image of Bailey flopping in the dirt.

Bailey heard this, but couldn't open his eyes. Heaviness consumed him. His limbs felt like cement. The rhythm of the panda's feet was mimicked by Jailin's necklace hanging around his neck. His stomach was churning and he was nauseated.

From behind them, Honovi was walking with Contardo. She had a chain in her hand that connected to a collar at his neck then fell to his feet. His hands and feet were also cuffed to the chain. Honovi consumed his mind so much that he didn't realize he was bound. "I remember you from when we were kids, you know."

"I'm sure you do, tough guy." She watched Adrian walking ahead of her. She enjoyed spying on him when he least expected it.

"I do. You were pretty then, but now you're gorgeous." Contardo was smiling his usual smile—a slight smirk which could only be read in his eyes. Honovi didn't say anything. She didn't even look at him. Everything she remembered about the past told her how much he actually hated her. The enchantments always confused her in that way. She wished all too often that the men held some truth within their fake devotion. They never did.

"Is that guy up there your boyfriend?" Contardo asked as he noticed that she never averted her gaze.

"No." She blinked longer than needed. Too often she had made that wish too.

"He's missing out."

"Try telling him that." She rolled her eyes and finally looked over at Contardo. She could get used to this.

"You know that guy on the bear's back?" He indicated the direction with his chin though he didn't need to, not many pandas were out strolling through the jungle with people on their backs.

"Not personally, no." She was intrigued to hear what Contardo knew of him. She knew his relation in this game and what purpose he was to serve, but could there be some secret that she didn't know?

"That's Anaba's. He belongs to her."

"That explains a lot. We were never told what the second reason was…" When Vernore had told Adrian and Honovi to kidnap Contardo Cloudtalker and Benjamin Bailey for experimental reasons with the M.S.s, he mentioned that a girl would come for them and they were to deal with her at that time. It was never said why she would come for them. They had always assumed it was her virtuous nature. Now Honovi knew it was because of her heart.

"Second reason? What does that mean?"

"It means she'll be on her way quicker than anticipated."

"You'll be in a lot of trouble if he dies."

"That's why you're here—to protect me." She winked and pouted her lips as if to blow him a kiss.

"With my life, beautiful." Contardo's pulse raced and he desired nothing more than to be alone with this woman. His wish jinxed him because immediately she was walking away from him—toward the man he hated for more reasons than he could count

"Adrian!" she called. "I've got a great idea!"

41

Cluce was a beautiful town. It was the newest town in all of Grundagon. It lay North West of South Central City. For many tourists, it was the cheaper version of Ecnamor Isle. Vernore had built it as a façade as a guarantee of loyalty to South Central City. His plan was to implement his influence over Grundagon one city at a time. North Central City was easily manipulated. Since Ronald Sterling had backed West Central City's economy, Vernnore's next target had been South Central. His office and business dealings took place in North Central City and South Central City unknowingly was a test site. Those that lived in South Central City and the surrounding towns, Klut and Cluce, had no idea they were Vernore's guinea pigs.

In the darkness of an overhang outside the largest building in Cluce were two figures, a man and a woman. "Deliver this to the yenena." He handed the woman a white envelope.

"Are you sure? They're not even here yet. What if something doesn't go as planned?" She was anxious and she gripped the envelope with both hands so the wind couldn't steal it away.

"Have faith. We will triumph over all of Grundagon. Our dreams will come true, my dear." He pushed her hair behind her ear.

"Are you positive?" She looked at the envelope. It shook in her nervous hands.

"You know I don't like it when you second-guess me. Perhaps M.S.-2 will serve me better." A smile was coded in his voice.

"No, sir. I'm sorry. I trust you with all my heart and soul." She inclined her head as if to ask for a kiss.

"Good girl." He took her hand from the envelope and kissed it as if it were royalty. Saddened, she ran off into the shadows cast by the buildings. As he watched her go, he whispered under his breath, "I will bring you back, Johanna. My heart belongs to no other. No matter how much they look like you."

Jailin's hut door swung open violently. "Oh, it's just you. I hate it when you do that." Meovi's heart was pounding against her chest.

"We have this for you." A woman held up an envelope and waved it back and forth. Her hair was a whisky-colored red. She was bone thin and her posture proved she held herself in high regard.

"Molly, you really must knock first. How do you know I'm not with someone?" Meovi was picking herself up out of an antique rocking chair.

"I always know." She looked around the room and her eyes rested momentarily on the mattress on the floor. Then she looked back to Meovi.

"Granted. I can't argue with you there." Meovi was a few scuffled steps away. An arm's length at most.

"Here. It's almost complete." Molly stretched her arm out with the envelope in it.

"You're never sent on errands like this unless he wants something in return. He has Ben and Contardo. What more does he want?" Meovi's voice was lethargic—drained from the previous night's concerns.

"The Munrow girl must be killed." Her eyes flashed to the bed again.

"I told Vernore I couldn't do that." Meovi's eyes were pleading with the wrong person.

"She's on her way to Cluce now with the cat." Molly bent down to pick up a dish towel that had fallen on the floor and handed it to Meovi. It was the only way to keep from looking at that pleading gaze.

"I knew she wouldn't wait." She tore the towel out of Molly's hand and slapped it down at her side.

"Did you bring another in on this?" Her eyes glanced toward the bed again. The man there made her nervous, even if he was snoring.

"Gabe? No. He's oblivious. I slipped him a sedative. He won't wake up."

"You and Masou have done well with the girl. Perhaps too well. Vernore will be pleased, but not if you don't follow through." She watched Meovi open the envelope.

"There's only half here." Meovi displayed the fanned-out money to Molly as if the woman had stolen it from the envelope and was going to get away with it.

"The other half will come when she's dead." She disregarded the accusation.

"But..."

"Vernore will delay the monorail as promised now that he has the boys. You must keep your secrets. When she's dead and Vernore gets her body, you'll get the rest of your money."

"That's not fair. For nineteen years I've raised Anaba. I taught her about her life. Sheltered her, kept her safe. Now he's saying I've only done half my job?"

"Think of it as an insurance policy." The woman left and Meovi stomped outside after her.

"Molly Stern, you backstabber! Tell Vernore I hope Anaba strangles him to death slowly!" she yelled. No one was in sight. And she didn't care who heard her.

42

"Where are we?" Jailin looked around. The town was peaceful. Only a few people were out walking. Some were playing with their children, others were enjoying the sun after all the days of constant rain. The grass was lusciously green and clear of the jungle's blue-eyed grass and springcress.

"This is Cluce. It's changed a lot since I was here last." Dierno sniffed the air.

"Changed how?"

"A lot more houses, stores, and people now. It actually looks like a nice place to visit and live."

"It doesn't seem like it was ever a dump." Jailin looked down at her feet and felt compelled to reach down and run her hand over the soft grass.

"Oh no, it never was. I didn't mean it like that. It just seems as if this town has more money to back it up. Like someone promised prosperity for servitude."

"I see. And the last time you were here was when you left my father?"

"I left him in good hands, I swear." Dierno's thoughts sounded as if he was guilty.

"I'm not placing any blame, but out of curiosity, who did you leave him with?"

"A family with a young girl. They looked nice and wanted to help him, I think. They didn't know I was with him. He seemed happy with them. Happy, but at the same time sad. I think the little girl reminded him of you."

"What did she look like?"

"She had strawberry-blonde hair, fair skin, and beautiful blue eyes. Skinny but very pretty."

"Are these people still here? Is the girl still living with them?"

"I don't know. Why?"

"I hoping she still does. Otherwise I think we have another issue to figure out. And Vernore has everything to do with it."

"I'll show you. Follow me."

They rounded the edge of the town so as not to draw any attention. When they came to a white privacy fence at the back yard of a gray house, Dierno stopped. "This is the place."

Jailin dropped down to look through a crack between two of the boards. A little boy was in the back yard playing in a sand-box. His hair was dirty brown and he kicked at the piles of sand. Jailin smiled and turned away from the boards. "They must have moved." The sound of a door slamming came from the house and Jailin turned her sight back to the boy.

"No. That's the same mother. The girl would be older now. Mostly likely she moved out or went to college." Dierno saw the mother scoop up the boy and take him inside.

Jailin was looking at the ground trying to catch her breath. "What's wrong?" Dierno asked.

"I think I've seen a picture of the girl. At least that is the woman in the picture I saw and you described the girl I saw with her in that picture."

"Where did you see this picture?"

"At the hospital when I broke in to steal my father's drugs."

"Why is this a problem?"

"The name plate didn't have a name on it. I think this family isn't real."

"Real in what way?"

"I think they foster children for Vernore, but they don't know they're raising monsters."

"That's crazy."

"Well, I'm going to go see how crazy I am. Be right back."

"Jailin, wait!" Dierno yelled in his mind. She was already over the fence and walking around the side of the house to the front door.

She tapped her foot and stood looking out at the cul de sac of houses while she waited for someone to answer. When the woman who had taken the child in came to the door she asked, "Can I help you?"

"Hello. I'm sorry to bother you. I was wondering if you could tell me about your son." The woman looked confused and started to close the door in Jailin's face. "I'm sorry. I didn't mean to sound crazy. Let me ask you another question, if I may."

The woman waited for Jailin's next question.

"Do you know Dr. Theodore Munrow?"

The woman's eyes went wide as she said, "Yes. Yes, I do. Why do you ask?"

"He's my father."

"Oh, you poor thing. Come in. How is your father?"

"Doing… better." Jailin followed the woman into the house.

"I never thought he was crazy, you know? He was so intelligent and so gentle."

"He still is. How long did he stay with you?"

"Only a couple of months. Six at the most, I think. I'd have to ask my husband. That was such long time ago." The woman sat on the edge of the off-white couch and nervously moved a few coasters around the glass coffee table.

Jailin sat on a rose-colored wing-back chair and made herself at home. Her eyes followed the woman's hands as they clumsily shifted items around on the coffee table. "He told me you have a daughter. That's why I asked about your son. I was surprised to see him."

"Oh, yes, well, that was a strange situation we had going on back then."

"Do you mind telling me about it?"

"I suppose it wouldn't hurt." The woman slid back on the couch and closed her eyes for a moment before she continued, "When Dr. Vernore bought this town and promised a better life for everyone—he came knocking on our door. He said he could help us. I never asked how he knew our problems. It seemed rude to ask any questions to someone who was offering to help. You see my husband and I couldn't conceive. He offered us a child to raise, making us foster parents, and he would make sure that in time we would be able to have children of our own. He said his company was working on a new fertility drug. I figured it would be good for us. We could practice raising a child, and then know what we were doing when the drug was on the market. By the time she was ten he came to get her. We haven't seen her since. She'd be about twenty now. I have no idea where she is or how she's doing. I hope she hasn't forgotten us."

"I don't know how she could." Jailin's eyes darted around the room. She noticed how clean and brightly colored the room was—defiantly a woman's touch. "When did you have your son?"

"He's five. Quite a handful too. Megan was a breeze to raise, it was like she was specially designed to take orders. What a kick in the face that not all children are like that, huh?"

"Yeah, sounds like a mean trick," Jailin deadpanned.

"I wouldn't have changed a thing if I could do it over again."

"Nothing?"

"Well, I would have adopted Megan."

"What's your last name?

"Stahl. Why do you ask?

"Just curious. When I see my father I want to be able to tell him that I spoke with you."

"My name's Susan and my husband is Joshua."

"I'm sure my father will be very happy to hear that I've met you." Jailin smiled warmly.

"He used to talk about you. I'm sorry I don't remember your name."

"Jailin."

"Oh yes, very pretty name."

"What's your son's name?"

"Benny. Well, Benjamin actually."

Jailin swallowed hard. "What made you choose that name?"

"Megan said she always wanted a little brother she could call Benny." Susan looked down as if taking a moment of silence for her lost child.

"Did you ever take the fertility drugs?"

"Oh yes, if it wasn't for that we'd never have had our little miracle."

"Have you noticed anything strange about him?"

"Strange? What do you mean?"

"Does he have many friends? How is he around pets? Can he smell or hear things before you do?" Jailin's voice was rushed and eager for the answers to her questions.

"I don't know what you're talking about. He's five years old. I think he's a very normal little boy. He just has a lot of energy."

Jailin nodded and averted eye contact with Susan. "Oh, it's getting late. I should go."

"Of course. Tell your father I said hello. We'd love to have you both for a visit."

"Thank you. I'll tell him."

They went to the door and Susan saw Jailin out. She walked past three houses before cutting through someone's backyard and hopping the fence. "Dierno, we've got a new problem. Vernore has a drug for women who can't conceive and it's implanting the altered DNA right into their offspring."

"So that girl is like you?"

"She's engineered like me. That boy is bred like Adrian, but better. A new race is upon us as promised."

"So what do we do?"

"It's getting late. It'll be dark in a few more hours. We have to find out where Ben and Contardo are and get them home."

"Where is this drug being made? That could be where they are."

"Can't be that hard to find. Vernore has his trademark on everything, right?" They set out in search of a building with the flowering V logo. It didn't take long to find the tallest building, with the brightest blood-red V in town.

43

Twilight was upon them when Jailin looked up at the building. It was four sides of tinted panel windows. The panes were reinforced with cement. The building resembled a downscaled version of Vernore Biotech and Pharmaceuticals in North Central City. "I'm guessing that's about fifty feet up," Jailin thought. She assumed that whatever was kept in that building she'd have to get to from the roof.

"I checked all the sides. There aren't any fire escape ladders." Dierno prowled around the edge of the building.

"I guess I'll have to do it the old-fashioned way." She grabbed the edge of a window sill and hoisted herself up.

"She's here," Digna thought. She was lying on a cot that was positioned in the corner of the large, open-floored warehouse.

Boxes were piled all round the warehouse, creating room divisions. All the windows were boarded up from the inside except for the very top row.

Honovi leaned one shoulder against the wall that Bailey was strapped to. His arms were above his head and his body lay limp against the wall. She petted him like a sick puppy. Sweat streamed from his brow, due to the additional exertion of his heart. He still felt nauseated. All his strength was gone and his head hung lifelessly.

Contardo was sitting on the floor. His neck was chained to the wall, but he was given slack like a dog chained in the backyard. The attention that Honovi was giving Bailey angered him. At that moment he only needed one word and he would happily tear out Bailey's heart.

"Don't look so upset. He'll probably die anyway. Then she can be all yours." Adrian watched Contardo's face twist with anger.

"You two look like twins. I may have to kill you too," Contardo said.

"Not likely to happen."

"Shouldn't you two be working?" Vernore said as he walked into the room. "How are his vitals?" he asked Honovi while he surveyed Bailey's condition.

"Increased heart rate and fever are at the expected levels. He's incredibly weak and he sleeps through most of the tests. Even the painful ones." Honovi wiped Bailey's face with a towel.

"We have to find the problem. The M.S.s are not expected to live past thirty at this rate."

"We may lose him too," Adrian added.

"Figure it out before you do. I'm heading back to North Central City. I have some matters to attend to personally." Digna got up and followed him out the door.

"You think father knows she's here?" Adrian asked Honovi.

"Probably." Bailey's head lifted slightly. "Oh look, some movement." She spoke directly to Bailey and said, "You think the love of your life can save you?"

His eyes fluttered open for a brief second. Adrian saw the anger on his face before he passed out again. "He doesn't like you very much, Honovi. It must run in the family."

"You only say that because of the M.S.s."

"Yeah, father's good ol' reliable infinite assassins. Glad I don't see them often."

"You wouldn't know what to do if you did."

Jailin reached the top of the building. She lowered herself into a hatch on the roof—a vent for releasing stale air. She was surrounded by storage boxes and packing material. It was musty, damp, and dark.

She found her way out of the storage attic to the unfinished room below. Rafters lined the ceiling and every ten feet a pillar reinforced the roof. The sound from faraway voices bounced off the white-tiled floor and plain cement block walls. She headed toward the voices, balancing on the rafters.

"If I unchain you, you'll be a good boy, right?"

"Anything your heart desires, I will give you." Contardo's voice vibrated through the room.

"I'll unhook you from the wall, but the chain stays on so I can put you in your place when I need to, got it?"

"The sooner the better, beautiful."

"Honovi, if you don't make him stop that, I will." Adrian sounded disgusted with Contardo's flirting.

"I should record you sometime when you're enchanted. You're no different." She smiled at Adrian, glad he cared enough to dislike it.

"Bitch," Adrian spoke under his breath.

Jailin could see Honovi standing over Contardo. He was closer to her than expected. His hands were free and clutching Honovi's thighs. Her head was turned back to Adrian who was sitting in a computer chair with his feet up on a desk. The panda was nowhere in sight. Neither was the wolf or Digna. A small monitor sat in front of Adrian. He touched the screen and an echocardiogram enlarged on the screen, displaying the quick successions of Bailey's heart rate.

"He needs more Ativan. Too many random spikes." Adrian opened a drawer and took out a pre-filled syringe.

Jailin noticed the monitor had wires running out of the back. Tracing the wires with her eyes, they disappeared into a dark corner. Adrian flipped on a light and Jailin saw Bailey strapped to the wall. Her heart sank to her stomach. He looked dead hanging the way he was. When Adrian slammed the needle into his arm she could see Bailey's face harden with the pain. She was relieved he wasn't dead, but she didn't know how much time he had left. She followed the rafters to move closer to Bailey. She needed to single him out from everyone else in order to sense his condition. She might even be able to smell whatever drugs were in him.

"Dierno. I need you to do something for me," she thought to her accomplice waiting for her outside.

"What?"

"Go back to Socrates. Tell him to get GIA here as fast as possible. Tell Meovi we need tea leaves by the bundle. And make sure Dr. Simon is on the helicopter with GIA."

"That may take a few hours."

"I know that. I'll have Ben out of here and still alive by then. I hope."

"I'm already on my way. Good luck."

Jailin put her mask on over her face and lowered herself to the floor with a light thud.

"So you've made it, I see." Adrian turned around to see her standing behind him.

"This will be much easier if you let them go," she growled.

"But that won't be any fun, will it Honovi?"

"You wait 'til I tell you," Honovi whispered in Contardo's ear, traced his angular face with her tail, then walked over to lean against the wall. She ran her finger down Bailey's face and traced his hard defined jaw line. "Anaba, this is our key. Our key to a new world and a new race."

"You're all crazy." She took one step forward.

"You don't get it, do you? Our master lost someone very important to him. Do you know what that's like?"

"Of course I do. Do you, Honovi? Or you, Adrian?"

"That's not the point. This is about getting back what was lost," Adrian rebuked.

"So give me Ben and Contardo and we'll call it even," Jailin growled.

Honovi laughed and Adrian sat back down with a smile that stretched from ear to ear. "That's not even a consideration. Ben here is special. So much like his mother. We've created an exaggerated effect of his tachycardia and fever. His symptoms were never as accelerated as his mother's, but now they are." Honovi said.

"You're killing him!"

"Don't be silly." Honovi ran her hand tenderly back and forth across Bailey's chest from shoulder to shoulder. "His vitals are stable with an increasingly high amount of Ativan. Johanna was doing well on an old weaker pill form. We need to figure out how to stop these symptoms so no one dies unexpectedly again."

"Why would it happen again? Johanna's dead and if you leave Ben alone now, I won't kill you… *unexpectedly*."

"Silly girl. Johanna isn't dead."

"What?"

"Well, she is now, but she won't be forever." Honovi examined her nails.

"Vernore can't play God. Tell him he can't replace what he's killed."

"He didn't kill Johanna. Nick did."

"You're lying!"

"Am I? Nick thought he could cure her just as Dr. Munrow accidentally cured some of Vernore's experiments in the wild. Nick messed up and Vernore got his revenge with a little help from Digna."

Jailin took one quick step closer to Adrian in the chair. From her leg strap she took one knife and held it to his neck. "Let them go and I won't hurt Adrian."

Adrian squirmed a bit, but not enough for Jailin to change her hold on him. He wasn't going to resist her touch, no matter how violent. Having Jailin dominate this confrontation made his heart pump a little faster. He remembered the night she had pinned him down on the roof of her hut. He smiled at the memory.

"He likes it rough, so don't tempt him. Although, I haven't had a chance to find out what his little brother here likes." Honovi placed her head on Bailey's shoulder and nuzzled her nose into his neck. She ran her palm across his chest from shoulder to shoulder. Slowly she draped her leg over one of his and then she kissed his jaw line under his ear. Her tail twitched with excitement.

"Stop that!" Jailin left Adrian in the chair and dragged Honovi away from Bailey by her dreadlocks.

When Contardo saw Honovi being dragged away he stalked over to Jailin with long powerful strides and viciously grabbed her wrist.

"Contardo, you're hurting me!" Jailin dropped Honovi's head.

"Don't touch her!" he yelled, inches away from her face.

"You're being controlled by a Minowa. I told you to be careful. Don't you remember?" Jailin begged for her friend to return to normal.

"That's ridiculous. Minowas don't exist," Contardo grunted.

"Wait and see. You'll feel it later," Adrian mumbled.

Honovi stood behind Jailin and met Contardo's stare. "Let's begin round one, shall we?"

"Round one?" Jailin breathed.

"Contardo here is going to kill you at my request. You have to kill him in order to stay alive for round two."

"And I suppose you would be round two?"

Honovi smiled and backed away. "Contardo, you may begin!"

Contardo swung his fist at Jailin but she stepped back and he just missed. "I won't fight you, Contardo."

"You can't run forever, Anaba."

"You can't chase me forever!"

Honovi sighed and took a syringe out of a drawer. "Do you know what this is, Anaba?"

Jailin sniffed the air. "Epinephrine?"

"Good nose. This will go into your little boy toy if you don't fight."

"I'll fight you. I'll fight Adrian. I'll even fight your damn panda! Just don't make me do this."

"My rules or your love dies."

Jailin looked back at Contardo. He was positioned and ready to fight. Jailin brought one foot backward, bent her knees, exhaled, and put her fists in the air. Every movement was a burden.

"No bo staffs? I'm disappointed." Contardo grinned.

"I know you'd like me to let Ben die, but I can't do that. I will stop you."

"Let's begin then."

They ran at each other and Jailin launched into the air. She spun as she descended and kicked out one leg, landing it into Contardo's jaw. His head snapped to the side and then his hands went up and grabbed her leg. He pulled her straight to the floor. When she hit, her free leg kicked between Contardo's legs and his one knee buckled under him. He was forced to let go of Jailin to break his fall.

"Wake him up. He needs to experience a new kind of pain." Honvoi pushed Adrian's shoulder to get him out of the chair.

"We'd lose all the work we've already done. If I use the hemlock saline it'll be like we never did anything tonight. My father will have your hide."

"He won't know anyway. We'll say she showed up and we had to tranq him while we took care of her. Then we resume the work and that's why we fell behind. Besides, if you only give him half the dose we only have to redo half the work later."

"Fine." Adrian walked over to Bailey and stuck another needle in his arm. "Wakey, wakey." Bailey's head nodded once as if he were trying to lift it. He was still too deeply sedated and his head movement was due to the force of Adrian's pat on the shoulder.

Jailin was doing a good job of keeping some distance between herself and Contardo. His reach was longer than hers and he was keeping up with her speed. She finally landed one punch into

Contardo's chin. His head went back slightly and she sidestepped him to get more leverage.

Bailey opened his eyes and tried to pick up his head. "Jailin?"

"Oh, you're awake now. Can you see how you're little jungle kitty fights to save your life?" Honovi held up his head. Bailey squinted to clear the blurring from his eyes.

Jailin was on Contardo's back, her arm wrapped around his neck. She thought if she could get him to pass out that perhaps it would be enough to end this whole thing. Contardo swung all his weight forward and tried to dump Jailin off his back. Her body rocked forward with the momentum and her feet hit the ground. Contardo snapped his body upright again and Jailin was left lying on her back. She got up quickly and kicked her right foot up. It missed Contardo's face slightly but she rounded her left foot and in a spin caught him in the side of the head.

Jailin's back was to Contardo for only a second after she got her balance, but that was long enough. He wrapped his arms around her from behind and she screamed under the pressure of her own arms squeezing against her.

Bailey's eyes shifted to the side. "Oh no, you watch her die!" Honovi jerked his head so that his eyes were back on the fight.

Contardo threw Jailin down and then kicked her leg. She squirmed backward. When she stood she couldn't bear all her weight on her left leg. The muscle throbbed, but she tried to ignore it. She took one step forward and fell to the side.

"You aren't doing too well, Anaba. You know you're stronger than me. Fight me for real!"

"I can't!"

"You will or he dies." Contardo pointed to Bailey. Jailin looked over and saw Bailey watching them. Seeing Honovi so close to him filled her with anger all over again.

She took out her bo staff and clicked it together. "No holding back anymore."

"That's my girl," Contardo said, and Honovi heard Bailey grunt gently with repugnance.

Jailin strode toward Contardo. Her leg hurt but she didn't care. Contardo picked up a bar of iron from a scrap pile close by. It was heavy, but he was confident. Jailin advanced with her staff twirling it on alternating sides of her body. Contardo lunged into the air and brought the iron bar down like a hammer. Jailin's arms raised and she lowered herself to the floor, distributing her weight for the impact.

When Contardo's feet touched the floor she angled her staff to the side and slapped him in the ear. He retaliated by poking the end of the bar into her face, but she caught it with one hand and pulled it toward her. As Contardo fell forward, her leg came up and her heel smashed into his nose. Blood sprayed everywhere. Contardo dropped the bar and both his hands went to his face.

"You enjoy that?" Adrian saw Bailey smile slightly. "I thought it was pretty hot too."

Contardo stood up. He started swirling the chain from around his neck in a figure eight and ran at Jailin. She moved to the side at the last second and slammed her interlocked fists down on his back. His momentum threw him into a table holding medicine and chemicals. Liquids and glass splashed up into the air.

"This is getting boring. Contardo is tired and Jailin's not going to kill him," Honovi said.

"Give it some more time," Adrian said.

"No. Bring on round two. I'm bored," Honovi demanded. Adrian shrugged, but obeyed her request.

"Anubis?" Adrian thought. "It's your turn."

Jailin looked at Contardo lying on the collapsed table. He wasn't getting up too quickly. He flopped over on his back and exhaled as if he was relieved to be lying down.

Nails tapped lightly on the floor behind Jailin. She turned around and saw a bear on all fours walking out of the darkness. When he was completely in the light, Jailin watched him stand up. A thick chain-link necklace was around its neck and a small skull lay at the center of it. Jailin smirked and popped the small spade out of the one end of her staff making it into a spear. She did a crow's hop and using all her strength, released the spear at the panda's heart.

It stopped two inches from its chest. The spear turned in mid air and headed straight back at Jailin. It traveled twice as fast as Jailin had thrown it. She closed her eyes and went down on her knees. When she opened her eyes, blood was pooling up on the floor around her knees. She turned around. Contardo was standing over her. The spear was sticking out of Contardo's chest. She caught him as he fell to the floor.

"No! Contardo..." She held him in her arms as he gasped for air and spit blood.

"I'm sorry… Anaba, I'm so… sorry. I didn't know… she was…"

"Shh. Don't talk. You'll be okay." Jailin cradled him in her arms. Water welled up in her eyes and she bit her bottom lip, hoping the pain would stifle the tears.

"Stop… Vernore. You can… only you. You're strong."

"Please don't go. I need you, Contardo."

"You.... need.... him." Contardo closed his eyes. "Love him... forever. The way he loves..."

"Contardo? Contardo!" Jailin's eyes became a river.

45

The sound of nails hitting the roof echoed through the warehouse. The backhand of thunder slapped Cluce across the face. The storm came quickly and intensified twice as fast. A curtain of water draped down the windows. The only other sound in the room was the muffled whimper of heartache.

Bailey caught a glimpse of Jailin holding Contardo in her arms. It looked as if he'd fallen asleep reclined on his back and Jailin was his crutch. As she held him against her chest, his head angled up toward the ceiling, cradled by her shoulder. She had taken off her mask and her forehead was pressed to his shoulder blade. Tears stained his back. Bailey shifted on the wall as if he could pull out of the straps and walk over to console her.

"Sorry, sugar. She's not done yet." Honovi kissed her finger and went to place it on Bailey's lips. He turned his head and she touched his cheek instead. "Aw, you're so rude."

"Let. Me. Go." He struggled to vocalize.

"Not yet." She turned her back to him and yelled, "Anubis! What are you waiting for?"

"She's not standing." A metallic voice echoed around the room.

Jailin's head raised slowly. Her face glistened in the light from her tears. Bailey's heart sank. She looked the same as the night Masou had dismissed her from the tribe. He wanted to hold her and tell her everything was going to be all right, although he wasn't sure he believed that himself.

Adrian walked over to her and bent down to pick Contardo up off her lap. She glared up at him. "Don't touch him!"

"I'm just going to move him out of the way." Adrian gathered Contardo in his arms and slung him over his shoulder. Adrian's body-width was half that of Contardo's and yet Adrian held him like a sack of flour.

Jailin stood and watched Adrian walk off toward a corner with a cot and lay Contardo on it. She turned her head back to Honovi and Bailey. She slowly squared her shoulders, made fists at her sides, and stalked toward them. Anger was written all over her face as she stared at Honovi.

She walked right past Honovi without another look and stood as close to Bailey as possible. He smiled as much as his strength would allow him and the anger in her body melted away. Honovi wormed her way in between them. "You're not finished. Get over there and fight or I'll kill you myself!"

Jailin never took her eyes off Bailey. Her hand went up and covered Honovi's small face. Before Honovi could say another word, Jailin slammed her head into the cement wall. Honovi was unconscious as she slid down the wall.

"Thank. You." Bailey exhaled each word. Jailin kissed him gently. Her hands held the sides of his face. As she felt his lips grow hard, she pulled away. He was losing more strength every minute. His eyes were closed as he whispered, "I love you."

"We're getting you out of here." She cut the thick leather around his feet with one of the small knives from her leg strap. Then she cut each of the straps at his wrists. He slid down into her arms as she rested him on the floor. "Can you walk?"

"Neither of you are leaving." Anubis stomped up behind Jailin. She stood up and turned around. Her head reached as high as the panda's breast plate.

"If we don't leave, then neither do you," Jailin threatened.

"You are my first one-on-one fight. I expect to enjoy this."

"Glutton for punishment, huh? You've got some impressive talents. Are you hiding anything else other than the ability to speak through a mechanical box in your throat and telekinesis?"

"Only one way to find out."

"As a little friend of mind might say, I concur."

Jailin bent down to kiss Bailey on the head. "Sit tight. I'll be right back." She followed Anubis to the same spot from which Contardo had just departed.

As Anubis stood on two feet, she took more notice of him. Red leather cuffs with black spikes wrapped around his wrists. Two strands of small chain links hung from a red band around his arm just below his elbow. He wore a red harness around his chest. Jailin assumed that this was what Adrian would use to ride him, and what Bailey had been strapped to on the way here. She wondered if the skull at his neck was human or animal.

"You're wondering about my skull. It's a humal."

"If you can hear my thoughts than your voice is purely for show. What's a humal?"

"You. A race of people, mostly human with animal aspects. Honovi and Adrian are also humal."

"Why is the skull so small?"

"It was a baby."

Jailin's eyes went wide. "If I'm a humal, what are you?"

"Anian."

"Vernore couldn't be a little more creative?"

"He didn't design us. He just brought a theory into creation."

Bailey grunted lightly and fell to his side. Jailin glanced over and saw him slide down onto his elbow. "Let's get this over with."

She ran up to Anubis and jumped straight up, alternatively kicking her feet into his torso. His paws wrapped around her waist and threw her to the ground. As she picked herself up, she noticed her bo staff only a few feet away.

Grabbing her staff, she got to her feet, but remained crouched. Anubis took a few steps toward her. She quickly stuck her bo between his legs and hit his left foot, then his right, to set him off balance. As she withdrew the bo she slapped it into the bear's pelvis. He roared and fell down on all fours.

Bailey's eyes opened at the sound and vibrations from the fall. He watched as the panda got up again and swiped his claws at Jailin's face. She blocked the blow by slapping the staff's right end against his paws. The extended end of the bo came back around and it cut down across Anubis's face. She spun out of the hit to gain more momentum, hitting his muzzle again before he could recover.

A loud growl came from the panda. He used his mind to move a lamp off the desk to throw at Jailin. She hit it with her bo and it sailed into the table Contardo had landed on earlier. The bulb broke and sparks flew onto the boxes drenched with chemicals. The area burst into flames.

Bailey pushed himself up, but couldn't move his legs. Trying as hard as he could, he slid himself across the floor away from the boxes and chemicals. The fire spread quickly.

Jailin had moved behind Anubis while he was beguiled by the flames. She cracked her bo into the back of his head. The impact caused him to lean forward enough for Jailin to run up his back. She launched herself off and jabbed her staff between his shoulder blades. It knocked him further toward the flames and she caught the bo as it rebounded off his back.

Anubis turned to face Jailin. Adrenaline was pumping through her. She knew Bailey would die without proper medical attention soon. The fire was going to engulf this warehouse in minutes. She glanced around the room while jumping back from Anubis's swipes. Adrian was gone. He'd taken Honovi with him.

Jailin focused back on Anubis. He had small objects floating around him. Cement blocks, scraps of iron, extra piping, chains, and more lamps started coming at Jailin. She ducked and blocked what she could. Moving closer through the debris, she was able to fake a strike to Anubis's left. She quickly brought the other end of her bo downward on his head and then, in a circular motion around her body, she struck his neck upward. She heard plastic crack.

"You broke my voice box," Anubis thought in anger.

"So you *can* communicate without it." She slid her bo behind his head and with all her weight pulled him down on all fours. She used one foot to push off his head, sending him further to the ground. Spinning up around her staff she reached the top and with all her weight and momentum smashed her feet down into his face.

Panting, she realized Anubis was unconscious. She ran over to Bailey. He was breathing into the crook of his elbow so as not to inhale smoke. She lifted him up off his back. "We should go, GIA should be here by now with Dr. Simon." Bailey only coughed in reply as she placed her shoulder under his arm. His temperature was higher than she had ever noticed before. His heartbeat was faint but fast. Pain thudded in her own chest.

Jailin supported Bailey's weight on the side of her good leg and walked him out through the large metal panel doors. Dierno was pacing back and forth. There was a fine mist in the air. The rain was letting up.

"Where's the helicopter?" Jailin thought.

"Coming. The ambulance is on its way from Cluce Community Hospital."

Wind picked up quickly in the parking lot. A patterned thudding was heard around the corner of the warehouse. Jailin walked slowly with her arm wrapped around Bailey's waist. She saw a thin man with a mustache in a suit with a light blue shirt jogging toward them with Dr. Simon.

"Agent Bailey? What happened?" Dr. Simon asked, as he saw the condition of them both.

"Hello, miss. I'm Commissioner Levin. Would you mind explaining what went on here?"

"That depends," she said without taking her eyes off Bailey as the medics laid him on a stretcher and hooked up intravenous fluids.

She thought she heard the medic say something about removing a necklace and Bailey grumbling. She saw Bailey knock the medic's hand away from his neckline. Commissioner Levin asked, "Depends on…?"

"If Ben lives or dies." She met the Commissioner's eyes only after the helicopter doors closed with Dr. Simon inside with Bailey.

"I don't plan on letting my best agent perish."

"You'd better not. Where are you taking him?"

"Dr. Simon says he needs to be at GIA's independent clinic. He'll be going back to Northpost."

"Dr. Simon would know best," she said but still looked worried that he'd be back in the same city as Vernore.

"No unauthorized personnel will be allowed in. With the exception of you, of course. You have my word."

"Thanks," Jailin said, not quite believing that they could keep him safe. She would be spending every night outside his room. Commissioner Levin ran off to the helicopter and she watched it take off into the north.

The Cluce ambulance rounded the corner with a fire truck. A medic asked Jailin if she'd like any medical attention. "Your medicines won't help me," she said, heading behind the warehouse to meet Dierno and head home.

Home wasn't as inviting as Jailin remembered it. A few huts were burned to the ground. Others had broken windows or roofs. People were scattered around helping one another rebuild their lives. She saw Meovi talking privately with Masou. She knew eavesdropping was rude, but she was curious about their efforts at secrecy in a public place.

"I know she'll be back soon. Call it mother's intuition," Meovi said.

"We won't get the rest of the money if she does. Look at our homes, Meovi. We've done our job. I even had to trade one of my women to get Contardo's body back for Darwishi. I've done enough in the last nineteen years. I'm tired of this."

Jailin had heard enough. She stepped out of the trees' shadows. Meovi's eyes connected with Jailin's. "Anaba! You're back!" She ran, holding up the hem of her brown skirt. As she got closer she slowed, "Well, you could look better. What's wrong?"

"Contardo's dead and Ben might not make it through the week. I just got back from GIA. Dr. Simon is working as fast as he can. Whatever they did, it's killing him. They unleashed the dormant gene and it's wreaking havoc in his body."

"Come inside. You could use a cup of tea and a nap."

"I can't sleep. I'm dying inside." Her head hung down and a tear fell to the burnt grass at her feet.

Meovi's mouth sloped downward and she interlaced her arm with Jailin's. She seemed older than ever before to Jailin. "I have something I need to tell you." They walked into the hut together.

"What do you mean all the information is gone?" Vernore was reclined in his puffy black leather chair. Digna was lying beside his highly polished ornate desk. He looked out at the city and swirled his glass of red wine under his nose.

"She took Johanna's son and ran, after knocking me out and beating Anubis unconscious."

"Honovi, I'm greatly disappointed in you."

"I am too, sir." Her tail twitched side to side with unease.

"How do you plan on fixing this?"

"I'll do anything you ask, sir."

"First of all," he spun around in his chair to meet her face to face, "you're going to break into that GIA facility and get me that boy back. Secondly, you're going to fix that warehouse. A lot of merchandise was ruined because of you and..."

"Me? Adrian is the sole guardian of Anubis. Let them fix it."

"It was your idea to press my best work into a fight. You will fix that warehouse and I may sever that tail of yours just for interrupting me."

"I'm sorry, sir." Honovi bowed her head in shame.

"As I was saying, you will increase the dosages on M.S.-1 and 2. Number 3 needs more training. They must be ready for the next phase."

"Yes, sir!" She turned to go.

"And one more thing, Honovi." She turned around to face him again. "Whatever anger you feel toward me, don't take it out on Adrian tonight."

A week had gone by and the sun was setting on another day. Jailin sat on Bailey's patio, watching the sky change colors. She was waiting for Gabe to return from a meeting with Bailey's landlord about the surplus of foliage in the apartment.

"This is quite an obscure assessment to make," Socrates thought.

"Why do you say that?"

"This decision can provoke all you have fought to prevent."

"I know, but he'll die if I don't do this."

"Are you capable of existing without regret?"

"I don't think I can live the rest of my life without him. Now that Commissioner Levin knows everything, I don't think anything will ever be the way it was."

"I was aware of that the initial night in the clearing."

She didn't say anything. Thoughts quickly ran through her head of every moment she and Bailey had spent together. "I gather that you do not aspire to conceal yourself with your father elsewhere?"

"Dierno told you about that, huh?" She rubbed her forehead, embarrassed that she had even considered it. "No, I'm not leaving him. *Ever.*"

"Hey." Gabe stepped out onto the patio.

"How did it go?" She turned her head up as Gabe loomed over her.

"No fines as long as we clean out the dead stuff. I also had to agree to put some lattices around the grounds and to donate a few ficuses to the foyer out front. I already tossed the dead flowers. Hope that's okay."

"Yeah, no big deal."

"Oh, and Dr. Simon just called. He says he needs to see you immediately."

"Is Ben okay?" Her pulse quickened with anxiety.

"No change." Gabe looked down at the pen he was playing with in his hands.

Jailin stood up and thought to Socrates, "I'll be back." She straightened Bailey's old soccer jersey where it bunched around her waist and then headed off toward GIA.

When she arrived at GIA, she swiped Bailey's keychain across the sensor plate. Sylvia smiled at Jailin and called Dr. Simon to tell him she had arrived.

Kishi met her at the first security door which needed biological codes for authorized passage. "How are you doing?" he asked her.

"Okay." She shrugged. "How about yourself?"

"Fine. Just fine." They walked the rest of the way in silence.

When they entered the lab, Dr. Simon rushed up to meet Jailin. "You are amazing!"

"Uh, thanks?"

"I hope you've made your decision, because your blood is perfect. You are O negative and not only are you a perfect donor for *anyone*, you are also a perfect healer."

"Meovi was my healer." She glanced to one side and found herself missing the woman who had told her that she had been an employee of Vernore for years.

"No. You're body regenerates on the inside. Whatever Meovi did for you was purely superficial."

"What are you saying?"

"I'm saying that with a blood transfusion from you, Agent Bailey will be up and running in no time."

"He'll be back to normal? Like he was two weeks ago?" Jailin's excitement peaked.

"No. Not exactly."

"Up and running like me, you mean. That's what he's wanted all along." Her heart sank as her voice fell.

"Yes. And perhaps even stronger."

"Stronger? Why is that?"

"He already holds this Vernore gene in his DNA. Yours is engineered. The combination of an inherited gene with that of an engineered one has been shown to lead to an incredible increase in abilities."

"Shown?"

"I went to talk with your father. I have his notes from years ago. He's a genius and he's figured out Vernore's formula."

"Can you reverse this then?"

"Maybe, but if we fix you and Agent Bailey regresses back to this stage, then no one can save him."

"Dr. Simon, may I speak with Ben first?"

"Of course, but don't be fooled by appearances." Jailin didn't know what he meant by that.

She went into the adjacent room where Bailey was being treated as if he were in a real hospital. He was asleep sitting half up in the bed. Starched white blankets and pillows surrounded him. There was a table that could be pulled up to the bed for miscellaneous uses, a chair for visitors, and a TV on a stand in the corner. Jailin sat on the edge of the chair and slid her hand into Bailey's.

His eyes opened and he looked at her adoringly. "Hi." He smiled as if he hadn't seen her in months.

"Hi." She met his gaze.

"Why are you way over there?" He pushed himself up in the bed.

"Are you feeling all right?"

"Each day is different. I sleep a lot and probably more in the last week consecutively than I have in the past two years."

She smiled. She was glad he looked better. Maybe he'd be all right if she didn't give him her blood, but Dr. Simon said not to be fooled by his appearance. She got up and sat on the edge of his bed. He adjusted himself to give her more room. She swung her legs up and nestled into him. Her head rested comfortably on his chest. He kissed her hair and inhaled her fragrance.

"They think I can save you," she confided.

"You already have."

"I mean Dr. Simon says you won't be better unless you get a blood transfusion from me."

"I know."

"You do?"

"You don't want to do that because it goes against everything you've been fighting for."

"It's not that I don't want to. And why do you sound like Socrates?" She turned her face up to his.

"You don't have to do anything you don't want to do." He smiled. His eyes reflected the same intense longing she always felt when she looked at him.

"I won't lose you," she whispered.

"I'm not going anywhere."

"You'll die if I don't do this." Her hand rested on his chest. Through the thin white shirt she could feel the pendant she had asked him to hold onto. She was glad she didn't have to rely on it for comfort anymore.

"I won't die today or tomorrow. Give it time. Think about it. Maybe there's another way."

"There isn't."

"How do you know that?"

"We've looked. Besides, I wasn't completely honest when I told you I didn't want you to be like me. I didn't tell you what I'm really afraid of."

"What are you afraid of?"

"That something inside you will change. That you won't love me anymore. That you won't be able to control all those horrible nights of nightmares, lust, and anger for no reason."

"I'm not getting a new heart or a monkey's brain or anything." He angled her chin up to him to read her face. "In fact, I'll have your blood intermixed with mine. The way I see it, I'll just want you more." His arms tightened around her.

"I hadn't thought of it that way."

"I've got a question for you. Actually, it's two questions."

"Okay."

"That night you broke into the hospital for your father's medicine, there was blood on you when you came back. What happened?"

"A man was delivering supplies. I smelled more drugs specifically for my father. When I tried to take them from him he fought back. I think my mask scared him and he was going to shoot me, but he missed and shot himself in our struggle. It was an accident."

"Good. I mean good that you didn't ravage him or anything."

"Oh no. He wasn't you." She tapped his nose with her finger.

"Last question." His eyes blinked away the tiredness. "Meovi and Masou thought that I could control your, let's call it desires. What did they mean by me controlling you? I don't understand."

"Let me try to explain it the best I know how. Minowas don't work on those who have already found true love. We found that out when Contardo..." She paused for a brief moment and Bailey tightened his hand around hers. "When he responded to her and you didn't."

"So you respond only to one person?"

"As long as I was distracted enough by you at the height of my... *confliction* during the rainy season, I wouldn't search out another mate. Meovi and Masou know I love you, and they used that to Vernore's advantage. They knew that I'd be loyal in a detrimental time—one they insured would happen in the middle of the rainy season, no less. When Honovi and Adrian came for you and Contardo, I knew my place in the fight. No matter how badly I ached for you that night, they knew I would fulfill my duty to protect my home first as long as you were part of that home. I was the liability. I am the weapon."

Bailey looked into her eyes and then kissed her forehead. "To me, you are Kafele. And you're breathtaking." He traced his hand from behind her ear along her jaw line and raised her chin. His lips met hers and she melted into his embrace. "Never lose this jersey," he worded through their kiss and tugged on the sleeve, "You're so damn cute in it."

She smiled and wrapped her free arm around his neck. In his arms she would always feel safe, secure, and at home.

Epilogue

The women's and children's tears fell harder and faster than the rain on the surrounding foliage. Each man in the tribe placed another rock on the mound before them. The last one to approach was carrying a small brown leather pouch. Darwishi poured the five white stones into his hand, then hooked the pouch back on his belt.

"Mo aberico. Adelino." Darwishi paused.

A single tear ran down Jailin's cheek. She kept her face to the sky and let the rain wash the salt from her face.

A strong slender hand slipped into hers. She smiled lightly and turned her head toward her friend.

"What's he saying?" Gabe whispered in her ear. Together they stood at the border of the trees and watched as the two tribes gave their respects to their departed young Primary.

Quietly, Jailin translated Darwishi's trembling words to the crowd, "My first son. The daring prince."

"Prince?" Gabe raised his eyebrows. "Makes sense. He was a little too confident, wasn't he?" He nudged Jailin with his elbow, while he held on tighter to her hand. A little smile was all he wanted to provoke.

"He was courageous in our time of need. He was a gift from God." Jailin repeated Darwishi's words as he bent to lay the five white stones in the shape of a pentagon where Contardo's chest would be.

"Jyn om caralipo tai sanjiv." Darwishi's hand waved out toward the graves behind him.

"In our saddened hearts they live on." Jailin shut her eyes. She couldn't look at all the death Vernore had brought on the tribes.

"You okay?" Gabe pulled at a leaf with his free hand. The trees were heavy with the sky's sorrow. Jailin opened her eyes when she heard the soft lyrical voices of the women singing their goodbyes to the dead.

"This is all my fault," she exhaled slowly.

"No, it's not. You did everything you could. They shouldn't be so angry with you," Gabe reassured her. He sounded as she had on the day Contardo's best friend drowned and he was held responsible for it.

Jailin felt eyes peering at her and turned her head to see Meovi slowly disappearing into the shadows of the teaks. She shook her head as she avoided having to watch another person she loved vanishing from her life.

"What are you going to do now?" Gabe asked.

Jailin unthreaded her hand from Gabe's and pried her fingers under the bandage at her elbow. She ripped it off and stared at the small drop of blood on the cloth. "First of all," she looked over at Gabe, "I'm going to do everything I can to help Ben get better."

"And then?"

"Then I'm breaking my father out of that hell hole and bringing destruction down on Vernore!" Jailin squeezed the cloth in her hand.

Gabe smiled to show his agreement and then looked around at the deserted graveyard. "But what about the tribes… and Meovi?"

"The shadows of my friends will watch over them." From her pocket she withdrew her necklace—Bailey's necklace—Vernore's necklace—and dropped it on a bed of damp leaves.

"We need to get back. He'll be awake soon and I know he'll want you there."

Jailin stood and looked down at the necklace on the jungle floor. "Ben," she whispered to herself. "You'll always be Kafele."

Gabe didn't ask her what she was mumbling. He assumed it was a private matter.

They walked back to Bailey's truck in the clearing by the boulder. Dierno and Sarana were lounging on the boulder and Socrates was sunbathing on the top of the truck. "We have a lot of work to do," Jailin thought. "And I'm gonna need all the help I can get."

ACKNOWLEDGMENTS

Many people have taken the time to help me with this endeavor. I greatly appreciate all that you have done. Thanks to: Richard Whitesell for his visual genius, which helped to bring my imagination to fruition. Bess Johnson for her gracious help with editing and proofreading. Pat Elsbree and Margaret Taylor for helping me become the person I am and for the review of my many drafts for clarity. Laura Whitesell for her reassurance and giving up some of her time for reading a "first" draft. Marisa Mann, for loyally answering all those silly questions I conjure up. Keith and Brian West, for their daily routines that most people would overlook. And of course Jim Ashley and Linda Elsbree, for being so loving and inspirational through everything that I set my heart to. Lastly, to the reader for you are giving me hope and reason to keep writing and loving the heartache of it.

ABOUT THE AUTHOR

J.T. Whitesell lives in Rochester, New York, with her husband, Rottweiler, Boston terrier, and a "love-bug" of a black cat. She is a medical receptionist and has a certificate in veterinary assisting. This is her first novel. You can learn more at her website www.jtwhitesell.webs.com.